The Confession of STELLA MOON

Shelley Day

CONTRABAND

"My very chains and I grew friends,
So much a long communion tends
To make us what we are..."

BYRON, *THE PRISONER OF CHILLON*

Prologue

In the NEWCASTLE UPON TYNE Crown Court

Case Number 70/003394

R v Stella Moon

Voluntary Statement by the DEFENDANT STELLA MOON relating to death of MURIEL WILLOUGHBY MOON.

My name is Stella Moon. I confess to the killing of my mother Muriel Willoughby Moon on 14th October 1970. I sincerely regret what I have done.

The day I killed my mother was the day I turned eighteen and the day I ceased being a Ward of the High Court of Justice of England and Wales. It was also the day I ceased being in the Custody, Care and Control of my grandmother, Ruby Willoughby. It had always been my plan, as soon as it was legal, to go and be with Muriel (I always called my mother Muriel).

That day I went to where she lived, which was at the Beach Hut on the dunes between Beadnell and Embleton. It was late afternoon. Muriel wasn't there, but the door was open and I went in. Straight away I saw the place had been ransacked. There was stuff all over the place, broken and spilled. Muriel's specimens – she was a taxidermist – had been attacked and mutilated. They'd been pulled apart, limb from limb, and lay in bits all over the floor. There were splatter marks in the distemper as though the half-preserved skins had been thrown against the walls. Bottles and jars of chemicals that Muriel used for preserving were smashed, and their contents tipped out and scattered. The place stank of formaldehyde, which is a preserving liquid and is volatile and pungent, and gets on your chest.

I am asked whether Muriel would have created that havoc herself and my answer is no. Anyone will tell you that Muriel valued her specimens above all else – she cared for dead things better than most people care for the living.

I went through to the back. A few years ago, Muriel had pulled an old lean-to down and Frank Fanshaw had built a new kitchen on. Now I saw it was all spoiled and there was a hole about three feet in diameter in the kitchen floor. Broken floorboards and piles of sand had been pushed to the sides.

The state of the place made me panic about Muriel. I was afraid something had happened to her. She would have been expecting me at the Beach Hut. I'd written to her to tell her what day I was getting out of the Home and said I would come straight from there to hers, so I was surprised she wasn't there. I shouted for her but there was no reply. I went out onto the dunes in case she was out there, setting her traps. I didn't find her. So I decided to go to the Saddle Rock. That was a place along the dune path just before you get to the castle ruin. Muriel especially liked that place. I don't know why, but she often went there: when she was feeling down or just wanted to think, that's the place she would go. The Saddle Rock is a ten-minute run from the Beach Hut. The tide was coming in that night, so I was against the clock. The Saddle Rock disappears under the water when the tide is in. It was already starting to get dark when I left the Beach Hut.

Muriel had always been prone to sudden slumps in mood. She would go off to be by herself, sometimes for weeks on end. Her own needs always came first. I was hurt that she hadn't thought me important enough to wait in for.

I ran along the dune path and cut across the golf course. As I came over the ridge I could see Muriel sitting there on the Saddle Rock, with the incoming tide lashing about around her. I shouted but it was stormy and the sea and the wind were too loud. Muriel was sat there like a statue. I ran down and came right up to her. She was soaked from the sea spray, her hair was stuck to her face and whipping out in the wind like snakes.

If I had been a normal daughter and if Muriel had been a normal mother, we'd have put our arms around each other. It was a good two years since I had seen her. But Muriel and I weren't a normal mother and daughter. When I looked into her face, she turned away. I pleaded for her to come back with me, but she wouldn't. Muriel was stubborn. She just kept staring out to sea, acting like I wasn't there. I was her daughter – her only daughter – it was my eighteenth birthday, and she was acting like I wasn't there.

I kept on talking. I wanted to prove to Muriel that I could speak. I wanted to convince her things between us could be put right. I wanted us to be normal, to put the whole ugly past behind us and start again. But at the same time I knew that wasn't going happen.

The tide was getting closer and I pulled at Muriel's coat to try to make her come away. The way she looked, it was like she was accusing me, as if I was the cause of whatever it was that was making her weird. A deep sigh shuddered out of her. Then she suddenly got to her feet, almost knocking me over as she pushed past me, and stormed off up the cliff path. She'd left a small grey haversack on the rock so I picked it up and went after her. I followed her along the cliff path, keeping up the best I could. Then we were in the lea of the castle, away from the open sea, and it was quieter and more sheltered.

It was then that she told me quite calmly to go back. Her voice was weary but insistent. I knew that tone. I shook my head. I told her I wasn't going anywhere without her. She began losing patience when I would not do as she said. She kept telling me to go away, to go while I still had the chance. She made it quite clear she wanted rid of me. It was very

3

hurtful, the way she spoke to me. She started swearing and calling me bloody awkward and insisting that I go away and never come back. She was treating me like I was a little kid. I said I would go back to the Beach Hut, but only on condition that she came with me. She flatly refused.

Then she was yelling and screaming and saying I had no idea about anything, and the whole bloody mess was all my fault. She got weepy and starting saying odd things about a baby being gone and she lost her temper totally when I said I didn't know what she was talking about. She said everything had gone wrong and it was all my fault. I honestly didn't know how I'd upset her so much. I was there trying to help her. But she kept on blaming me, and going on about a baby being taken away. I couldn't make sense of it because the only baby Muriel ever had was me.

Eventually she flew into a full-on rage, screaming that I was pig-ignorant and stupid and useless. She said she had never wanted me, she cursed the day I was born, it would be better if I had never existed…etc, all of which I had heard before many times, because that is how she was. In the middle of it all she turned and went fast up the steep sheep track. By then it was dark and a gale was howling. My chest was burning and my heart thumping all over the place with the emotion and with all the effort of trying to keep up with Muriel. I stumbled over the rough ground: I wanted to make her stop. I wanted her to say she was sorry. I wanted to tell her I never asked to be born. It wasn't my fault her life had turned out such a mess, that everything was a terminal disappointment. I grabbed her jacket from behind but she wrenched herself away from me. She screamed for me to get away from her.

I refused to believe she was telling me to leave her alone – after all this time, after all that had happened. I couldn't take it in that she just wanted rid of me.

Anger took me over. Years of my mother's rejection and contempt, her ridicule and neglect – it all condensed in that moment. It made me desperate with need for her and full of

4

hate for her, all at the same time. Everything was all mixed up and nothing was real. Things started happening in slow motion. My limbs no longer obeyed me. I felt myself grab Muriel by the hair. I clung on, refusing to let go as she struggled to pull away, and clumps of her hair were coming out in my hands. There was a fight. We grabbed at each other, we punched and kicked, each of us as desperate and determined as the other. Our feet slid about in the mud. Muriel had me by the back of the neck, like she used to. She was forcing my head down, forcing me by the neck to the ground. As she scrambled to get up, I pushed her. I pushed her hard, as hard as I could. Her hand left my neck and then she was gone. Muriel had gone over the edge of the cliff. I pushed her right over into the sea. I killed her. I killed my mother. She didn't scream. I don't remember anything after that.

This is the statement of the DEFENDANT STELLA MOON made under caution 18th October 1970 at Bolam St Police Station, Newcastle upon Tyne. Interviewed by Senior Investigating Officer: Detective Superintendent Anthony Hutchinson. Present: Detective Sergeant Nicholas Webber

SIGNED: Stella Moon
Dated: 18 October 1970

Chapter One

Stella Moon shivers in the draughty queue. The clothes she has chosen for this occasion – the faded silk dress, once a pale sage-green, the fine lacy cardigan of almost the same colour, the gold lamé sandals with the kitten heels, all old-fashioned, all a size too big – are entirely inappropriate for the season, for the weather, for everything. Marcia had advised against it. She should have listened to her. But Stella had been determined, and hadn't been much in the mood for listening. Yesterday, Marcia had helped her pack her things into the little blue suitcase and Stella had gotten carried away with the sudden luxury of choosing, being quite out of the habit: out of the habit too, of taking account of the weather – out of the habit of most things. Marcia had watched her laying aside the dress and the cardigan and the shoes for the morning.

'You might as well go the whole hog,' she'd said, a strange rasp to her voice, 'go the whole bloody hog. Put her knickers on while you're at it.' It wasn't like Marcia to say hurtful things. 'I'm gonna miss you, Stell,' she'd said straight after. Had almost hugged her.

Stella shuffles into a window seat, glad of the fuggy warmth of the coach. Other passengers are dumping their bags, heaving stuff onto the luggage racks, jamming it under seats, but not Stella. She keeps a tight hold of hers, up-ends the little blue suitcase on her lap, her fingers gripping the handle gone shiny with wear. A bit battered now, this suitcase would have been the very thing in the fifties, when Muriel spent half her wages on it for her three-day honeymoon on Skye. It's Stella's now. She lays it down flat, smoothes her hands across the soft blue leather and brings them to rest, fingers splayed, palms flat.

The window is too steamed up to see out. Stella tugs down the cuff of the cardigan and clears a patch. The window's dirty on the outside too. London grime. Seven or eight hours and she'll be in Newcastle. Plenty of time to make proper plans.

The doors fold shut, the engine whines and the coach judders a bit as it starts to pull away. Stella sits up straight and makes a determined effort to see out, to see past her own reflection. No-one has sat next to her. She pushes her hair back from her face but it won't stay there: it just springs back again. The coach edges its way through streets solid with traffic; tall red buses, squat black taxis, motorbikes, scooters, cyclists weaving in and out. Look at all those people. Going about their lives. Ordinary people. Ordinary lives. Each avoiding everyone else's eyes. Lean back in your seat, Stella. Relax. Rest your eyes, soften your mouth, be aware of your hands. Breathe out. Come on. Right out. In again. And out. In. Out. Stella has never been good at relaxing. The flat of Marcia's hand between her shoulder blades. Steady now. In. Out. That's it. Keep going.

Stella pushes her hair back from her face again. People will recognise her by the hair: wild, red, very curly hair. Why hadn't she thought of that? She pulls an elastic band from round her wrist, scrapes her hair back from her face and fastens it tight. The clothes as well, they make her stand out. She shouldn't have worn the clothes. What was she thinking of, wearing clothes that don't even fit? She looks ridiculous. She should have listened to Marcia. She should have put on the normal jeans, the plain black jersey, the baseball boots – not this stupid dress, not these stupid kitten heels. Marcia had warned her she would feel conspicuous.

'It's normal,' she'd said, shrugging, laughing. Everyone feels like they're the only one. 'Don't think about it – you'll get used to it and it'll go away.'

It will go away. If you refuse to think about things, they do go away. *This is a whole new life now, Stella. Get out there and make the world your own.*

She'll have her hair cropped like Mia Farrow in *Peyton Place*, she'll dye it black and she'll cover up her freckles with Pan-stick. There will be No Looking Back.

'There's no point in dwelling, Stella,' Marcia had said, 'Put the past behind you. And pray to God it stays where you put it.'

OK. But some of the women – those who'd been in and out a few times – had said it wasn't that easy, and freedom wasn't all it was cracked up to be. Stella hadn't understood. Surely, she'd thought, surely you can't wait to be your own person? But she's getting a sense now of what they must have meant. Is it elation or terror that is making her hot and queasy? She's forgotten what sensation belongs to what. She pulls at the neck of the cardy. She can feel sweat running down her back, down between her breasts, and she's glad she hasn't got that big black jumper on after all. It's started to rain. She rubs the window again with her cuff but still can't see much. Stella needs a smoke but she's not sure if it's allowed. She looks around. No-one else is smoking. Maybe you've got to go up the back, like on the school bus. She's no idea. After seven years, she's got no idea how normal people do normal things. She'll get her ciggies out all the same, keep them handy, light up if anyone else does.

Stella undoes the catches of the little blue suitcase, letting them click open. She lifts the lid. There, lying on the top, the present from Marcia, neatly wrapped in pale blue crêpe paper. Stella scratches at the edge of the Sellotape with her nail – it's a shame to spoil the lovely paper. She teases the parcel open. Inside, a beautiful notebook with a cover of fine turquoise Indian silk, embroidered with tiny coloured glass beads and silver and gold sequins. Stella lifts the book to her face and breathes in the soft, clean smell of the silk. She holds it against her cheek.

The last person to touch this book was Marcia. Stella thumbs through soft blank pages of handmade paper. They're thick, they feel almost like cloth. They're torn rough around the edges. Marcia has slipped a card inside the front cover – a postcard, a retro photo, a line of women in long baggy shorts holding onto their sit-up-and-beg bicycles, fists raised in the air. The women are beaming smiles out of broad, healthy-looking faces. 'We have nothing to lose but our chains,' it says across the top. Typical Marcia. Stella smiles. She turns the card over. On the other side,

Marcia has written in her curly script,

You know what this notebook is for, and there's a pen to go with it, and a letter you're not to open till you've done what you promised you'd do. Meanwhile, all love and luck, Marcie xx

Stella feels about inside the crepe paper packaging. Yes, here's the pen, a dark green Parker 'Lady' fountain pen. And yes, there's a letter too, in a slim blue airmail envelope. The envelope is sealed. For a brief moment, Stella is tempted to tear the envelope open, but she doesn't, and she won't. It's a question of trust. Respect. Trust and respect. They'd talked a lot about that. The bedrock of any relationship worthy of the name, Marcia said. Stella fingers the edges of the card, looks down at Marcia's writing on the back of it for a long time before she slips it back between the pages, claps the book shut, and sits with her palms flat against the beaded cover. Stella looks out the bus window through the grime, watching London going by.

She's on her way now, the journey has begun. A pale autumn sun is trying to shine through uniform grey drizzle. The whine of the bus's engine, the rhythmic scrape of the wipers, the faint sound of Radio One playing in the driver's cab, all around her the smell of damp people.

This is it. This is now. This is Your Life, Stella Moon.

Stella folds the crepe paper back round the book and re-sticks the Sellotape as best she can. She lowers the lid of the little blue suitcase and presses the clasps shut. She lays her head back against the bristly velour of the seat and closes her eyes. Stella breathes. In. Out. In. Out. Bless you, Marcia. Stella doesn't think she can do what Marcia asks, but she'll give it a go. Let nobody say she didn't even give it a go.

Chapter Two

Newcastle, and Stella gets off at Worswick Street bus station. The big clock says nearly five to eight. It's dark, cold, drizzly. Stella pulls the cardigan about her and clicks around the corner in the kitten heels. Somehow she's going to have to get a coat. She's looking out for the number 61, but any of the 60s will probably do. Everything looks the same – not what you'd expect, after seven years. But places don't change that much, not really: it's you that changes. What you see is where you're at. Who said that? Stella can't remember, but there seems to be some truth in it. She'll take a chance with whichever of the 60s comes first.

Coming round the corner, Stella sees there's a 65 already there with its doors wide open and its wipers humming. Stella steps on and slides some coins under the glass.

'Chillingham Road, please, far end.' Her own voice unfamiliar, far away, yet its loudness surprises her.

The bus man doesn't seem to notice. Stella takes the ticket and pockets the change. She sits down near the front, the little blue suitcase on her knee. On the wall behind the driver's cab there is an advert for Brook Street Bureau, a recruitment agency. New life means job. She'll have to get a job. She'll need a reference. Marcia. Marcia's not exactly the ideal person to give a reference, though, is she? But there's no-one else. It wouldn't look very good, would it? A prison warder for a referee. Stella will have to think about that one. But not just now. First things first. Grandma Willoughby.

Even if she hasn't got a free room at the boarding house, Grandma Willoughby will make space for Stella. She'll let Stella stay until she gets something sorted.

'Forgive and forget,' Grandma Willoughby will say, 'let bygones be bygones.' She'll make a pot of earl grey – Ruby Willoughby always adds the bergamot to the black Indian leaves herself – she can't be doing with any of this new-fangled, ready-made rubbish. She'll set out the china cups with the primroses on. The two of them will sit down at the big oak table with the thick chenille cloth, the brown glass vase overflowing with powdery mimosa the colour of egg yolk. A biscuit barrel with gypsy creams and home-made shortbread with bits of almond in. Stella can almost hear the clink of teaspoons against china, smell the scent of the flowers and feel the warmth of the fire burning in the grate. She'll hug Grandma Willoughby for a long time, resting her cheek against Grandma Willoughby's, soft and papery, breathing in the smell of rosewater, lavender and a hint of rouge.

She'll go on hugging and hugging until Grandma says, 'Away with you now, our Stella, and let me get on,' as she pats the back of Stella's hand with the pads of her fingers. 'You stay as long as you like, our Stella,' she'll say, disappearing into the scullery. 'My home will always be your home. I think you know that.'

Our Stella.

Grandma Willoughby will not have washed her hands of Our Stella. Not like she washed them of Our Muriel.

But Stella hasn't heard from her grandmother in seven years. No replies to any letters. Some had even come back 'not known at this address'. Stella had received no Christmas wishes and no Many Happy Returns. But it will all be different when Grandma Willoughby sees Stella – when she sees Our Stella. When she sees her in the flesh, the past will melt away as if it had never happened. All that will be forgotten. Forgiven and forgotten. Because Grandma Willoughby is not one for bearing grudges. That's what she always says: 'Blood's thicker than water.' Yes, that's what she'd said when Stella was sent to that convalescent place and then to that children's home. 'Blood's thicker than water.' That's what she'd said as the weeks turned into months and still Stella couldn't speak, couldn't get a single word out by way of reply. Grandma Willoughby had been there, in the background. But she didn't often visit. Not after the first few times. After a while it no longer seemed important, and the doctors said that it's probably for the best.

11

Now, it's going to be different. This time it's going to be alright. A long time has passed. Seven years. And blood is thicker than water. It's going to be like old times, like Stella never went away.

The bus is crawling along Shields Road, stopping at every traffic light, taking forever. The street is desolate, the shops all closed and their mesh shutters pulled down and padlocked. A streetlamp that's lost its yellow covering flickers in the rain. The air is foggy with coal smoke. The bus stops outside the Apollo and an old couple gets off. *Gone with the Wind* is on. Muriel loved that film. She said Clark Gable was the perfect man and the spit of Stella's dad.

'Where's my dad?' Only once had Stella suddenly dared to ask the forbidden question. The words had blurted themselves out of her mouth before Stella had time to stop and think. There'd surely be ructions. Even now, Stella feels herself shrink at the memory of it. Muriel had hesitated before she replied. To Stella's surprise, Muriel hadn't gone off the deep end. Muriel had just shrugged. She said nothing, but Stella saw that her mother's eyes had gone blank. Muriel's eyes could go blank and stay blank, like she'd gone off far away and somewhere else, and couldn't or wouldn't come back. Stella resolved never to ask that question again. A silent pact had been made between mother and daughter, and it would never be broken. As if in recognition of Stella's respect and compliance, Muriel had crouched down in front of her and, holding tight to the tops of her arms, had planted a loud kiss on Stella's forehead.

'I love you, Stella Moon,' she said, 'I always have and I always will, so don't you ever forget that.' Then the strangeness had passed and everything went back to normal and life was full of all the ordinary sounds again – Grandma Willoughby banging about in the scullery, Baby Keating screaming his lungs out, Frank Fanshaw lurking in the passageway before clumping away up the stairs.

The bus turns left into Chillingham Road. At last. At long last, she's nearly there. Stella just wants to get to the boarding house, get to Grandma Willoughby and back where she belongs. She can't wait to see Grandma Willoughby! What a surprise she'll have when she opens the door and sees Stella standing there! Our Stella. Home again after more than seven years.

By the time Stella gets off the bus, it's raining good and proper and she's dying for the toilet. She gets drenched walking the fifty yards from the bus stop. She covers her head with the little blue suitcase but needn't have bothered. There's a wind and it's blowing the wet everywhere. Stella walks as quickly as the kitten heels will allow, the thin dress clinging to her bare wet legs, rain running down the back of her neck, stinging at her eyes. Nearly there, Stella turns the corner, looks up to cross the road, and cannot, cannot, cannot believe what she sees in front of her.

Only a few seconds ago Stella had been tempted to sod the shoes and run the last bit right to her grandmother's door. But now she stops dead on the far side of the road. Grandma Willoughby's house is boarded up, deserted, derelict, condemned.

Chapter Three

Stella can hardly bear to look at the house. Wooden boards have been hammered over every window. The garden – once Grandma Willoughby's pride and joy – is spewing tangled weeds and brambles, broken beer bottles, crisp packets and soggy newspapers. She looks up at the top of the house, at the little attic flat where Stella lived with Muriel, the little flat that was home to the two of them in the days before Stella was old enough to know anything different, too young to know anything was wrong, the days before Grandpa Worthy passed away, before Baby Keating was even born, before he disappeared, before Muriel was banished from the house altogether. Nobody's bothered to board the window up and the glass is smashed, the soaking tattered curtains flap-flap-flapping in the rain.

Home. Look at it. Abandoned. Derelict. Grandma Willoughby's house has been left to rot. Stella should have listened to Marcia, she shouldn't have come back here; she should have made proper plans. But it's hard to plan anything when the future is just a great, gaping hole.

Grandma Willoughby's hostility, yes, Stella might have expected. Her rejection even, Stella could understand. But this, this nothingness, this terrible dereliction – this is something Stella never imagined would be waiting. Where is her grandmother? How long has the house been like this? Stella should have done like she promised Marcia, done things properly, made proper plans. It's late. It's dark. It's cold and it's wet. She hasn't got a coat, she's already soaked and she's nowhere to go. And she's completely worn out. Stella stares across at the boarded-up house and it sinks in how utterly worn out and exhausted she is. Marcia and everything that matters, a whole world away.

Stella's been foolish. You can't just go back to a place and expect everything to be the same as it was before. Things move on, even if you don't. Mistakes once made are made forever. You can't undo them. If you could turn the clock back – God knows, Stella would have done that long ago. She'd have done it the instant Muriel died. She would never have pushed her.

You've paid for that, Stella. You've paid your dues.

Without checking for traffic, the rain in her face, the wet dress clinging to her body, Stella wanders out into the road. Oh, to disappear, this moment, to dissolve into the smell of wet pavements, into the wafts of coal smoke from a thousand-thousand chimneys, to dissolve into the sound of tyres on tarmac, of water rushing along gutters, gushing down drains. Oh, to dissolve with the rain.

Come on, Stella. You have to keep going. There are no other choices to be made. Do it for Marcia.

Don't wander in the road. There's traffic. Get onto the pavement. At least get onto the pavement.

You've come this far. You have to keep going. You promised Marcia. You promised her.

She's got money, Stella's got money – at least she's got some money, they give you money when you come out, to last you till you get signed on. And Marcia, bless her, had given Stella three quid out of her wages. Stella puts a hand up to her chest. Still there, three pound notes, folded up, tucked safe in her bra. Marcia told her the Probation will sort accommodation – that's their job, they do it for you. But she's missed her chance now. It's far too late to go to the Probation. She'll have to stay in the house. She'll have to break in.

The front gate is rotting off its hinges and it's padlocked. Stella puts the little blue suitcase over first, then hitches up her dress and climbs over, scraping the inside of her thigh as her foot slips on the wet wood. She catches the dress on a nail as she lowers herself down the other side. The old silk tears as she wrenches it free. Stella hears the tear. Over the sounds of the city, the noise of the traffic and the beating of the rain, Stella hears the cloth tear and she cries and cries as though her own flesh had been torn. She cries and she doesn't know what she is crying about.

Stella sits down on the top step and fumbles to light a Number Six with wet hands and a damp box of matches. The matches are almost all gone before she can get the cigarette lit. But she manages, she smokes it quickly, and lights a second before flicking the dump over the gate and into the road. Be logical. Be practical. Tomorrow she'll find out what's happened to her grandmother. There's nothing she can do about that tonight. There's nothing she can do about anything tonight. Stella lights a third cigarette and registers that her hands are shaking. It's probably just the cold. She'll smoke just one more.

Ruby Willoughby had been like a mother to Stella, effectively brought her up, what with Muriel always so unreliable – unfit's the word, Ruby always said, make no bones about it, unfit is the only word. Muriel was headstrong, unpredictable, had no regard for others, gallivanting off God knows where. Muriel, away with the pigeons, away with the fairies, selfish through and through – that was Muriel. The boarders all loved Ruby, of course they did: her homely eccentricities called forth a kind of loyalty that made them all feel special, made them feel – sad, lonely misfits that they were – that they belonged. On Ruby's cue they too shunned Muriel – 'Poor Muriel,' they called her, imagining their fear of her was safely concealed, their dread nicely hidden behind a façade of concern. To call her 'Poor Muriel' gave their hatred a benign edge. But they didn't feel sorry for Muriel, not one little bit. No, their eyes looked at her with fear and with longing, not concern or pity. Poor Muriel had a strange charisma nobody could stand or cared to understand.

The atmosphere in the house when Muriel was around filled little Stella with a terrible dread. She didn't know where it came from or what it meant. Everyone was on their guard and trying not to show it. Blank smiles, empty eyes, tip-toe politeness, watchful concern. And all that sly snickering as soon as Poor Muriel's back was turned. Always the bleak expectation that Ruby Willoughby would 'do something about it' – she was the landlady and the wretched Muriel's mother, after all. But if Ruby Willoughby was going to do anything about anything, she'd do it in her own time and in her own way. Stella, forever watchful, would feel their eyes penetrating her, judging her as they judged Muriel. A child, aware of the distrust and disgust of others, their silent condemnation, as though she, Stella, should be held to account for Muriel's imagined misdeeds, as though Stella too were tainted with some unfathomable curse.

Muriel came and went at the boarding house seemingly as the mood took her. Every time she showed up, Ruby was at pains to act normal. Ruby set great store by Normal, and there was always a chance that things had somehow righted themselves – might still right themselves – if nobody meddled, if nobody aggravated Muriel. The trouble was, nobody – especially Ruby – knew how not to aggravate Muriel. And once Muriel was on her high horse, well, Ruby could no longer turn a blind eye. The veneer of normality would collapse as Ruby bustled, lifting things up and banging them down in exaggerated motions, her eyes quick and averted, her mouth set. In the end she'd speak through clenched teeth, she'd tell Muriel to go and be quick about it. But Muriel was every bit as stubborn as Ruby. She wouldn't leave on command, not without a fight. Ruby would end up threatening legal action.

'Just go,' she'd insist. 'And no, our Stella's not going with you. Over my dead body. Stella's staying put. Here with me.' And when still Muriel didn't leave, Ruby would start yelling and screaming. 'I'll go back to the solicitor, I'll take it to the High Court. I'm warning you, don't you force my hand, our Muriel.' That final threat was the one that always made Muriel go. Till the next time.

It hadn't been so bad when Grandpa Worthy was alive, but things got worse after he died. Then, when baby Keating was abducted, that was the last straw. Ruby told Muriel to keep away from the boarding house, or else. After that, Stella saw little of her mother and was never allowed to go away with her, not even to the Beach Hut, though Muriel tried many times to take her. Stella found Court papers stuffed behind the doilies at the back of the sideboard drawer. But Stella did see her mother on some Wednesdays, when Muriel was permitted to collect her from the dancing class. Back at the boarding house, Ruby Willoughby had better things to do: Wednesdays she conducted her weekly Sittings – her fixed appointments with the dead.

Those Wednesdays, trouble always brewed and Stella didn't always get to the dancing class as a result. She would sit on the back step, the cat on her lap, her hands buried deep in his warming fur, pretending not to listen. She never quite made sense of why it was her name the two of them spat back and forth. Sometimes the cat would jump down and make off, his ears back and Stella would sit there, staring at her shoes. She could lick her finger and rub imaginary spots off the patent leather shoes Muriel had brought, which were causing the latest ructions. Or she could recite psalms backwards under her breath. She knew backwards was the devil's work and she shouldn't be doing it, but she didn't care. She also knew the longer she kept it up, the sooner the parting would happen – Muriel turning tail, swearing and slamming and spitting on the floor, Grandmother Willoughby cursing in a language Stella couldn't understand. Then, when the house had gone quiet, Grandma Willoughby would sit in her chair by the fire in the back kitchen, her eyes closed and her chest heaving, the herb-cupboard door gaping open.

Stella finishes her cigarette and flicks the dump into the front garden in among the brambles. She's stopped crying and wipes her nose on the cardigan and her wet face with the back of her hand. She gets to her feet. Muriel is dead. Seven years, and she hasn't got used to Muriel being dead, not really. Grandma Willoughby is probably dead as well. And what about Frank Fanshaw? What if there's nobody left?

There is no point in speculation. Marcia talking. Deal with the here and now. Do what has to be done. Action.

Then when the time comes to make sense of it all, write it down.

Stella looks down at her soaking clothes and nips together the faded green silk where the dress is torn. How can a dress be sad?

Chapter Four

Stella pushes at the front door, knowing full well as she does that it's locked. The big bay window is boarded up with plywood. Someone's sprayed it with graffiti – a big jumble of colours and strangely shaped letters Stella can't read.

Tomorrow she'll knock at the dentist across the way and find out what's going on. Mr Cohen will know: he always makes it his business to know what's what. Or there's Mrs Carson, if she's still there. Probably not a good idea to knock on the Carsons, though – it's unlikely they'd talk to Stella, not after what she's done. Mrs Carson is – or was – a religious woman. Chapel, one of the brigade who'd written to Stella when she first went to prison, making their feelings known. Mrs Carson's was not a friendly letter: she was one of those who thought Stella had gotten off too lightly. Should have got life, evil little madam, a hanging is too good for the likes of her. Bad lot, others had chimed, those Willoughbys, they're as queer as they come. But Oh Dear God, think of it, think of that poor Muriel – as bad as she was, she didn't deserve to die. No, not a good idea to knock on the Carsons. Stella picks up the little blue suitcase and walks round into the back lane. She has to find somewhere to pee or she's going to wet herself any moment. She's going to have to climb in.

At the back of the house is a wall – a brick wall – eight or nine feet high. Stella used to climb over this wall when she ran away from school. Grandpa Worthy would be in the house, consulting with his clients. Or he'd be in the back kitchen, putting up his medications, in which case he wasn't displeased to see Stella, who could help with the pouring and measuring and writing names on bottles. But if Grandpa Worthy was down in the basement doing his procedures, the back door would be locked and Stella would have to wait outside until she saw the lady going away in a taxi, and she'd have to make sure there wasn't another waiting in the queue. It's a long time since Stella's climbed that wall and she's not sure she can still get over it. Plus someone's cemented sharp shards of broken glass all along the top. Stella finds a dustbin to stand on and pushes the case over first. She hears it drop: she'll have to go now or say goodbye to the little blue suitcase that contains everything she owns. She starts to heave herself up the wall. It's more difficult than she remembers, and now there's the broken glass to contend with. The dress rides up and her bare knees and toes scrape over the bricks as her hands grip the smallest of holds between the bits of glass. Then she's balanced on the top, lowering herself down the other side. She drops the last couple of feet, wipes her hands on the dress, pushes her straggly wet hair out of her eyes and looks about her.

Bugger it if the back windows aren't all boarded up as well. She might have known. In the back yard, the old coalhouse and the outside netty have big rusty padlocks. Faded green paint is peeling off the doors. Stella remembers that paint. She remembers her grandmother slapping it on with a brush that was meant for wallpaper paste, scrubbing the coalhouse out with Lysol and fitting the big padlock on and locking it up. She gave Stella sixpence for sweets and sent her down the back lane to drop the key down the drain beside the swimming baths. Then she planted geraniums in tubs and window boxes and arranged them around the yard. Where they once stood, and where seed trays of lettuce and beetroot and carrots sprouted under old panes of glass to keep the pigeons off and where the cat used to stretch out to soak up the sun, now Stella sees there is only neglect: straggly weeds barely hanging onto life between paving stones gone wonky with worms. Grandmother Willoughby must have been gone a long time, judging by the state of the place.

Stella badly needs the toilet. Something about being here is making her even more desperate. The padlock on the netty won't budge. She'll have to pee in the yard. It won't be the first time. Stella lifts up the sodden dress, pulls her pants down and squats in the corner, suddenly aware of her own heart missing beats and her own breathing: too fast, too shallow, too high up in her chest.

If this is freedom, Stella doesn't want it. She wants Marcia with her fat black arms and her crooked teeth and her cackly laugh and her smell of peppermints and coconut oil. Stella would never have got through that stint without her. Marcia in her rough dark uniform, her broad hips bulging in the navy trousers with the ironed crease, the giant bunch of keys dangling from the thick black belt and little pearls of sweat on the sides of her nose. It's best not to think. It's better to get on with things.

No point in dwelling ... Put the past behind you. C'mon, Stella, me lass – cheer up now, it might never happen.

Stella pulls her pants up and tries the back door. Locked. Of course it's sodding locked.

How the fuck Marcia expects her to write, to fucking write any fucking thing when it's going to take every ounce of everything simply to survive...

She'll try a window, prise a board off and smash the glass.

Get on with it. Come on, Stella. Focus on the task in hand. Do whatever it is you have to do.

Through the lean-to and round the side of the house, Stella stops and listens. Traffic on wet roads. In the distance, a siren. The heavy taste of coal smoke in the damp air. Then Stella stops breathing. She stops breathing because she sees it. Someone's been here. In the pale glow from the back lane street lamp, Stella sees clearly that the board on the scullery window has been pried off. It's lying on the ground in bits. The window's been smashed as well, the broken glass shoved in close to the wall. Whoever did that could still be here. Or on their way back. Stella looks back at the wall. There's nothing on this side to stand on. There's no way she can climb back over. The only way out is through this window, along the passageway, and out again by the front door.

But even Stella Moon hasn't got the bottle to do that. There could be anyone in there.

Or no-one, Stella. There could be no-one. Chances are, there's no-one.

OK, there's probably been a tramp. Or a wino. Or a druggie.

Rough sleepers have been here, that's all. They've sheltered for the night. A night or two. And why shouldn't they? The place is empty. They've been and gone. Or they'll be off their heads. Fast asleep. They wouldn't harm you anyway. Just remind them you're a killer. Don't forget you're a killer, Stella.

Stella listens at the window, convinced she can hear something. But it's nothing. Her imagination in overdrive. Everything's actually quiet. Even Stella's own breath, quiet.

Stella knows this house, she knows it, and it knows her. It wants her back, like she belongs. She feels the pull.

She'll wait a bit longer, listen a bit harder. Still nothing.

Marcia. Go for it, Stella. You're nothing if not a survivor.

You have no choice, Stella. Unless you want to stay in this sopping yard indefinitely and catch pneumonia. Stella looks up at the Carsons' back windows. No lights on, either upstairs or down.

You're on your own, Stella, and you've got to make the best of it.

Stella climbs in at the scullery window and drops down onto the lino, the suitcase in her hand. She listens, hearing only her own blood swooshing past her ear drums.

A flash of fascination for the circulation of blood, the pumping of the heart, the miracle of life. The way Marcia throws her head back when she laughs.

In the scullery, Stella scans the room, her eyes adjusting to the dark. Everything is drained of its own colour and tinged a pale yellow. She knows this room, it's just like it used to be, only it's draped with cobwebs, sticky looking dust, dead flies and it smells rancid. The blue Formica cabinet is falling to bits. How do things, left on their own, start dropping to bits? The stove, covered in grease and dead insects. The ceramic sink chipped black along the front. Lino on the floor, styled to look like parquet, now sticky underfoot and blackened with mould where it curls up at edges just shy of the walls. The insipid light makes the room uniformly colourless. It smells of damp, of grime and rodents.

Stella listens hard, hears the rain on the lean-to, the slosh of water escaping from a broken downpipe. The light switch doesn't work, obviously. It's sticky. Everything is sticky.

The door into the back kitchen is standing open. Grandma Willoughby's pinny is still hanging damply on its plastic hook. Stella pushes the door wide open and a pale shaft of jaundiced light falls across the floor. The maroon patterned carpet, so filthy the pattern is no longer visible. Stella remembers it new, bought with the insurance after the distraught Hedy Keating wreaked havoc that time, the day her baby went AWOL. The furniture's all like it was, even the chenille cloth still covers the table. Stella used to hide under there, peering out at people's feet from between the tassels, observing socks, stockings, the shapes of ankles, earwigging on conversations she couldn't make sense of, making notes all the same and storing her secret observations inside a giant bible she'd hollowed out with Mr Fanshaw's Swiss Army knife that week he nipped off to Skegness with his floozy and forgot to take it with him. Stella had hung onto the knife for ages, knowing he wouldn't dare say anything.

Stella can hear herself breathing. Breathing in the same smell of soot from the back kitchen chimney, the same clamouring smells of camphor, belladonna, pleurisy herb, chloroform and God knows what else from Grandfather Worthy's cupboard under the stairs. She can smell it all, though the door is tightly shut and probably there's none of that stuff left in there now. Stella won't go near that door. Won't even look at it. She should not be here. She can't think what possessed her to come back to this place. All she wants now is to get away, get along that passageway, out the front door and never come back.

Come on, Stella. Get going. The longer you stay here the worse it will get.

She listens hard, breathing shallow, and begins to edge along the passage, her back to the wall. Grandma Willoughby's bedroom door swings open as Stella draws level with it. The dark figure of a man stands in the doorway.

Chapter Five

Mr Frank Fanshaw is a bold one – bolder, yes, than Stella remembers him.

'I knew you'd come back,' Frank says, 'I knew it.' He settles himself on the stair next to Stella.

The familiar smell of his greasy hair. All the time that's passed and the smell still the same: she'd know it anywhere. Keep your wits about you, Stella. Stella says nothing, just pulls the little blue suitcase closer in, sets it on her lap and puts her arms around it.

'Cat got your tongue?' Frank says, flicking his lighter on and leaning round to peer into Stella's face.

'Ah, I get it. Giving us the silent treatment, eh? The same old trick.' Frank sniggers and comes right up close to Stella's face. 'Silly old Frank. He thought you'd have grown out of that.'

His breath smells of old meat pies. Stella pulls back and tightens her arms around the case.

'I've been waiting for you,' Frank says, leaning back. 'I says to myself, I says, Frank, I says, if you're not mistaken, Stella will be getting out round about now, done her time, free as a bird. Now, Frank, I says, look at it this way. Stella comes out, where does she go? And I apply a little logic.' Frank interrupts himself to pull Stella's face round to face him, but immediately he lets go and she turns away. 'Why, Frankie boy, I says, she'll come out of yon prison, and I reckon she'll head straight to Newcastle. She'll go straight to that grandmother of hers. That's what I says to myself. And I was right, wasn't I? Spot on.'

Frank stands up and plants himself at the foot of the stairs so he's right in front of Stella. He flicks on his lighter again.

'So I comes here, and I wait. I wait patiently. Patience pays off. But you wouldn't know much about that now, would you?'

Stella gets to her feet, wanting to get to the bottom of the stairs, and tries to push Frank out of the way, but he grabs the banister and stands his ground.

'Now you listen to me, missy,' Frank prods Stella hard on her breastbone, hard enough to make her sit back down. 'Now you be a good girl and listen. Uncle Frankie hasn't finished what he was saying.' Frank pulls a packet of Number Six out of his pocket, undoes the cellophane, lights two and hands one to Stella. 'I usually smoke Embassy, blue,' he says, changing his tone. He inhales deeply. 'But I got these for old times' sake, specially for you.'

Stella stays silent. She accepts the lighted cigarette without looking at Frank.

'Why, thank you very much, Mr Fanshaw.' Frank mimics a high-pitched female voice. 'That really was most kind of you. Your friendly gesture is much appreciated.' Frank's mimicry dissolves into snorts of laughter.

'I've actually got a torch here,' Frank says, pulling a heavy looking object out of his pocket and fiddling with the switch. 'The electric's off, in case you hadn't noticed. No point in wasting the lighter.' He shakes the torch and shines an uncertain beam into Stella's face. She pushes it away with the back of her hand.

'You're looking a bit peaky, if you don't mind me saying,' Frank says. 'Didn't they feed you in yon place? I thought them places were supposed to be holiday camps.'

Frank puts the torch under his own chin and pulls a face, but Stella doesn't look. 'Gargoyle,' he says in a stupid gargly voice. 'C'mon, kiddo. You used to laugh at that.'

Stella snatches the torch and lays it down on the stairs, where it lights up a patch of once flower-patterned wallpaper, now scuffed into a uniform grey.

'I've even got food,' Frank says.

'I don't want anything,' Stella shakes her head. 'I'm going. I'm not stopping here…'

'Ah, it talks, does it?' Frank interrupts. He picks up the torch and shines it on Stella again. 'Now there's a turn up for the books. It said something. It actually said something. Go on, say something else! Prove it can talk!'

Stella stands up and moves a step down. This time Frank doesn't try to stop her. There's nothing save a few yards of passageway between her and the porch door that leads out the front. But she needs to watch out. She knows Frank Fanshaw. And the inside door could be locked.

'I broke the board and the window so's you could get in,' Frank is saying, now standing next to her at the foot of the stairs. 'By rights, you should be saying, "Why, thank you very much, Mister Fanshaw. That was very kind of you, Mister Fanshaw."'

'You did it for yourself to get in, you mean.'

'Now doesn't that show how little you know, little Miss Clever,' Frank snorts, 'I happen to have the key.'

Frank pulls a grubby bit of string out of his top pocket. A key dangles in the air, glinting in the torchlight. 'I broke the window, I pulled the board off, I put myself in danger of getting arrested, and all on your account, my dear. And you can't even say thank you. Ungrateful little besom. I might have known I'd get no thanks from the likes of you.' Frank nods his head. 'But it was all worth it. I knew you'd be here in the end. Where else has she got to go I asks myself...'

'You said that before. Where's my grandmother?'

Stella backs off a few steps, but Frank closes in.

'Old Mrs Willoughby? Now how am I supposed to know? Since when was I a mind reader? You're the one who's supposed to be clairvoyant,' Frank sniggers a snorty laugh, drops his cigarette end onto the hall lino and grinds it to bits with his boot.

'You shouldn't do that,' Stella says. 'It's disgusting.' She stubs hers out on the sole of her shoe and keeps hold of the dump.

'Oh, disgusting is it?' Frank mocks, 'Disgusting?' He's imitating Stella's voice with exaggerated scorn. 'Still Miss High and Bloody Mighty. Just like your mother. Haven't changed a bit, have you?'

Frank lights another cigarette, just for himself this time. He's standing right beside Stella now. She may have lost her chance.

'I'll tell you what Disgusting is,' he continues, 'you killing your own mother, that's what I call Disgusting. That's what most Normal people call Disgusting. You're in no position to lecture me ...'

'Is that what you came here to say?'

'You might as well get used to hearing it. It's what Normal people say.'

'What is it you want?' Stella asks. 'Why've you come here?' She edges half a step further towards the porch door.

'Oh no you don't!' Frank wrenches Stella by the arm and puts himself between her and the porch door, 'I know your game. Sly as ever. You'll go when Frank says. And not a minute before. And you'd better get used to that, girlie, if you and I are going to get along.'

Frank is a big man. He gets hold of Stella's shoulders, turns her around and marches her along the passageway to where the step goes down into the back kitchen. He pushes her into the room and shuts the door behind them. He sets the torch down on the mantelpiece.

'So you want to know what I'm here for? Well, I've asked myself the same question,' Frank says.

'So what's the answer? I'm all ears.' Stella sits down on the chair by the fireside that used to be her grandmother's. Best to act normal. Don't rattle his cage. 'You don't know where my grandmother is, then?'

'Dead, for all I know.' Frank throws his half-smoked cigarette end into the fireplace. 'Aye, dead and buried. Long since.'

Stella feels herself flinch inside. But it's really not wise to let on to any emotion of any kind. Keep it to yourself, Stella.

'Why come here, then, if she's dead and buried?'

'I told you. I came for you! I knew you'd come back. It was only a matter of time. I knew when you'd be out. And I was waiting. Then, bang, there you were, and I says to myself, Frankie boy, you're a genius, you've not lost your touch. I was there all the time. Heard you creeping along that hallway, skulking about like a sewer rat...' Frank's voice trails off into chesty laughter. 'But if I may say,' he resumes after a bout of coughing, 'you've turned into one fine young woman, Stella Moon.' He picks up the torch and shines it at Stella, moving it up and down her body, and nods. 'Yes, one fine young woman. All that time inside must have done you good, you're starting to fill out in all the right places...' The beam of the torch has come to rest on Stella's breasts, where the thin, damp dress clings to her shape. 'What is it, seven years? That must make you the ripe old age of...what? Twenty-five?'

Stella finds herself pulling the cardigan about her, though it too is thin and wet and it reveals more than it conceals. Marcia was right. She should not have come back here. She should have gone straight from the coach into a B&B and so on to the Probation, like Marcia had made her promise. She shouldn't have been such a pig head. But it's too late now. She'll have to make the best of a bad job. Act normal. Take control. Come on, Stella. You know how to handle this creep.

'You still haven't said what it is you're after,' Stella says, standing up now and looking Frank in the eye.

Frank lights another cigarette.

'You smoke too much.'

Frank exhales smoke slowly.

Stella sighs, picks up a brass candlestick from the mantelpiece, rubs it on her sleeve and puts it back. She picks up a ceramic spill holder. 'This,' she says, 'you brought from Skegness. I remember. You had a dirty weekend with your floozy, and you brought this back.' It's Stella's turn to snigger.

'That floozy, so-called, happens to have been your mother,' Frank gives Stella a satisfied smirk. 'Come to think of it, Muriel would have been about the same age as you are now, when she got started. Ha! Now there's a thought!'

'You're a liar, Frank Fanshaw. I can't say as you've changed.'

Stella's going to have to ride this one out. There's no way she can get to the front door, not now.

'Funnily enough,' Frank says, 'I was just thinking the very same thing about you. Great minds think alike, eh?'

Stella looks around the room. Frank follows her gaze.

'Everything's still here,' he says, 'Whatever it was that caused old Ma Willoughby to do a moonlight, she didn't trouble to take much with her. Pretty obvious to me that one's gone to meet her maker...'

'It's like the Marie Celeste,' Stella interrupts. She walks over to the cupboard under the stairs and rests her hand on the round brass door handle. It feels cold and inert. It can't be… but it is. Could the handle be moving, turning against her palm? Stella snatches her hand away and stares down at the doorknob. Just an ordinary brass doorknob. Perfectly still. Stella looks at her palm. Just an ordinary palm.

'Who? Who? Who are you talking about?' Frank is insistent, 'What was that you said? You said a name before you drifted off onto Planet Stella.'

For a few moments nothing makes sense. Stella continues to stare at the handle on the cupboard door, but nothing is moving.

'Oh…I'm sorry, what was I saying? Yes, yes, the Marie Celeste,' Stella struggling to pull together her thoughts, 'The Marie Celeste. It was a ship. A mystery ship, found floating on the sea, the dinners half eaten, the drinks half drunk, all the people – the crew and everybody – vanished…'

'Old wives' tale, that,' says Frank, 'a lot of old baloney.'

'It's true. It's a true story, Frank, an unsolved mystery.'

'Well, old mother Willoughby's no mystery, she's snuffed it, that's what I reckon.'

Stella will not rise to that bait. The old fool knows no more than she does. If he did, he'd have said.

'D'you want something to eat?' Frank nods towards the back kitchen window sill, where Stella now sees he has some provisions stacked up. 'I've got some left of a loaf and half a tin of pilchards…'

How long has he been here? How long is he figuring on them staying here?

'Thanks, but no thanks. I don't want anything. You have what you like.'

'Oh, anything I like, is it?' Frank titters. 'You sure about that?' He rubs his hands together.

Chapter Six

Stella is still standing by the cupboard under the stairs. She is completely aware of her resolve not to go near that cupboard. Yet here she is, standing right next to it, her hand reaching out towards the door. Suddenly she grabs hold of the handle and wrenches the door open so hard it bangs back on its hinges, releasing the most horrible smell into the room. The smell is pungent, herbal, sour, but there are volatiles – ether, chloroform, formalin – and there's something sulphurous, and there's the smell of something dead in there, something long dead and rotting.

'Christ almighty, the stench coming out of there…' Frank gasps, getting to his feet and covering his nose and mouth with his hand. 'Shut the bloody door, for God's sake!'

But something's stopping Stella from closing the door. Like she can't close it, won't close it, she doesn't know which. She's holding the door wide open and is just standing there, leaning forward, straining to see inside.

'For fuck's sake, Stella, shut the bloody door.' Frank sounds genuinely alarmed. 'You don't know what you're doing. There's good reason why that door's kept locked… I would've thought you of all people…'

'It's not locked now,' says Stella. 'It just came open. Honestly, I hardly touched it.'

'That's the whole damn point.'

'I swear I hardly touched it…'

'Get away from there, I'm telling you. There's poisons in there. And Christ knows what else. What the hell old Mother Willoughby – God rest her soul – was wanting with all them poisons I'll never know, but that's what's in there, and you'd be best getting that door shut Stella and leaving it shut.'

'You said "God rest her soul" – are you saying my grandmother's dead, then?'

'I'm surmising. Open your eyes, girl. Why else would the place be all boarded up if the old stick hasn't popped her clogs, eh? Now shut the door. There's a good girl. Let's leave all that where it is.'

'She'd only just be eighty. She could have gone away somewhere.'

'I'm not answering any more of your questions till you get that door shut. I mean it. Or do I have to get up and do it myself?'

Stella makes no attempt to close the cupboard door. Frank strides across the room, gets behind the cupboard door, gives it an almighty kick and it slams shut. But Frank's no sooner sat down in the chair again than the door's sprung back open.

'Would you shut that fucking door, for Christ's sake, Stella?! And put the fucking catch on.'

Stella's made him angry now, Stella and the cupboard. Stella should know better than to make Frank angry. She tries to shut the door but it keeps springing open. The catch won't hold. Maybe it's broken, but it looks alright.

'Remember Baby Keating?' Stella says out of the blue, apropos of nothing. She hardly remembers the baby herself and has no idea why Hedy Keating's abducted infant should suddenly come into her mind again. The police had spent ages tracking down Hedy's estranged 'husband', but hadn't found the baby. Frank is silent. 'Do you remember Baby Keating, Frank?' Stella repeats, 'Dunno why he suddenly came into my head, but he did.' Frank's still not answering. Why's he not saying anything? Stella turns and looks at Frank. He looks peculiar. 'What's up with you, all of a sudden?' she says, 'Are you ill?'

Frank sits down, elbows on his knees, his head in his hands. Stella comes over and puts her hand on his shoulder. He shakes his head and pushes her away. He can't be crying. Surely he can't be crying. Why is he making those noises? He seems to be having trouble getting his breath.

'What's the matter? Shall I fetch a doctor?'

Frank shakes his head again. 'Just let me alone. Let me alone. I'll be alright in a minute.'

Stella backs off. She's never seen Frank like this before, she can't make sense of the sudden change – unless he's ill, unless he's about to have a heart attack or something.

'Open the window,' he says, breathless.

Stella could leave now, while he's poorly – he won't be able to follow. But doing that doesn't seem right. It's not right to leave someone who's been taken ill. Even when that someone is Frank Fanshaw.

Stella opens the back kitchen window. 'Is that better? Your face is the wrong colour. It's gone all grey.'

'It's them smells. From that cupboard,' Frank says after a while. 'They've turned my stomach. I told you, they're poisons. I told you, you should shut the door and keep it shut.'

So Frank's getting back to his normal self. She'd never have guessed he'd be so scared of a few smells from a stinking old cupboard.

'I can't smell anything now,' Stella says, 'I could before, but it's faded…'

'Shut the bloody door, can't you?' Frank's yelling now, getting to his feet. He looks to Stella very unsteady. 'Can't you do anything right? I told you to shut the bloody door.' Frank staggers across the room and slams the door shut himself and before it can come open again, he wedges one of the chairs under the handle and kicks it into place. He slumps back down in the chair.

'Pass the tabs,' he commands.

Stella takes one for herself and passes the box to Frank. No point in antagonising him.

'What did you say you wanted to see me for, Mr Fanshaw?'

'Frank,' he says, 'why's it suddenly "Mr Fanshaw"? I told you, the name's Frank. You're a big girl now.' Frank's gripping his cigarette so tightly he can hardly get a draw on it. 'There's something you'll be interested in, that's all,' He shrugs, 'How about it?'

'How about what? What might I be interested in?' Frank Fanshaw hasn't changed one bit. Stella knows exactly what he's going to say next. He seems to have completely recovered. She should have taken the chance and run while he was acting the sick man. 'I came here to see my grandmother. She's not here. So I'm not staying. I'm going elsewhere…'

'Ask me nicely, there's a good girl, and I'll tell you everything you need to know.' Frank is fiddling with the cigarette lighter, flicking it on and off.

'The Zippo,' Stella says, 'you've got the Zippo.' She reaches out to catch hold of the lighter in Frank's hand, but Frank snatches it away and holds it just out of her reach. 'That's not yours,' Stella says, 'that was Grandpa Worthy's.' She's not going to play Frank's stupid games.

'Aye,' he says, 'Any objection? I found it upstairs. Amazing it still works. Nice one. Always fancied a Zippo. Dear to buy, these are.' He flicks the lighter on and off a few times more, then puts it into his trouser pocket.

'You've no right helping yourself to stuff that's not yours.'

'It's mine now,' Frank says. 'Finders keepers.' Frank pats the outside of his trouser pocket in a gesture that makes Stella wince. 'Ask me nicely, like I said, and I'll tell you everything I know. I might even show you,' he adds, 'if you're specially nice.' He puts a pointed finger under Stella's chin, but she moves away before he can tilt her head up and make her teeth crash together.

'I read all about you in the papers,' Frank says, 'Yeah, you were famous. Stella Moon's little hour of fame.'

Frank Fanshaw pretending to be nice is worse than Frank Fanshaw being naturally nasty.

'Nobody at the work would believe we were acquainted,' he went on, 'or that a slip of a lass like you could do a murder. But then I described how I'd…how I'd come to know your mother, and what a nasty bitch she was…'

'Don't you say that,' Stella interrupts. 'There's no need to say that.'

'Oh, I should know better than to speak ill of the dead, should I? Well, missy, let me tell you. I don't give a piece of shit about the dead. And I don't give a piece of shit about your bloody mother. I happen to know first-hand what a bitch Muriel was, so don't come all high and mighty on me. There's no law against speaking the truth.'

'What do you know about the truth? You wouldn't know the truth if it jumped up and smacked you in the gob.'

'Oh, touchy-touchy all of a sudden, are we? OK. What'd you go and kill her for then, if she wasn't a bitch? The papers all said you said…'

'Shut up, will you?!' Stella jams her hands against her ears. 'I don't know what I'm doing here with you anyway. You're weird, you are. You always were weird. God, when I think…' Stella grabs her little suitcase and goes towards the door. 'I'm going,' she says, 'and I'm not coming back. I'd rather sleep on the streets than spend another minute in this stinking hole.'

Frank jumps up and pushes in front of Stella, standing with his back against the door, his arms outstretched across the opening.

'Not so fast, missy,' he says. 'Frankie hasn't finished yet.'

'Well, Stella has.' Stella tries to push past him but he stands his ground. 'Let me past,' she says.

'I'll let you past when I say, not when you say. Who the hell do you think you are?'

'For Christ's sake…'

'That's right, you're going to need Christ before I'm finished with you, you little bitch, you nasty little murderer! What kind of person is it that kills their own mother, eh? I ask you, what kind of person is it who goes and does something like that?' Frank prods his finger in front of Stella's face. She can smell his breath again, and feels droplets of his spittle landing on her face.

'What is it you want?' Stella says, backing off, 'I haven't got anything. I've no money, nothing…'

'I don't want bloody money! What makes you think I want money?'

'Well, what do you want?'

'I told you, there's something I have to talk to you about. It's in both our interests. Trust me.'

'Something? Like what? Why not just say it here and now and get it over and done with? Then we can go our separate ways. I want to get on with my life, Frank. I mean that. I actually just want to get on with my life.'

34

'Look, Stella,' Frank says, 'a lot's happened. You and me, we're on the same side. We shouldn't be fighting. We've got to trust each other. Or we're both in the shit.'

'It's you that's fighting. I'm not fighting.'

'Come with me to the Beach Hut and I'll explain. You have to see for yourself,' Frank says. 'We'll go up to the Beach Hut and get it all sorted out.'

Stella is suddenly very weary. She'd intended to get started on a whole new life. And instead…this. More of the same. More of the bloody same.

'Tomorrow,' she says, 'tomorrow, when it's light. We'll go to the Beach Hut. But please, get out of the way of the door. I'm all in. Let's just leave it for now. I'm absolutely dropping.'

Chapter Seven

That first night, in the cold of her grandmother's abandoned and derelict lodging house, Stella spends crouched on the stairs drifting in and out of sleep. Frank is somewhere on the first floor, probably in his old room, but Stella didn't know where, and is too weary to care. He'd smirked as he locked the porch door from the inside and shoved the key back into his trouser pocket. He'd gazed at Stella for a long moment before trudging up the stairs. She'd kept her eyes closed, her breathing steady and her arms round the suitcase.

Frank may not have realised it, but Stella was ready for anything. Then he was gone and Stella spent a long time listening to him pacing about upstairs, back and forth, back and forth, like he couldn't settle either, not until the early hours. Something was eating him. Stella didn't know what. She was thirsty, so thirsty, but there was no water to be had and she had to get used to it. No electricity, no light, no nothing except the smell of the past that seemed to renew its intensity with every pacing footstep of Frank's on the floor above.

Morning, and here's Frank standing beside Stella on the stairs, shining the torch into her eyes.

'Wakey, wakey,' he says, his hand nudging into her shoulder.

Stella flinches and stands up, her back stiff, her neck aching. Strategy in place after the long night.

'Can't you pull some of these boards off, Frank?' she says in a small voice, 'Let some light in?'

Frank shakes his head. 'Not a good idea, missy,' he says, 'not a good idea at all.'

'But this dark's depressing.'

Frank shakes his head again. 'People will see. We don't want all and sundry nebbing in now, do we? Seeing that we're in here. They'll have you back inside for breaking and entering.' Frank laughs. 'And bang goes your parole! There's no point anyway,' he adds, 'we're off to the Beach Hut. Remember?'

'Well, the back, then,' Stella says. 'Pull the boards off at the back. Nobody can see in there. Go on, Frank, please – for me. I'm getting claustrophobia. And I'm not on parole.'

'Alright. Have it your way.' Frank sighs. He clumps down the rest of the stairs and opens the door of the room that was Ruby Willoughby's.

'Not that one,' Stella says. Too late. Frank's already gone in, he's opening the sash and banging at the plywood board with his fist.

Stella stays standing in the doorway, another threshold she doesn't want to cross. It's important to sound normal and act normal. But now she's breathing in her grandmother, breathing in rose water, rouge, laudanum.

'You'll need more than your fist,' Stella manages to say, still hovering in the doorway. Is Grandma Willoughby dead? How could she have died without Stella knowing, without her having some kind of feeling?

Frank has produced some tool from his pocket. It's the Swiss Army knife, and he's prising the board off the window with it. The plywood cracks and splits, and eventually gives way. When the pale morning light comes in, Stella has wandered into the room and is staring at the bed she used to share with Grandma Willoughby. It's covered by a large sheet of the sort decorators use, but it's all stained and there are clusters of rodent droppings piled up in the dips.

'Nice bed for you there,' says Frank, 'just like old times, eh?'

Stella hadn't intended to think of old times and she's not going to start now. She goes back towards the door, but Frank is pulling off the top sheet, letting it fall to the floor in a cloud of dried droppings and dust. Underneath, the paisley patterned eiderdown is good as new. But the air's old and full of dust, dust that accumulates in thick woollen blankets, starched cotton sheets, feather pillows, dust that accentuates the absence of a person.

'There you are,' Frank says, 'a lovely comfy bed, all made up. All nice and ready.'

In the unaccustomed light, Stella looks at Frank and sees him as if for the first time: a man grown older than she remembers him, his face gaunt and veiny. A grubby checked lumberjack shirt bulges round his swollen belly, his trousers are stained, greasy and shapeless – he's obviously been sleeping in them. He stinks of sour sweat. It's hard to believe this is Frank Fanshaw, the self-confessed ladies man who prided himself in looking dapper. His hair, once slicked and dark, has gone grey, thin, lank, and there's more than a week's worth of greying bristle over half the mottled skin of his face, the face of someone fond of a drink. Is that what's happened? Is that why he lost his job? It's hard to imagine that Stella had been so afraid of him. But back then she was just a bit bairn. He was a man. He had the authority that men had: big, bullying, overpowering, men who couldn't stand not getting their own way. He had to have what he wanted, like a spoilt kid. Only kids don't have that kind of power, do they, the power to demand? Kids don't even have the power to make themselves heard, let alone the power to say No.

Now Stella observes a frailty about Frank, a neediness she hadn't realised was so close to the surface. Either she's changed, or he has. Frank Fanshaw is no longer the monster Stella once took him to be. He's nothing but a pale, pathetic copy, a sad, lonely old man. But Stella must not let down her guard. Sad old man he may be, but right now he's got the power.

Frank Fanshaw has never belonged – not here, not anywhere – that's why he's never had enough to lose. Just one of Ruby Willoughby's lame dogs. Muriel had never approved of Stella living in a household full of Ruby's misfits, but there was nothing she could do after Stella was made a Ward of Court and Muriel was declared Unfit to look after her own daughter. In her turn, Stella had made the best of it. She'd had to learn how to handle the lonely men who came and went through Ruby's doors. They weren't all like Frank, and he was the only one who'd stayed any length of time. But it was through Frank that Stella learned how not to rock the boat.

Frank stares at Stella, like he always did. She avoids his rheumy eyes and sees now he's a man who got himself lost a long time ago.

She looks at his hands, those big, reddened, callused hands. Those hands that grabbed her and gripped her and held her. Hands that pushed her head down and held it there and kept it there until she thought she would be sick. Now they're the hands of someone desperately clinging onto the thinnest of ledges.

What does he want? Surely he's too old and weary to be thinking about sexual favours. His hands are filthy, his nails bitten to the quick. On his feet, the same old cracked and dusty black boots, steel toecaps showing through where the leather has worn away, laces kept together with knots. Stella takes it all in: she could almost feel sorry for him. But she won't forget he's got that Swiss Army knife, and who knows what else. Stella knows Frank well enough to keep that in mind, to remember he doesn't like his desires thwarted. He's told her often enough, the one thing he can't abide, people not doing what they're told. He's a big man. Stella needs to be wary, needs to find out what he wants, why he's come to this derelict place. She forces herself to look directly into Frank's eyes. They're bloodshot and yellowing, like the nicotine stains on his fingers, like his filthy teeth.

'Just what is it you're doing here, Frank?' she says, 'I really don't understand why you're here, of all places. Haven't you got a life of your own to go to?'

Stella has said the wrong thing. As soon as the words leave her mouth, she knows she's said the wrong thing.

'A life of my own?' Frank sounds incredulous. He snorts briefly and shakes his head. 'My God. You people. You just don't get it, do you?'

'Get what, Frank?'

'How the hell do you expect me to have "a life of my own" – as you put it – after what your precious bloody grandmother did to me? After what your filthy bitch of a mother put me through? You're unbelievable, you lot, you really are.' Frank slumps down on the bed and sits with his head in his hands. 'I hope Ruby Willoughby rots in hell,' he says after a few moments, 'which is better than she deserves.' Frank splutters something else but Stella can't make out what it is.

'You're not making much sense, Frank,' Stella says. She's not sure if he is angry or crying or both or neither.

'Why am I here, you ask. Because here is as good a place as anywhere, that's why.' He bounces a few times on the bed. 'Mattress good as new,' he says, patting a place next to him, 'Howay, bonnie lass. C'mon, try it.'

He's changed his tune. That's what he does, that's how he puts you off guard. Stella's remembering it all now. She truly should not have risked coming back to this place. Frank shuffles further back on the bed, puts his head on one side, patting the space beside him.

'While we're here, might as well make the most of it, eh, bonnie lass? What do you say, eh?'

The thin October light in the room now strikes Stella as eerie. But no, she must not think like that. It's daylight out there. She needs to be practical. The street lamp in the back lane is still on, so it must be very early. Stella goes over to the dressing table – Grandma Willoughby's since she was a girl. Stella sits down on the stool and tilts the mirror back a bit so she doesn't have to look into it.

Stella Moon is afraid of mirrors. She knows how they can swallow you up.

Every night without fail, Grandma Willoughby sat Stella down in front of this very mirror to brush her hair a hundred strokes, not one more, not one less. Stella's tightly spiralled, flame-red hair was a curse, she said, nothing but a curse. A cross she would have to bear forever and the least she could do was keep it clean, keep it brushed, it would be fatal to let that ugly mop get the upper hand. A hundred strokes, every night, then the whole lot done into tight plaits piled up and fastened on the top of Stella's head with as many Kirby grips as it took to keep them in place. The roots pulled and ached all night, but that was a small price to pay, according to Grandma Willoughby, to stop that awful hair taking over. Stella always had to grope her way to the stool with her eyes closed for fear of catching sight of her reflection in the mirror. Or worse than seeing herself was the chance that the mirror would be blank, that it would be empty, that there would be no reflection in there at all. So Stella kept her eyes tight-closed. Impatient as always, Grandma Willoughby pushed Stella down onto the stool by her shoulders and began brushing with long strong strokes.

'One, two, three, four…count out loud, our Stella, one hundred times…five, six, seven, eight…' One by one, Stella counted the strokes, certain that at any moment she could be sucked into the mirror and transported to whichever hateful place it is that mirrors take you. Stella's hands gripped tightly, one on either side of the stool. When Grandma Willoughby insisted Stella open her eyes and stop being stupid, Stella became an expert at opening them but seeing nothing. She discovered that all you need to do is look into the middle distance; everything is out of focus and, after a short while, it's all one single blur.

Now Stella straightens up the mirror, her eyes wide open. She knows Frank is sprawled across the bed behind her, his belt undone, his right hand moving rhythmically inside his trousers. But she doesn't see him. He thinks she's watching him but she's not. Instead, it's Marcia – Marcia's face – Marcia that looks out at her from the mirror. Stella hears Marcia's voice, a soft voice, almost a whisper, 'You alright, hon?'

On the dressing table – focus, Stella, focus. Grandma Willoughby's hairbrush, its spiral of bristles, the worn wooden handle, varnish peeling off, a few grey hairs. Stella picks up the brush, pulls her hair free of the elastic band and begins brushing, one, two, three, four. The lavender and rosewater smell of her grandmother fills the room. Five, six, seven, eight. A musty, scalpy smell from the brush. Nine, ten, eleven, twelve. Her grandmother's left hand resting on Stella's shoulder.

Frank's moans bring Stella back to the present. She puts the brush down and backs away from the mirror. She needs to say something. Act normal.

'Has my grandmother died, then? How come nobody told me?' Stella turns and looks directly at Frank, who is now propped up on his elbows on the bed, his erection obvious inside his trousers. He rubs his palm on his crotch in a circular motion. She moves

41

towards the door. She remembers the porch door is locked from the inside. He has the key in his trouser pocket.

Frank pats the bed again, undoes his flies, exposes his penis.

'Howay,' he says, touching himself, 'never you mind about the old lady, we'll find her after. Just you come on over here. Come on. For old times' sake. Make an old man happy.'

'Leave it out, Frank,' Stella shakes her head. 'Do it yourself. Looks to me you're pretty good at it.'

Stella, still standing in the doorway, can't quite believe how easy it is to stand up to him. But she's on her guard still.

'All that's in the past, Frank,' she hears herself say, as if from far away.

'You know how to make an old man happy, bonny lass, don't pretend you've forgot...'

Frank shuffles his trousers down so his erect penis is fully exposed. He puts his hand around it and pulls back the foreskin. She knows it's the wrong thing to do but she looks away.

'Don't, Frank,' she says. She can smell its ugly, filthy smell from where she is standing. She closes her eyes and breathes without breathing, the same old sick feeling welling.

'Ah, now I get it,' Frank nods, 'seven years down among the women turned your head, has it? Now, I don't mind that, I don't mind that at all. In fact...'

'Leave it out, I said. I'm not that child any more. I stopped being that child the moment I killed my mother.'

Stella's hand is resting on the door. She could slam it shut and lock it from the passage side before Frank could even get off the bed, he'd be tripping over, his trousers round his ankles. Stella could get away, she'd have to smash the glass in the porch door and climb through, but she could do that, make a run for it. He's clearly still after the sordid stuff – she'd be better off getting away while she can. But no, he's moaning, he's finishing. She doesn't look. She hears him fumbling with his clothes, zipping himself up.

'You shouldn't have looked the other way,' Frank says, shaking his head. 'You know that's bad. Frank likes Stella to see what he's doing... Frankie likes little Stella to watch. But the naughty girl

42

was looking the other way. The naughty girl might have to have her bottom smacked... Frankie's going to have to think what to do about that.'

Carry on as normal, Stella. As if everything was totally and completely normal. It's the only way.

'How do you find out if somebody's died, Frank? There must be a way...'

'Old Mrs W? As it happens, I knocked Mr Cohen Thursday,' Frank says, doing up his belt, 'but I'm none the wiser. Said he didn't know where she'd gone. One minute there, the next, vanished. "Looked like a death, I'm sorry to say," was what the man said. A few weeks after, the council comes and puts these boards up, and them bits of glass along the back wall. They do that, apparently, when somebody's died. Or so Mr Cohen said.'

'Oh. What about the Carsons? Did you ask Mrs Carson?'

'Old bag told me to mind my own business. Slammed the door in my face. Stinking old crone. Who does she think she is?'

Stella will tread carefully. Frank doesn't like being shut out. Especially doesn't like women getting the upper hand.

'Frank,' she says, 'see if you can get that board off the back kitchen window?'

'Aye. If it'll make you happy. But we're not staying long, mind. Beach Hut. Remember.'

He hasn't got a clue, has he? Stella shrinks as he comes towards her, but all he does is tousle her hair as though she's six again.

'This house must be somebody's,' Stella says, standing back for Frank to go through the door, 'if my grandmother's died. Or maybe she's sold it. I wonder whose house it is now?'

Stella can't believe her grandmother is no longer alive. She would have known. Surely.

She lingers a moment longer in the doorway and looks back into the room. From this safe distance, she dares to look at the big oak wardrobe, with its full-length mirror, the diagonal crack right across the glass. Stella made that crack. She made it the day her grandfather died. Stupid kid, she thought she could hide in a crack in the mirror and no-one would find out what she'd done.

43

Marcia. It's going wrong. It's all going wrong. This isn't how it was meant to be. This isn't what you meant for me.

Follow Frank into the back kitchen, Stella. Then get away as soon as you can. Leave the past alone. Leave this house alone. Go away and never come back. Do things right, like Marcia said.

In the back kitchen, Frank has opened the window and is using the tool to lever off the board.

'Ah, light,' he says, 'that's better. This place was giving me the heebie jeebies. Starting to give me the creeps. Like old Ma Willoughby's watching through the walls.'

'How about getting us something to eat, Frank?' Stella says, 'I don't much feel like going out, not just yet. I must look a right sight.' Stella puts her hands to her head and tries to flatten down her half-brushed hair.

'The Beach Hut,' he says. 'You said we could go to the Beach Hut.'

'Can we go in a bit?' Stella says, 'I'm starving. Get us something to eat first, Frank? I'll tidy myself up while you go. I don't want to go out looking like this.'

Frank wrenches the last of the board free from the window, turns and looks at Stella. The light falls on her thin, pale face, her hair half brushed and all over the place, Muriel's faded clothes hanging off her. She's far too thin, a proper little waif. To think, that little thing's got it in her to murder somebody.

Stella thinks she sees a change in Frank's face. But no, he's not to be trusted. Be careful, Stella.

'Anything to oblige,' Frank says, putting the tool back in his pocket and wiping his hands on his trousers. 'I'll go and get us some breakfast. Then Beach Hut, right?'

'Right. Get Vienna buns and butter and a bit of ham and... some pease pudding. My God, Frank, I didn't realise till now how much I'd missed all those. And something to drink. Orange juice,' Stella says, her voice suddenly light. 'Not the squash, the real stuff. Have you got money? I'll pay you back, I can pay you back.' She's really starving now she comes to think about food. And so very thirsty. 'Go on, Frank, be as quick as you can, before I starve to death. I'll make us a fire, I'll warm the place up. It'll be cozy, like old times,' she says. She rubs her hands together like an excited child. Frank will want to please her.

But the minute he's gone, Stella reaches into the cupboard under the stairs, right there above the door and unhooks the secret key. There's a second bunch of keys there as well. She takes those too. She picks up the suitcase, looks around, undoes the lock on the porch and lets herself out of the house. Before the door slams shut behind her, Stella is running across the road.

Chapter Eight

Stella is jittering from foot to foot at the bus stop, praying the bus comes before creepy Frank Fanshaw comes back with the food and twigs she's done a runner. What an idiot, falling for that cheap little trick. Or else he's desperate. For what? Sex? Surely not only. He'll come looking for Stella, bound to. That's what he's like. Hates people having one over on him. But it all depends what he wants, and Stella hasn't worked out what that is. He's been acting restrained; not normal for him and therefore dangerous. He's let her get away once. There won't be a second time. She needs to get well away.

Frank Fanshaw is the past and he can stay there. Stella Moon is moving forward – moving forward in her new life. She will put Frank to one side and concentrate on more important things. Focus. Hurry up bus.

Main thing: Grandma Willoughby. Find out what's happened: when she died – no, whether she's died. Maybe she hasn't died at all. Anything could have happened in seven years. Ten, if you count the three before, when Stella was in the convalescent place and the children's home. Grandma Willoughby is the only family Stella's got, anyway. You'd think she'd have got used to being without her grandmother, after all those years. She had got used to it. She'd been coping fine. It's just this coming back to Newcastle, stirring everything up. And Frank being at the house, with whatever unfinished business, and him trying to rope her in, pull her back to the very place she thought she'd got away from. She'd never expected he'd be there, not in a million years.

Stella, you need to focus on practicalities. Don't start letting memories get the better of you. So before Grandma Willoughby: accommodation, get that sorted.

Stella is starting again, doing things by the book, like she promised Marcia. She'll go to the Probation. Number one priority is the probation/accommodation. That Clara who answered the phone when Stella rang from London said she could definitely get her a hostel place. Not ideal, but it'd do for now; it'll have to do, better than a kick up the arse. Here comes the 61. That'll get her into town. Away from the horrible house. Away from Frank Fanshaw.

Stella gets on the bus, pays the fare, goes straight up to the top deck and lights up a Number Six from Frank's packet using Grandpa Worthy's Zippo. She smiles to herself as she flips the lighter shut and exhales. She blows some smoke rings, watches out the window. As the bus goes by the pork shop, Stella sees Frank just going in, going for the ham and the pease pudding, the Co-Op package with the buns and butter under his arm and a bottle of Brown Ale sticking one out of each jacket pocket. Stella could just fancy a nice ham sandwich. But she doesn't fancy all what goes along with it. She never wants to set eyes on Frank Fanshaw again. But this Number Six, it's good. Thanks, Frank.

Stella rummages in the suitcase and pulls out the keys from the boarding house, both lots. A Yale on its own, on a bit of baler twine – boarding house, front door, she recognises it. She unzips her purse and stuffs it in. Hopes she won't need it again. But just in case. The second bunch has six keys in all, including two deadlocks. Stella has no idea what these are for. She fingers them one by one. Padlocks, maybe. The garage, the netty, can't be the coalhouse. Stella looks at them again before dropping the bunch back into the suitcase and clipping it shut. She might as well hang onto them. Just in case.

Stella lights another cigarette, she blows some more smoke rings and she watches through the window. There's a funny little sense of freedom, just for a moment. Even a bit of sun is coming through. People. Ordinary people, doing ordinary morning things – cycling to work, dragging kids to school, queuing up at Greggs to buy stuff for their bait. Stella could murder a hot sausage roll. She's out now. She can do as many ordinary things as she pleases. Ordinary things suddenly look strange, odd and peculiar, not quite of this world, as though Stella is seeing them for the first time, like she's an alien just landed. She'll have to get used to this. Disorientation. Marcia had warned her coming out wasn't a bed of roses and had advised her just to focus on the practical things when the world started looking weird, which it would, inevitably, Marcia said. You're right, Marcia, the world's looking really weird but it's as it's meant to be – there's nothing actually weird about it.

Focus on the keys, Stella, think about the keys. The Beach Hut. These are the keys for the Beach Hut. Stella fishes the bunch out of the suitcase again. Has she got the guts to go to the Beach Hut? Probably not – certainly not now, maybe not ever. Quite apart from slimy Frank Fanshaw evidently desperate to get her there… Well, Frankie boy, you can go and whistle. Stella Moon is going to the Probation, and she's going to get proper accommodation sorted. From now on, she's going to do everything by the book. And she's avoiding that Beach Hut like it was housing the plague.

Stella hasn't been back to the Beach Hut, not since the day Muriel died. She thought she could say that without flinching – 'the day Muriel died' – thanks to Marcia's coaching. 'The day my mother died.' She'd repeated those words again and again for Marcia – she thought they'd lost their force. 'The day Muriel died.' Marcia says they're just words and shapes – letters of the alphabet. Stella had felt a small sense of triumph as she'd reeled the words off for Marcia, almost chanting. She'd smiled and smiled afterwards, a massive sense of pride. But now, 'the day my mother died,' the very thought of those words, and Stella's smile stops before her muscles move. She's not sure any more that trying to empty words of their meaning is altogether a good thing. And the words are in fact no longer empty, if they have ever been. And now she notices there's a strange feel to the keys she's turning over in her hands, a tingling feeling, a vibration, a kind of current. She must put the keys away, put them away now. Put them in the case and leave them there and don't touch them. Stella fumbles to get the little case open, her thoughts crowding in. The case won't open. The clasps are stuck.

The keys belong to Muriel.

Muriel is dead.

You killed her, Stella.

You killed your own mother.

Oh, yes, you've done your time for it, you might well have paid your dues. But time is never going to be enough, is it? You'll never pay the full price for what you've done, not ever. The guilt and the shame of it will be yours for always, Stella Moon. It will shrink you, make you smaller, smaller, smaller and smaller till you are no more than the size of a lentil.

Under Stella's shaking hands, the clasps on the suitcase suddenly ping open. She stuffs the keys in and clamps the suitcase shut again. She's sweating. Nauseous. She'll have get off the bus.

Stella presses the bell and gets off the bus. She sits down on Byker Bridge, her back against the wall. It's better out in the air, even if it is cold and damp and noisy and stinks of traffic fumes. As soon as she feels a bit better, she'll walk the rest of the way into town. She'll be alright in a minute. People are passing, all looking like they're going somewhere with a purpose. No-one so much as casts a glance at Stella. She must look a sight. People must think she's a beggar. She should get up and start walking. But in a minute. Just a few more minutes and she'll be alright. Everyone is avoiding looking at her, like she's not there at all.

The police hadn't been interested in the whys and wherefores, only in the fact that Muriel was dead and that Stella had killed her. Stella had confessed, she'd made the voluntary statement, she'd told them everything she could remember. She'd signed her name at the bottom. And that was that.

Her eighteenth birthday. No longer a Ward of Court, Stella had come to the Beach Hut straight from the Children's Home. No Muriel. She'd panicked, run along the cliff path, the darkness closing in. Afterwards, night, she'd come back to the Beach Hut – she must have done – because that's where they came for her – a hand on her shoulder, a voice asking her what had happened, asking if she was alright. She'd been sitting by the stove, how long she'd been sitting by the stove she didn't know, the only light the glancing beam of the lighthouse on the Farnes, swing, swing, swinging through the black, diagonally across the walls.

The lighthouse – there for the safety of seafarers. Safety. What safety has there ever been for Stella Moon?

They said she'd phoned Emergency from the Coastguard telephone down by the dune path. Stella doesn't remember. They said she was hugging a small grey haversack, she wouldn't let go of it. Stella doesn't remember. They said all that was in the bag was an empty Kilner jar. They showed her the bag. Was the bag Muriel's? they kept asking. And the jar. Was that Muriel's? What was in the jar? Whose was the bag? What was the jar for? Stella didn't know. But it was important to Muriel and she'd kept it.

It was from the Beach Hut they took Stella away.

She could have kept on running, stumbling among stones, running all angles in the tipping sand. Run as fast as you can, as far as you can, for as long as you can – run away from yourself, go on, Stella, see if you can. Stella had stopped, she'd stood on the beach, looking out through the black to the drop of the cliff shining luminous under the moon, the white cliff that plunges vertical into the sea.

It was from the Beach Hut that they took Stella away.

Now, sitting on Byker Bridge, Stella hears not the sounds of a city coming alive in the morning, but the churning rage of the sea like it was on the day Muriel died.

Stand up, Stella. Stand up tall. You're on the bridge. Walk across the bridge and go to the Probation Service. They're expecting you. They will help you. Go on. Do it. Stand up and go.

Stella picks up the case and walks over Byker Bridge towards the city centre.

Marcia said it's normal for memory to blur and fade, to disappear altogether. Memory disappears for a purpose. Let sleeping dogs lie. What if memories come back? That's worse than when they disappear. Stella has learned not to listen to the screams of memory. Now it's memories' whispers she's finding it harder to ignore.

Stella may have the keys but she's not going to the Beach Hut, not with Frank, not with anyone. Frank can whistle. Stella's off to the Probation. Marcie will be proud of her, doing things by the book. Getting back on track.

Chapter Nine

It's strange how a place can become part of you, take root inside you and take possession of you, like an unwanted ghost. A place can, one day, be perfect and be everything you want it to be. But when it turns on you, there's no relief, no magic formula to exorcise the hold a place can have on you.

The Beach Hut had been in the family all Stella's life, and much of Muriel's. There were photographs – one of Muriel and Grandpa Worthy, with their sun hats on, lounging on stripy deck chairs on the veranda of the Beach Hut, grinning for the camera. Muriel is about ten years old, her bare, sun-browned legs swing over the bar of the chair. Whoever stuck that one into the album has written 'Happy Days' beside it, white ink on the thick black paper. Sometime after, the words have been scribbled over and then scratched out, but they still show through.

Another photograph – this one loose, creased, faded – Muriel, about fourteen, pouty, wearing a sundress, sitting with a handsome young beau, side-by-side on an upturned boat, the Beach Hut just visible on the dunes behind.

'Who's the hunk?' Stella had asked. 'Is it my dad?' She thought it might be because he looked like Clark Gable. From what Stella saw in pictures, a lot of young men in those days had the look of Clark Gable. Muriel had snatched the picture from Stella's hand.

'Don't be daft,' she said as she straightened the crumpled edges of the photograph. 'Don't be so bloody stupid.' Muriel looked at the photograph for a long time. 'It's only my brother,' she'd said eventually, shrugging and making a tight smile with her lips closed. 'It's only our Billy.' Stella had wanted another look at the picture, but Muriel wouldn't let her. Instead Muriel slipped the picture inside the back cover of the album and clapped the album shut.

Stella never saw that picture again. The next time Muriel was out and she'd looked in the album, the photograph was gone. Stella knew, though she wasn't supposed to know, Muriel's brother Billy had taken his own life when he was only twenty-seven, which must have been not long after the picture was taken. Grandma Willoughby said she would never forgive Muriel, not as long as she had breath in her body.

Then everything went upside down and no-one went to the Beach Hut any more. Grandpa Worthy took to his bed with the bad chest that would eventually kill him. All hands were needed on deck, Grandpa Worthy was not to be left by himself, not even for half a minute, even Muriel was needed to watch him and to help at the boarding house and even Muriel couldn't be galli-vanting off every second minute, shirking her duties and getting up to God knows what. The Beach Hut was left on its own, with Muriel more than content to be near her beloved father.

Then, after Grandpa Worthy passed, the Beach Hut became the sole property of Ruby. She made it known it was hers and hers alone, nobody else's, and she wasn't having Muriel or anybody else taking liberties. Nobody was allowed to go there without Ruby's express permission. Especially not Muriel.

These keys that Stella now has are the keys for the Beach Hut, Stella's sure of that now – they used to hang in that secret place in the cupboard under the stairs where no-one but Ruby was supposed to set foot.

When Grandpa Worthy died, he left behind a whole basement full of materials and ledgers relating to his healing, his herbalism and his taxidermy – specimens in jars, and glass domes and locked tin boxes, instruments, chemicals, a dusty old manual of *Practical Taxidermy* bound in crumbling brown leather, which had belonged to his father and his before that. The whole lot was, by Grandpa Worthy's last Will and Testament, inherited by Muriel. But Ruby took it upon herself to dispose of the ledgers straight away. She said she wanted nothing of the sort. She wanted rid of everything, said she couldn't abide any of it. Morbid, it was, and quite beyond her why anybody in their right mind would hang on to the wizened remains of creatures long dead. Even so, she wouldn't allow Muriel – now its rightful owner – anywhere near. Until Muriel was in a position to take the whole lot away, it would remain in the cellar, strictly under lock and key. Ruby, as Executrix of her husband's Last Will and Testament, would dispose of whatever she wanted whenever she wanted, and as she saw fit.

But Grandpa Worthy was hardly cold in his grave when Ruby discovered the keys to the Cellar and the Beach Hut were going missing and Muriel, damn her, was taking liberties. With men. With that damned Frank Fanshaw. And with the stinking specimens.

It all blew up worse when poor Mrs Keating's baby was stolen from his pram outside the boarding house. A plainclothes policeman was stationed at the house for a time in case Mrs Keating's estranged husband should put in an appearance, but he never did, and the policeman eventually went away. After he left, Muriel was finally given her marching orders, told to get out and stay out, and to take the blasted stinking specimens with her, remove every one of them, every single one, and don't come back. Ruby declared she could no longer abide the reverence of rot, the worshipping of mutilated specimens in jars of stinking formaldehyde – it wasn't normal, it wasn't right. Indicative it was, indicative of Muriel's mentality, the warped mentality of a damn fool who couldn't let go, not of anything, not even the dead.

Muriel meant to hang on to as much as she could. Those specimens had meant something to her much-loved father and, him gone, they were the world to her. Muriel refused to leave the boarding house till she'd got the specimens organised. She locked herself in the basement, she packed and pickled and labelled for days on end. Then suddenly Muriel and Mr Fanshaw were emptying out the basement. Stella had sat on the stairs, watching them cart off all Muriel's carefully labelled jars and cases and boxes, dumping them into the back of an old munitions truck Mr Fanshaw had somehow got the loan of, leaving a trail of packing straw like in *The Babes in the Wood*. At the last moment, Mr Fanshaw had shoved Stella into the back of the truck along with the stinking specimens while he drove the whole lot clattering up the road to Embleton and dumped it at all angles outside the Beach Hut. Muriel would stay there and sod to bloody Ruby. Frank shrugged and left Muriel to carry it all in. He took Stella by the hand and helped her back into the truck. They drove back to Newcastle, more slowly, and in silence, Mr Fanshaw shaking his head and crunching the gears and occasionally scratching at his crotch.

So, contrary to Ruby Willoughby's wishes, Muriel stayed on at the Beach Hut, where she tackled the taxidermy with a renewed enthusiasm and had a new kitchen built with shelves for all the specimens and chemicals. But still Muriel kept on coming back to the boarding house, turning up unannounced and taking Stella away with her, trying to keep her. By then, Stella had gone right off the Beach Hut. It was creepy. She didn't like the smells of the chemicals and the dead animals hanging by their feet from the rafters with blood dripping out. She couldn't sleep, knowing there were wizened specimens of innards and jars full of eyes on the other side of the wall from where her bed was. She was scared to go into the new kitchen where she knew eyes could watch her. And Frank Fanshaw was often there, his braces dangling, his grubby vest sweaty, his underarm hair escaping like crippled spiders. Stella would be glad when Grandma Willoughby came storming up in the A35 and, without saying a word, she'd grab hold of Stella's wrist, manhandle her into the back seat of the car and fetch her straight back to Newcastle.

One day, out of the blue, a large brown envelope came through the post. Grandma Willoughby had stopped what she was doing, wiped her hands on the dishtowel and torn open the envelope.

'Right,' she said, 'Right. I'm going to put a stop to this whole blessed malarkey.'

'Have you got a bee in your bonnet?' Stella asked.

'You just wait and see,' Grandma Willoughby said. 'I've got a lot more than a blinking bee.'

Grandma Willoughby was always saying how she had right on her side. Now she was very pleased with herself and saying she had the full force of the law behind her. The Judge had agreed with her and had made an Order of the High Court of Justice. The Order said Stella was a Ward of Court. Grandma Willoughby waved the official paper in front of Stella.

'See,' she said, triumphant, 'it's all there in black and white. I'll fettle that Muriel if it's the last thing I do.' She'd folded the paper into four and put it back in its brown envelope. She put the envelope into her handbag.

'From now on, our Stella, the Judge says you've to stay put here with me. No more gallivanting off with Muriel to that Beach Hut. Is that understood?' Without waiting for a reply, Grandma Willoughby clicked the stiff black leather handbag shut.

Chapter Ten

That day, Grandma Willoughby cleared the breakfasts more quickly than usual. She bustled about, stuffing empty sacks and baskets and boxes into the back seat of the Austin. She ordered Stella to get in and be quick about it. She drove off at great speed with a determined look on her face and her hat at an angle – she'd been in such a rush of purpose she'd forgotten the hat-pin. Stella, squeezed in the back seat among the packaging, had watched her grandmother's set face in the rear-view mirror. She knew better than to ask questions. Grandma Willoughby was clearly not in the mood for talking. They sped up the Great North Road in silence.

After an hour, they were bumping too fast along the muddy track that goes along behind the stone cottages at Low Newton, round the corner, past the back of The Fisherman's Arms. With a scattering of stones, Grandmother Willoughby pulled up in the area where the fishing boats are kept in winter and where cars are not supposed to park. She yelled at Stella to get a move on and help her with the bags. She straightened her hat, locked the car, picked up as many packages as she could carry, and set off along the dune path with Stella stumbling behind carrying her own load, a sharp wind in their faces. There was nobody about. They wended their way through the dunes and through the little colony of wooden beach huts that stand here and there at angles, mostly closed up for the coming winter. Grandmother Willoughby puffed and panted up the last steep slope but didn't slow down. Stella followed.

When they got to the Beach Hut, Grandma Willoughby banged at the door. It was locked. She pulled a bunch of keys out of her pocket, shoved the big one into the deadlock and flung open the door so hard it banged against the wall and caused the whole place to shudder. Muriel was nowhere to be seen, though it was clear she was living there and was perhaps still about. Ruby went straight through to the kitchen and gave a grunt of satisfaction before scanning the shelves where Muriel kept all her jars and bottles. The smell turned Stella's stomach. She could hardly stand to be in there. In the front room, she looked around at Muriel's taxidermy materials, all laid out neatly. A dead swan hung by its scrawny legs from a meat hook attached to the ceiling, its throat cut and a basin of congealed blood with bits of feathers underneath collecting drips. A dismembered hare was pinned gaping open on a plywood board on the table, its bones in the process of being removed. A bloodied scalpel and an open jar marked Arsenic, POISON sat beside it. Coming through from the kitchen, Ruby cursed, readjusted her hat, picked up a lid and screwed it back on the arsenic jar. She breathed out loudly and threw the jar roughly into the sack she was holding open with the other hand.

Stella followed her into the bedroom. There was no sign of Muriel there either. The room smelt stuffy, of bedclothes that needed changing. The bed was a mess of sheets and blankets and the paraffin heater was on. Ruby turned it off and yanked the thin curtains back on their wires. Grey autumn light seeped into the room and made it look abandoned. Muriel's little travel clock that she took everywhere was on the bedside table, propped up in its case, saying ten to two and still ticking. In the other bedroom – the smaller room where Stella used to sleep – the bed had been stripped and Muriel's clothes were strewn all over. The window was open, the curtain billowing. Ruby banged the window shut and screwed it tight. She stormed about, picking up items of clothing and throwing them back down. Grandma Willoughby seemed to be looking for something, but Stella didn't know what. There was a pair of man-size wellies beside the front door, but Grandma Willoughby didn't seem to notice those. In the little bathroom she picked up some shaving things and both toothbrushes and threw them into the sack along with the poison.

'I'll set fire to the place,' she said. 'That'll fettle her. And Him. Whoever He is.' Grandma Willoughby knew fine well who He was.

But Ruby didn't set fire to the place, she just went round grabbing randomly at Muriel's taxidermy things – the dead swan and the hare included – and stuffed them at arm's length into the old coal sacks they'd brought.

'Get that basin emptied out, our Stella,' she said, kicking the enamel one that was catching the blood, 'and get a move on.' Ruby held a sack open with one hand and stuffed things in it with the other, all the while muttering and cursing. Bluebottles, disturbed from the dismembered bodies, buzzed against the skylight.

Stella couldn't lift up the enamel basin; it was stuck to the floor. When she finally pulled it away, it came unstuck with a jerk and semi-congealed blood splashed over the edge and onto her hand. Her instinct was to drop the whole thing, but she didn't dare let go of it. She held the basin out at out arm's length, holding her breath, trying not to breathe in the smell of the blood or feel the touch of it on her hand. It was like in *Treasure Island* where you're given the Black Spot and then you die. A horrid feeling swept over her – just for a moment – a horrid, horrid feeling. Then it passed. Stella went into the lean-to and turned on the tap. There was no water. She stood there, helpless. A loud sigh and Grandma Willoughby stomped in, dumping the sack she was carrying at the door.

'For pity's sake, our Stella, get your wits about you,' she said as she snatched the basin from Stella's hands, now splashing more of its vile contents on the floor. 'See to it you get that floor wiped,' she commanded as she wrenched open the back door and threw the whole basin and everything in it outside so it disappeared among the marram grass and dead bracken. Slamming the door shut again, Grandma Willoughby turned the key in the lock, removed it and shoved it deep into her coat pocket. 'And you can put your face straight, our Stella, or there'll be Trouble,' she said.

Stella watched Grandma Willoughby unfold a copy of the Court Order and fix it on the wall above the stove. She fixed it with a nail in each corner and she hammered them in with the thick end of the poker. Then she stuck it round with parcel tape for good measure.

'Come along, our Stella,' she said, gathering up the sacks and baskets and boxes she'd stuffed all the paraphernalia in and dumped them on the creaky veranda outside. 'Come along, and get a move on.' They left the sacks and baskets and boxes there, leaking blood and formalin. The only thing Grandma Willoughby brought away with her that day was a small Kilner jar with some hateful wizened specimen in. She'd stopped on the way to the car, taken it out of her bag as though she meant to throw it into the hedge, but she hesitated and put it back in her bag. She grabbed Stella by the wrist and pulled her all the way back to the car.

'That's that,' Grandma Willoughby said with finality as she started the engine. But of course it wasn't. And Stella had to travel all the way home with the congealed blood still on her hand.

The Beach Hut. Stella hasn't thought of any of that for years. She has the keys for the Beach Hut, but she won't go there. Not yet. Not with that Frank Fanshaw panting after her, in that way he does.

Clutching the suitcase, Stella wonders why Frank was waiting for her at the boarding house, why Frank wants to go to the Beach Hut, why he wants Stella to go with him.

Stella opens her case and feels around for the envelope from the prison. She pulls out the introductory letter to the social worker. Newcastle upon Tyne Probation Service, it says at the top. She'll have to ring that Clara up again. Ask for more concrete help. She's entitled. Marcia said. Entitled. Don't forget, Stella. They're expecting you. You're entitled.

Chapter Eleven

Stella, standing outside the YWCA in Clayton Street, waits for Probation Officer Gareth Davies to show up. It's cold and she pulls the thin cardy about her, but it's damp and she can't get warm. They'd said she could wait inside if she wanted, but Stella would rather wait out here. She shifts from foot to foot, one either side of the little blue suitcase, her bare feet grubby and wet in the gold lamé sandals. It's October and these shoes are for summer. Marcia should not have let her get away with wearing them. Stella has proper clothes in the case but there's nowhere to get changed. Plus there's a part of her that still doesn't want to put the proper things on, a part of her that wants to keep these clothes on, stupid as they are. Marcia would have understood that, bless her.

On the phone the social worker man said he'd be straight over, but there's no sign of him. Maybe Stella's in the wrong place? She might have got it wrong. The place, the time, the date – anything – she could have got something, anything wrong. Stella looks around. No. This is the YWCA. This must be right. This is where she's meant to be. She'll wait a bit longer and see if he comes. If he doesn't come, Stella will make a new plan, decide what to do. Meanwhile, she lights a Number Six – the last of Frank's. She crumples the empty packet in the palm of her hand and chucks it into the gutter, feeling a surge of guilt. Stella, the kid, in big trouble for throwing litter. She should pick it up, pick it up now, you bend down and you pick that up right now, our Stella. Stella can't understand why she's thrown it down, why she can't pick it up, why she's acting like a person she knows she's not. It can't seem to be any other way. Where's this Gareth man? Stella's suddenly not sure she wants to wait any longer in this place.

Stella used to stand right here, right on this spot, on the Wednesdays Grandma Willoughby did her Sittings, and Muriel was allowed to pick her up from the dancing class. Stella half liked those days and half hated them. Muriel was never on time and Stella could never be certain she would come at all. She'd wait and wait, yet she might end up having to get the bus, or walk back to Grandma Willoughby's by herself. If it was dark or wet, they might send Mr Fanshaw. Stella would much rather walk alone in the dark than go in the car with Frank Fanshaw.

This place doesn't have pleasant memories for Stella. She could have gone directly to the Probation Office – the receptionist, Clara, had suggested it – but Stella had found herself holding out to meet the Probation Officer at the YWCA. She couldn't explain it to herself, how it was she found herself doing things she didn't want to do, saying things she didn't believe in. But it happened all the time. And now she's waiting here for the man from the Probation and she's trying not to think about all those Wednesdays she helped with the preparations for the Sittings – cleaning out the grate, setting the fire with newspaper and kindling, pulling the little green baize card table into the middle of the room, covering it with the starched white cloth, and lining up the pairs of little white cotton gloves along the sideboard. Then, when all that was done, she was allowed to go off to the dancing class, and afterwards, there'd be her mother, come to fetch her home. And Grandma Willoughby and her Ladies might still be at it when Stella and Muriel got back. Or they'd be massing in the passage, doing up their bristly coats that smelt of mothballs, progging in their hat-pins, murmuring insights, nodding, nodding, nodding, another successful session over. Muriel had no time for any of it. She'd drop Stella off, a quick peck on the cheek, and she'd be gone, the garden gate swinging behind her.

Stella remembers little about her childhood, hardly anything compared to Marcia who could, and did, reel off tale after tale of what life was like in the Caribbean before her family brought her to London when she was fifteen. That was 1958, when Stella was only five. Marcia had Stella enraptured with her stories and Stella, hearing them in all their colourful detail, could only wonder how it was that so much of her own past was either only sketched out in black and white, or had been entirely forgotten.

'Maybe it's not lost,' Marcia used to joke, 'just temporarily mislaid.' Marcia remembered everything, not just events, but loads of minute detail, before, during and after. Her stories were full of sounds, tastes and smells. They transported Stella far away to distant places and right into the heart of Marcia's life. Marcia brought the world alive. She brought Stella alive. The sad stories made Stella cry, and Stella wasn't one for crying.

'They're only stories, Stell,' Marcia would say, rocking with laughter. 'Don't believe a word I say! They're stories, I make them up as I go along... C'mon honey, see the funny side...'

Looking down at her cold feet in the lamé slippers, Stella thinks about her mother. Part of her shrinks from any kind of remembering, but there's another part that, since she's been out, seems to want to build up a picture, a more complete picture of Muriel, wants to find out how Stella fits into that picture, if anywhere.

'Everyone wants to fit in, to find their place, to belong somewhere,' Marcia said. 'You can't spend your whole life on the outside, looking in.'

Sometimes Stella thought she couldn't wait to grow up, couldn't wait to take her rightful place in Muriel's magical shoes. Other times she wasn't so sure, she was never exactly sure what being grown up might mean for her, beyond a longing for the lovely things. And now, the gold lamé slippers with the kitten heels, the lovely slinky silk dress and the lacy sage cardy – they're all Stella's. The little blue honeymoon case. All hers. There was a time when Stella would have sold her soul for those slippers. It's strange how longing turns inside out when it's satisfied...

Stella wishes the Gareth man would get a move on. She's fed up waiting in the cold outside the YWCA. She wouldn't have worn these clothes if she'd known how cold it was going to be. She wouldn't have come back to this place if she'd known it was going to drag her backwards and make her remember all the things she preferred to forget.

Let the thoughts wash over you, Stella. Acknowledge them then let them pass, let them go on their way.

But Marcia hadn't killed a person. Marcia didn't know what it was like to be stuck in that place where you had killed someone, and that person still had a hold on you like you were stuck to them and they wouldn't let go and they'd been there so long they were a part of you and they were eating away, eating away all the time inside of you, because that's what happens when you kill someone, they're yours forever, you're tied to them, you can never let go. No, Marcia didn't know any of that. And when that person is your mother and you can't work out where it went wrong and why it went wrong and you try and you try, but your memory's fucked and you're fucked and there's nothing makes any sense any more...

Calm down, Stella. The man from the Probation will be here any minute, you don't want him to think you are some kind of Crazy.

'Your shadow's bigger than you are,' Marcia says. 'It can be walking right in front of you. But that's only because the sun's behind.'

Little Stella, just thirteen, waited here for Muriel to collect her from the dancing class.

Muriel's always late. Muriel's always smartly dressed. Muriel, so different from other people's mothers who wear clothes you never even notice. Muriel stands out, doesn't like to be the same as anyone, doesn't like even to be the same as herself.

Little Stella, waiting, plays a game with herself: What will Muriel look like this time? The scarlet lipstick – they colour it with cochineal, made from beetles' blood – beige trench coat, belted tight at the waist, open at the neck, accentuates Muriel's breasts and makes men look; Muriel, her head held high, never a hair out of place. Pretending not to notice. Wafts of Muriel, the faintest hint of Nina Ricci. Little Stella, holding the blue suitcase tight between her feet, uses both hands to flatten down her own hair. She needn't worry. Grandma Willoughby has tied it back tight in a ponytail with a stiff Alice band at the front for good measure. It's digging into Stella's skull, pulling her hair at the roots. Stella daren't touch it for fear of getting her wild hair all over the place and out of control and hell to pay. Stella stands up straight, an invisible string pulls from the top of her head like a marionette. She wishes she were taller. Like Muriel.

Muriel leaning against a grand piano in an up-market night-club, lights dimmed and candles. She's wearing a floor-length slinky dress – deep purple and satiny – that clings on Muriel's curves and falls away in soft folds, trailing behind her across the polished floor. A gesture to the pianist with her long ciga-rette holder, the sweet, sweet scent of the smoke from the Balkan Sobranie, it curls elegantly towards the ceiling. The pianist, in a dinner suit and a black bow tie, slicked-back hair, shiny, well-de-fined eyebrows, thin moustache and a faint blue shadow across his chin. He tugs once at each shirt cuff, flicks his tails and takes his seat at the piano. He looks at Muriel. She half closes her eyes and starts to sing in that special husky voice she saves for telephones and parties. The piano plinks in to join her in the fourth bar.

Little Stella, so very proud to have such a mother: elegant, sensual, remote, beautiful. And waiting outside the dancing class that day, Stella had been certain Muriel was soon going to be very proud of her: Stella had been awarded the treasured dancing certificate, has it tucked away safe inside the pocket of the little blue suitcase. Awarded to Stella Moon, it says, Grade One, with Merit. Stella, jigging about from foot to foot, can hardly wait for Muriel to get there.

But that was the day everything turned inside out. Muriel was unusually late, even for her. Stella had begun to wonder if her mother was coming at all, or would it be the vile Frank Fanshaw? Please, God, if you're real and if you care about me, don't let it be Frank Fanshaw. Stella had waited and waited. A trolley bus swished by, squeaking on its cables, drizzle visible in the headlamps. An old man shuffled past, wheezing like poor Grandpa Worthy, confined to his bed with emphysema of the lungs, brought on by years down the pit breathing in filth and living in damp. Then there was a woman, expecting, enormous, waddling, like poor Mrs Keating, a rattling bag of nerves Grandma Willoughby said, cursing the big Silver Cross pram that blocked the hall at the Boarding House.

That day, when Muriel eventually came striding towards Stella, it was obvious something was wrong. Already she was shouting for Stella to stand up straight, or did she want to end up like Quasimodo? And Muriel didn't have the trench coat on. Or the lipstick. And her hair was a mess. How could Stella have been so wrong? Muriel's hair had escaped from its pins on one side and was flapping with wet. With one hand Muriel caught hold of Stella roughly by the wrist and with the other she picked up the case. She pulled Stella across the road to the bus stop. One car had to screech to a halt to let them get by and the driver leaned heavily on the horn. Muriel ignored him. Muriel walked fast along past the shops and all the way to the bus stop, pulling Stella behind her. Stella didn't dare mention that she needed the toilet. And she didn't dare mention about the certificate. When they got off the bus, Muriel grabbed at Stella's wrist again but she let go half way across the road. Stella had to run to keep up, Muriel was rushing so fast back to the house. Stella soon found out why. Back at the boarding house, Muriel's precious father lay dying.

There's a young man talking to Stella, he's touching her on the shoulder, he's looking into her face and asking if she's alright. He's saying his name is Gareth Davies, he's holding out his hand. Stella has some trouble re-orienting herself. She looks at him. He has black hair and blue eyes with thick lashes. He's wearing a suit but the tie's a bit loose and his top button's undone. Stella has some trouble finding her voice.

'I'm sorry', she manages to say. 'Yes, yes, I'm Stella.' She holds out a damp, cold hand.

Chapter Twelve

Stella and Gareth are sitting in Mark Toney's in Grainger Street. He's bought two milky coffees and produced an open packet of Garibaldis from his bashed leather briefcase. He's been over the road to buy cigarettes for Stella. He came back with twenty B&H, the classy kind. Stella is smoking. Gareth is eating biscuits, leaning back politely.

Sometimes Stella has trouble speaking, the words don't or won't come – it's just how she is. Today is one of those days. Five minutes after she's sat down with the Probation Officer, all thoughts have congealed inside her, like old gravy. She's stuck in the day her grandfather died, like he's claimed her and is not letting go.

Sitting in Mark Toney's on the plastic padded bench seat, warming her hands round the coffee mug, Stella has given up trying to talk. Strangely, the Gareth man seems not to mind. Is he nice? He seems to be. At least it's warm and dry in the café and he's paid for the coffees. He brought biscuits. Is that why men have briefcases, to carry their Garibaldis? Stella can't eat those. The currants are like dead flies.

Gareth is saying he'll get Stella somewhere to stay, but not to expect too much, it won't be a hotel, and it's not going to be easy. He says it like he's making some kind of a sacrifice, like it's got nothing to do with his job. He's smiling along with it, like making sacrifices is just something you do, like he's happy to do it. Is Stella supposed to feel grateful? Does he expect her to bestow a ton of grateful thanks? Stella looks at Gareth's face over the rim of her coffee mug. He's not too sure of himself. He keeps rubbing the side of his nose with his knuckle. He bites his finger nails. He can't be that much older than Stella.

The YWCA won't have Stella. They said they were full up, which is not what they said to the Clara woman when Stella phoned. They must have realised who she is. Backed off. Don't want a murderer.

'You can't blame them,' Gareth says, smiling. 'They're just full up. Don't take it personal.' He's trying to be kind. He's eaten all the Garibaldis, and puts the empty packet back in his briefcase.

'Mustn't think like that,' Marcia says. 'No-one's out to get you.'

People who tell you how to think, they mean it kindly. They're trying to help. They don't think about what it's like to be told how to think, how not to think and what to think. When.

Muriel put thoughts in Stella's head. There's her lipsticked mouth, set tight, her lips all but disappeared, only the twin peaks of the scarlet bow showing: you're not paid to think. When I want you to think, I'll let you know. Muriel hisses. Muriel's script.

Stella sips at her coffee. Gareth is shuffling papers. He looks like he's been saying something, something consequential. Stella looks round the room. The smell of coffee and damp people, the clink and clatter of cups on saucers, the scrape of chairs on the floor-boards. Too many people; couples, friends, people who belong, others who come and go. The Italian man behind the counter, whistling through his teeth as he rubs the insides of coffee cups with his tea towel and hangs them up on little hooks. They chink and sway. A little line of coffee cups, making music, dancing above the Italian man's head.

Gareth is asking questions. He doodles on a spiral pad and waits for Stella to nod or shake her head. Her gaze remains fixed on him. When he looks up she is staring into his eyes. He looks away. He makes notes, underlines things and scrawls heavy circles around something he's written. Stella, still waiting for the words to come back, come back and fill the spaces in.

'Shouldn't be long now,' Gareth says. He pushes his pad to one side and pulls a pile of forms out of his briefcase. They're crum-pled at the edges and he flattens them out with the side of his hand. He fills in boxes with his biro. He's left-handed and has to sort of curl his hand back on itself to get the flow. He seems to know what to put where.

'Can you sign here?' Gareth smiles and pushes a piece of paper towards Stella, handing her the biro and points to where she is to put her name.

Can she sign? It's as though he expects all she can manage will be a cross, an anonymous generic cross, which he will then witness as the genuine mark of Stella Moon. Maybe she will put a cross, a giant X, right across the page, corner to corner to corner to corner. She'll do it again and again and again, pressing in harder and harder till the biro digs through the paper. But no, Stella promised Marcia. No wallowing, no acting out and no destroying for the sake of destroying. Dignity. Remember. Dignity. Stella opens her own little case and lifts out the fountain pen, the one Marcia's given her, the dark green Parker Lady, exactly like the pen Stella had at school. She must have told Marcia about it. Marcia must have remembered. Stella removes the cap from the pen, slowly and with purpose, and she signs her name in the box on the form in her finest copperplate.

'Great,' Gareth says, picking up the form and blowing on the ink.

Is he surprised that she can write? That she owns a fountain pen? That she has rather nice handwriting for a specimen of the underclass?

Gareth puts the form to the back of the pile and takes out the next one, fills out some boxes and chews on the already very chewed end of his biro.

'Address?' he says.

Stella looks at him and laughs, almost spitting out a mouthful of coffee and has to put her hand over her mouth. Gareth laughs as well.

'Oh, I'm sorry,' he says, sounding like he means it. 'I don't know what I'm thinking of.'

Gareth has a lilty Welsh accent. Stella likes it. It's musical. His eyes are very blue, and they crinkle up when he smiles; thick black lashes and white even teeth. And Stella is suddenly self-conscious, aware of her dirty wild hair, her grubby nails, the browning nicotine stain on her middle finger, her tatty misfit clothes that aren't even hers. One time these clothes looked so elegant on Muriel

– but she could have worn a coal sack and looked lovely.

Stella is not Muriel. Stella is Stella. As Marcia says, Stella, you're different altogether. And thank the Lord for that.

A wave of nausea, a tightening in her chest: it's too hot in the café, there's no air. Stella stubs out her cigarette half-smoked, pushes her half-empty coffee mug to one side and wishes she could just get up and walk away and keep on walking, walking, walking.

'It says here,' Gareth is talking, pointing at the page with the biro, 'former address?' He smiles, a genuine kind of smile. 'These forms aren't made with people like you in mind!' He laughs the kind of laugh like he wants Stella to join him, to agree the whole system is ridiculous, like they're conspirators, in this together. Stella smiles back, a tight, closed-mouth smile. She needs to get a toothbrush.

People like you. Stella is a certain kind of person now. The kind of person the YWCA doesn't want. Yet they're known for taking down-and-outs, winos and junkies. But no place for Stella Moon. No room at the inn.

'It should be alright,' Gareth is saying, draining the last of his coffee. 'I'll just put "care of the Probation Office", if that's alright with you?'

Stella nods, shrugs.

'I just need some financial information, then I can get this form in, and you'll be up for council accommodation. They'll put you in one of those half way places to begin with, but only temporary. With my recommendation, you'll be up the top of that list in no time.' Gareth stands up and picks up the empty cups. 'Another coffee?' he says, going over to the counter. 'You sure you're not hungry?'

Financial information? Stella tips her purse up on the table so all the money she has comes out.

'That's what I've got,' she manages to say when Gareth comes back with two coffees and two Danish pastries with apricots and custard in. Gareth stops, the tray still in his hands, and looks at her.

'Thanks,' he says. 'That's really good. Thanks a lot, Stella.'

He's thanking her for talking. They've probably taught him how to deal with people like her at college.

Gareth takes Stella to get her signed on for social security. He puts her address again as c/o the Probation Office. He waits with her and speaks when she can't. He doesn't ask why she doesn't or can't or won't talk. He looks over the forms the social security woman fills out and indicates when it's OK to sign. Each time Stella signs her name with her own fountain pen. Gareth must think she's worthless, useless, a waste of space, just another one of those, straight out of prison and hasn't got a clue. She does the copperplate signature more painstakingly and more perfect each time. Gareth negotiates an emergency payment on Stella's behalf. Stella gathers it up, stuffs it in her purse and nods thanks to the woman behind the unshatterable glass. Gareth touches her elbow as they cross the road. He walks with her to the housing office, the forms in his hand. The office is closed. Gareth looks at his watch. Ten past five.

'Dammo,' he says, 'It's closed. We missed it. I'm sorry.'

Stella shrugs. She doesn't know what this means, what anything means.

'It's my fault,' Gareth is saying. 'We should have come here first, instead of going to the Social. But I knew you'd be needing money.'

'No, it's alright, it's OK. I'm OK, really,' Stella finds herself saying, words now pouring out. 'No, it's my fault, I should have come earlier, I shouldn't have waited so long to do things the proper way, I shouldn't have messed around with Frank Fanshaw, I shouldn't have got off the bus...' Stella, suddenly lost in a torrent of words. 'I can go back to the boarding house, Chillingham Road, I'll get the bus. I've got the key...' She opens the purse, pulls out the key on the dirty bit of string and holds it up for Gareth to see.

'Messed around with who?' Gareth asks. 'What did you say just then?'

'Nobody. Well...Frank...just Frank Fanshaw... He was there, at the house when I got there yesterday. He's alright. He's OK. Just a bit weird, that's all. Harmless, really. Used to be one of the lodgers at my grandmother's boarding house. I've known him ... well, since I was a kid and ...'

'The one you said was... I thought you said on the phone there was someone there who was...er...a bit dodgy... You couldn't stay there because...'

'He won't be there. Not now. He'll have gone.'

'You sure about that?'

Stella shrugs. She's biting the inside of her bottom lip. She can't tell this social worker what Frank Fanshaw is actually like. They'd get it all wrong. They'd mess everything up.

'You don't look very sure,' Gareth says.

But Stella's made up her mind. She nods. 'I am sure,' she says, 'I'll be alright. It's no problem.' She shouldn't have mentioned Frank. She doesn't want to go into all that.

'You absolutely certain?' Gareth says again.

Stella's nodding. She's making as if to walk away. 'Thanks,' she says, 'thanks for all your help, Mr Davies.' Stella picks up the little blue suitcase and pulls her cardy around her.

'You'll have to come back to the housing place tomorrow,' he says, 'say 10 o'clock? I'll drop these forms in, so they'll know to expect you. I'll leave a note for Geoff. That's Geoff Burns. You're really his case and not mine. You've got that card I gave you? Just give Geoff a ring on that number if you get any problems. Alright?'

Stella nods again. And off she goes.

That Gareth man was itching to get away, Stella sensed it. She can't face going back to that boarding house, not alone, not tonight. If Frank Fanshaw's still there, he'll be angry, she'll be punished, he'll make her pay and she can't face him, she's run right out of guts.

But that place is Home, Stella. It's the only place she has ever called Home. And Home wants Stella back. Stella feels the pull of it in the pit of her stomach.

She'd rather sleep on the streets than go back there. She could take her pride in her hands, her courage in her hands, she could go back and ask that Gareth man... Stella turns, and she sees the back of Mr Probation Officer Gareth Davies, he's bending over, he's doing something at the door of the housing place. Go back,

Stella. Ask him about a B&B. There's nothing wrong in that. But no. There was something about him. And now he's hurrying away. It's too late to change anything. In any case, Stella should be managing on her own, she should be managing better than this. The Gareth man couldn't wait to get away from her. He's supposed to help, but clearly that's not going to happen. Marcia was wrong. There's no-one that can help. Stella's on her own. Like it always was. Only this time, she's not at all sure she can cope.

The house wants Stella back. It's calling her to come Home. That house is the one thing in this world that wants Stella Moon.

Marcia. This isn't how it was supposed to be. This isn't what you said would happen. First Frank, and now the house, pulling Stella back into the past. She's never going to be able to restart her life, never.

Chapter Thirteen

Gareth Davies had suddenly become aware of an intense desire to get away from Stella Moon. He'd felt a malaise creep over him, he'd tried to ignore it, but it got the better of him and he'd had to get away. It was, at first, only a vague discomfort he put down to tiredness and the anxiety of dealing with a case that wasn't his, and the peculiar, almost exhilarating anxiety – if he was honest – of dealing with a killer. He'd told himself it was all part of the job, that he should put his feelings to one side and just get on with it, but he'd started to feel it, whatever it was, in his stomach. Then the vague desire to free himself from Stella at once became a pressing need. In moments, it had overwhelmed him. Gareth felt his bowels turn to liquid, which set him onto the verge of panic and a horrible claustrophobia closed in. He'd rushed through the forms, hardly knowing what box he was ticking.

It pained him – even in the midst of panic – it actually hurt Gareth to know Stella was none the wiser. She looked trustingly on whatever he did, and appeared to have not a clue that something abnormal was happening. Yes, it hurt Gareth to know she was putting her trust in him and to know he was letting her down. The forms completed, Gareth had looked at Stella; those eyes, those great big staring too-pale eyes. He would never have been able to explain how he'd had no choice but to get well away.

Gareth had never been prone to nervous ailments before, not really, nothing like this. Whatever it was, every bone in his body told him to get away from Stella, as if she was a danger to him. And yet he felt drawn to her, he felt concerned for her, protective of her – yes! He felt responsible for her. Yet there was no reason on earth why Gareth should have felt any of those things, and felt them in the way he did. And on top of it all, Gareth couldn't get it out of his mind that the girl was a killer, a dangerous killer. Round and round the panicked thoughts went, clamouring inside his head, and in the end, making him want to be sick. His heartbeat jumped all over the place, it had completely lost its regular rhythm, and he was having trouble getting his breath. Gareth's overwhelming instinct was to put as much distance as he could between himself and the killer. Then, and only then, he would be able to breathe again. Somehow – he has no idea how – Gareth had made it to the Housing Office, he'd managed to get rid of Stella and managed not to go to pieces completely.

In the cold and the damp of the autumn evening, the Newcastle rush hour, traffic nose to tail, headlamps flickering, tail lamps red, red, red, exhaust fumes belching, and there's Gareth, still stood outside the Housing Office. He inhales deeply and breathes out a long sigh of relief. Stella's gone. Gareth fumbles as he stuffs the forms into the large brown envelope, his hand is shaking and he can hardly grip the biro to scribble a quick note on the outside. He tucks the flap in and pushes the envelope through the letter box. All his insides are vibrating. Gareth waits for a moment to watch the envelope drop onto the doormat on the other side of the glass. That small separation is enough to calm him a bit.

'Thank Christ,' he says aloud. 'Thank Christ that's over with.'

Stella is gone and Gareth will be OK in a minute. He can't think where those feelings came from. They weren't like anything he'd ever known before. The girl's inscrutable, bloody hard work and something about her had drained it out of him. Half the time she's clammed up silent, then out it all pours, a load of gush and ramble. She veers from very obviously not normal to completely normal, like she switches on a coping mode. All of which would be fascinating if it weren't so disturbing. Stella Moon makes Gareth feel disturbed. Gareth's not used to feeling disturbed, especially by clients. He can feel sorry for them, annoyed by them, angered even, but his reaction to Stella Moon is in an altogether different league. Please, God, he won't have to deal with her again.

As he walks away, Gareth starts to calm down. The panic subsiding, Gareth has to wonder what it was all about. He knows about panic attacks, but he's never had one before, and now he has, and he doesn't know why, and the whole thing's scary, terrifying, actually. What if it happens again? He's got away with it this time, but what if it happens again? And why? What's made him suddenly start feeling like – like what? Troubled. Unhinged. Vulnerable! Like one of his clients? It felt like he was having a heart attack. And Stella apparently hadn't even noticed there was anything awry.

Now, in the calmer light of day, Gareth has to admit privately to himself that he's made a cock-up as regards Stella Moon. Well, at least as far as the accommodation. And possibly other things. Leaving her alone – she's vulnerable, he has to keep reminding himself, vulnerable – but he left her alone to go back to that derelict house. Now that's all preying on Gareth's conscience. OK, she had a peculiar effect on him. But still, now Gareth's calmer, he's no longer entirely convinced that Stella Moon – straight out of seven years inside – can look after herself. At the end of the day, however, it's not Gareth's bogey. But still. She's a human being and he feels sorry for her. Stella Moon is not Gareth's case. She's Geoff's. Plus the fact she's twenty-five. She's a big girl now. She knows what's what. She's done time, for God's sake. She should be able to look after herself. Gareth's done his job, done everything he's supposed to, mostly. OK, yes, he's messed up on the accommodation front.

But it's not like she's got nowhere to go. She said so herself. She'd be alright. She wasn't at all bothered when they got to the housing place and found it was shut. She took it in her stride. Just said she'd go back to the grandmother's place. And off she went. Some clients would have freaked. Not Stella Moon. She might not look it, but she's made of tough stuff. She's obviously a coper. Come on, Gareth. It's home time. You've done what you could. End of.

But tonight Gareth can't relax. He keeps thinking about Stella Moon wandering the streets of Newcastle on her own in those stupid, flimsy clothes. He keeps seeing the skinny little shape of her in those wet clingy clothes that are too big for her and Christ knows where she got those from. And he keeps thinking about her being a convicted killer. She doesn't seem like a killer, not that he's met any killers before.

The training's supposed to prepare you for all sorts, for

75

criminals being 'real people' as well as criminals, which is all very fine – separate the person from the crime, etc. But that's not the entire story, is it? It doesn't end there. Far from it, Gareth now sees. He's on a learning curve. They tell you how to think about this, that, or the other crime. They tell you what to think, what leads to what, they give you ways of dealing with different personalities and categories of mental illness, etc. They tell you a whole load about underlying factors, background influences, personality disorders, psychiatric syndromes – you name it... But as to how you feel – as to how you, as a Probation Officer, might actually feel, as someone who confronts a criminal, a killer, face-to-face – well, that's a different story. The effect they actually have on you... nobody tells you sod all about that.

Gareth's not sure what he's feeling now the horrible panic has subsided: tiredness and turmoil, relief to be away from her, that's the predominant feeling. But there's worry as well, worry that she'll not make out alright tonight, worry that Frank man she mentioned might do something... Guilt that Gareth has made a single mistake as regards the accommodation that might have massive consequences, for himself as well as Stella. It must be worry that's causing the adrenalin that's still churning his insides up.

Is Gareth scared of Stella? He doesn't really believe so, but being 'reflexive' in this line of work is all the rage and, as a professional, he must ask himself the question. Gareth sighs. He needs a drink. It's the only thing that'll stop this nausea. He'll stop off for a quick one on the way home. Or maybe not such a good idea. Never drink to drown a sorrow, his Da always says, and look at where he's ended up. No, he should make do without the drink. The fact of the matter is Gareth is going to be effing bloody useless at this particular job if he can't even cope with the clients without getting pissed. He's got to get his wits about him a bit more and be more professional.

All the same, the powers that be don't realise how these things affect you: they don't appreciate how, day in, day out, dealing with criminal mentalities, it shifts the ground from under you, it does. Churns you right up. This job is Stressful. Stressful with a capital

S. Gareth hopes it'll get easier once he's finished his training, but that won't be for another year at least. He'll feel better after a good, hot shower and something to eat. He'd best get on home.

But no, Gareth can't face to go home. Neither can he face going to the gym. And the pub's out. He could do, he should do, one or the other or something, but he doesn't. Instead, Gareth finds himself heading back to work. He tells himself he is going back to the office, yes, this late in the day: he'd been called out at short notice to deal with Stella Moon, so he needs to clear up his desk, prepare for tomorrow, oh, yes, and leave a note for Geoff re: the Moon case. Concentrate on work, on helping other people, and that's the best way of dealing with anxieties. Gareth begins to compose the note for Geoff in his head as he walks.

Geoff, in yr absence this pm I dealt with the Stella Moon business on yr behalf. I got her signed on at the DHSS and the emergency accom forms have been filled out and left at the housing office. She'll meet you there at 10am tmrw but if you can't manage it, I can cover for you. Gareth.

'Cover.' That's suitably ambiguous.

Decision made, Stella out of sight, Gareth's step is more jaunty. Hands deep in his trouser pockets and tie flapping as he strides along, improvising on the theme from the film *Dirty Harry* – it's not a tune that's easy remember, even when you've heard it as many times as Gareth has. Gareth heads back to the office, encouraged by images of his hero. Like Harry Callahan, Gareth will rise to the occasion, rise to the challenge of the dirty job that's happened to come along… Gareth Davies has done a good day's work and it'll be over to Geoff now.

One of these days, Gareth will take a trip to Harry Callahan's patch, San Francisco – the City by the Bay. He wants to see those places, those rooftops and dark alleyways, he wants to see what the SFPD cops are like, he wants to hear their voices. In the meantime, he'll write the note for Geoff, put it in a sealed envelope, mark it 'Confidential' and leave it on Geoff's desk. Gareth doesn't want Clara prying. He'll get the Stella Moon file out of the cabinet and put it in Geoff's drawer, just in case Clara is tempted to nose into it again. Clara's always stepping over the boundaries of her professional capacity. The Number One Sin in this business. What is it about criminals that makes people so goddamn curious?

P.S. Geoff, you need to say something to Clara, she's been snooping in the Moon file.

All the lights are out when Gareth gets back to the office. He's not used to being here in the dark and fumbles to find the switches. He puts all the lights on: he hadn't noticed before what a nasty, bare, cold kind of light those fluorescent tubes give off – and flickery, they could make a person feel sick. Gareth switches them off one by one, till the flickering stops. He turns his Anglepoise on instead. He won't be long getting off home. Gareth gets the Moon file out of the filing cabinet, but he doesn't put it straight into Geoff's drawer.

The file, in faded pink cardboard, is bulging and heavy, come down to the Probation Office from Newcastle Crown Court, evidently. R v Stella Moon. Case Number 70/003394. Gareth holds it open and looks in, sees papers and reports grouped together with treasury tags, staples gone rusty, newspaper cuttings held together with old bulldog clips. There's a 'Brief to Counsel' page at the top of a bundle tied up with pink legal ribbon, counsel's hand-written jottings; it's all there. Gareth sits down at his desk, adjusts his Anglepoise, loosens his tie and pulls a wedge of papers out of the file. He sifts through seemingly randomly ordered official court documents until he gets to Stella's confession, the 'voluntary statement' that formed the basis of the charge, the conviction, the sentence.

Gareth reads about the Beach Hut, the cliff path, the sea, and all that happened on the night Muriel died. As he turns the pages, he can hear Stella's voice in his head as though she is sat right next to him. Gareth's chilled, he's fascinated, and he reads on, getting more and more of a sense of something not right, something uncertain. He can't put a finger on it but he feels it drawing him in, gnawing at him somewhere deep down. Reaching the end of the statement, Gareth realises he's been holding his breath. He breathes out long and loud, and pulls his tie off. He flicks through a few more papers from the file.

Unpredictable. Violent. Borderline. Words jumping out at him, none of them words he'd have used to describe Stella Moon.

It's very hard to square all he sees in the file with the silent, brooding, waif-like young woman he'd had coffee with in Mark Toney's only an hour or so ago. There seems a million miles between the Stella on those pages and the Stella Gareth saw. Gareth lays the papers down, takes off his glasses and rubs his eyes. He was chilled before, but he's sweating now; he really could do with a drink, just one. He could murder a cigarette as well, but he quit smoking months ago. He reaches into his briefcase before he remembers he ate the last of the Garibaldis at Mark Toney's.

Gareth sits back. 'Christ almighty,' he says out loud. 'Christ all bloody mighty.' That skinny little thing. She pushes her mother over a cliff. Just like that. She'd sat there in Mark Toney's, chewing on her fingernails, she'd sat there and watched him eat all the biscuits. What the hell makes somebody murder their own mother? It makes Gareth feel cold even to think about it.

79

Chapter Fourteen

Frank doesn't bother to search all the rooms. As soon as he walks back in the door he knows Stella's done a runner. He might have guessed. She's the same sly, crafty little bitch she always was, exactly like that bloody Muriel. Like mother, like daughter. And he's the same stupid fool. Frank could kick himself. A missed opportunity. And he had been waiting so long, all the time Stella was inside, waiting, and even before that, all that time not knowing if she's going to drop him in it big time. He should have shut her up there and then, this morning, whilst he had the chance. Frank had allowed his better nature to get the upper hand for once, and serves him right, it's backfired.

He thought he'd give her a fair chance, find out what she knew or at least what she remembered – if anything – about the baby's death, because chances were Stella didn't remember a thing, not a dickie bird. Chances were all that from nearly ten years ago has been lost to oblivion, like so many of Stella Moon's memories, vanished without trace. Or so she'd have you believe. Frank has often wondered – had those memories really disappeared? Or – and this always seemed to him more likely – did Stella know more than she was prepared to let on? Was she just keeping schtum for reasons best known to herself? Frank had never been able to work her out. Stella Moon didn't seem to have any trouble remembering every detail about how she killed her mother, she could tell you every sordid detail of that particular episode. Frank can't afford to take any chances, not after waiting nearly ten years to get himself in the clear. He has to err on the side of caution. Assume the worst. He needs to find Stella, he needs to find her quick, and he needs to deal with her, one way or the other.

The whole thing's turned out to be much more urgent than Frank thought, but he's not going to panic. Not only is Stella back on the loose, but the grandmother's gone AWOL, and with her gone, what's to stop Stella grassing him up big time? What's to stop Stella dropping Frank right in the shit? He's a fool, he shouldn't have fallen for her wily little tricks. She's a dark horse, that Stella, always was. It's impossible to know what's going on in that hot little head of hers, impossible to make out what she knows and what she doesn't – whose side she's on. When he thinks back, Frank should have known better than to trust her, nasty little killer. She must know she could drop him right in it, she's not stupid. Far from it. Nasty, creepy, devious, sly – but not bloody stupid.

And what if that grandmother's not dead and buried? What then? What if she's still alive, festering away with her secrets? What if some journalist – or worse – gets to her and makes her talk? Eh? Where's that going to leave Frank? Old Ruby Willoughby has no loyalty to him. She could spin no end of a tale about him and that poor dead baby and it'd end up her word against his, and Frank has a pretty good idea who they'd believe, and it wouldn't be Frank Fanshaw. What if she's gone gaga and is sprouting no end of accusations and insinuations right now, at this very moment?

Frank needs to calm down. Think rational. Logistics. Discipline. What needs to be done, when, where and how. Formulate a plan of action and stick to it, Frank. Think logical. Which is a bit difficult in this fusty old place, the unholy stink of it stops you from thinking.

OK. So Frank's original plan has backfired, that much is obvious. Softly, softly, catchy monkey didn't work. Give Stella the benefit of the doubt, get her on Frank's side, that's how he was playing it. Now: impossible. Solution: find her. Make her realise she has too much to lose, make her keep her mouth shut by whatever means proves necessary. It's possibly too late for that. What if he can't find her? Surely there's not that many places she can go? Frank will go after her and next time, there'll be no escaping. And when he gets his hands on her he'll wring the truth out of her, then he'll do whatever he has to do to get himself off the frigging hook once and for all.

Frank needs food first. Then decide. Find Stella first. Or Ruby. One's as bad as the other. Or mebbies he should tackle the evidence first. Get rid of it properly. He can do that by himself. He doesn't need Stella and mebbies it's better if she's not there.

There's a fair chance Stella remembers nowt of any significance about Baby Keating. She'd asked Frank if he remembered, and he'd come over a bit queer and hadn't been in the frame of mind to take it any further, which was a pity. He had missed a chance there. Anyhow, Stella had gone all that time – two, three years, was it? – without saying owt. In fact, without uttering a syllable about anything to anybody. And if Frank had understood it correctly, according to the medical people, loss of memory was part of Stella's 'condition'. Frank couldn't remember what name they gave it. So, yes, there was a chance Stella had nothing to tell that could implicate Frank. But who knows, Stella Moon could just be a bloody good actress. Who knew what she was thinking all that time she was giving everybody the runabout with the silent treatment? And who and what's she already told while she's been inside? Eh? Frank can't be sure, and as long as he can't be sure, he can't take no chances. Now the little madam's buggered off God knows where, she thinks she can call the tune. Well, Frank's the organ grinder now, not the bloody monkey. He'll not let her get away the next time. No-sir-ee. And to cap it all, the little besom's nicked off with the rest of his fags. And the bloody Zippo.

Frank sits down at the table and makes himself a sandwich with the ham. He throws the tub of pease pudding into the fireplace – he can't stand the stuff. He opens the bottle of Brown with the thing on his Swiss army knife and takes a few noisy gulps. That's better. He leans back in his chair, wipes the back of his hand across his mouth and takes another long swig. He could get some more beers in, wait it out a day or two, see if Stella comes back. He's waited more than a week already. It hasn't killed him. He could wait a bit longer. It could be worth it. Chances are she's nowhere else to go. He could wait. He stuffs what's left of the ham into the second roll, tears a chunk off with his teeth and washes it down with the rest of the beer.

Thinking logically. Frank decides Stella has most likely gone to try to find the grandmother. Alive or dead, he hasn't a clue. It'd be a helluva lot easier for Frank if the old stick has passed away. One less mouth to talk. There's Hedy Keating of course, but given that it was her baby, she's unlikely to want the authorities prying into that. That was all bad enough back then, when the baby went 'missing'. If Hedy was going to say anything, surely she'd have done so long before now. Frank may not have to worry about Hedy Keating. Frank's not sure what to do first, what's most important, whether he should stay on a bit or wait it out for Stella. Or try to find the grandmother. Or go and sort the evidence.

Let's see if he can get the water turned on, the electric even. He might be able to fiddle it. If he's going to stay here for a bit he'll need water and leccy. Frank picks up the torch and goes into the scullery. He lies on the floor, wriggles his head and shoulders under the sink and feels for the stopcock. His hand touches something, it's an ancient bar of Fairy all stuck up with mouse shit. He can just about reach the stop-cock, but it's jammed up with rust. He wraps a rag around it the best he can and tries to turn it, but it's not budging.

Lying on the scullery floor, Frank Fanshaw is fed up with his life and sick to the back teeth of being messed around by blasted women. They think they know it all, always have to be one step ahead. But this time it's going to be different. From now on things will be a whole lot bloody different. Frank will not be ordered about, organised, or told what to do any longer by effing know-all women who think they know better than he does. Lying on his back on the cold lino of the scullery floor, twisting at the stop cock – half the handle has already broken off – with cold wet hands, Frank's thoughts turn to his mother. The original culprit. God damn her, he hasn't thought about her for months. She could be dead and buried long since for all he knows, stone-cold dead and six foot under, like old mother Willoughby, the both of them, rotting under the ground. And good bloody riddance.

On the other hand, if she's still alive and kicking, Frank's mother could possibly be of some use for once in her life – if she knows anything about old mother Willoughby's movements, for example. Or if she knows where Hedy is to be found. Frank hopes it won't come to that. There are other avenues to explore first, but he has to think logical. Make plans.

In the old days, when Frank first came to old Ma Willoughby's place, she used to pry and neb on about his mother. It seemed she couldn't keep her nose out of Frank's personal affairs.

'And what about your Mam?' old Ruby had asked. 'Is she…?

'Oh…passed away.' Frank had shrugged, shaking his head and arranging a suitably sad look on his face. A moment had passed before Ruby had looked up and said, 'Oh dear, dear, you poor man, I'm very sorry to hear it…' But there was something in that look Ruby gave him that made Frank think she hadn't altogether believed him. He'd felt obliged to elaborate.

'Passed away', he said again, frowning this time. 'Aye, passed away when I was just a lad.' Ruby tipped the dirty water from the washing-up bowl down the sink and turned to dry her hands.

'Oh dear,' she'd said again, looking Frank straight in the eye. 'That's an awful shame, a little lad losing his mother…' Was there a note of sympathy in her voice? Frank couldn't tell.

'I wasn't that little,' he'd said, getting into the full swing of telling a story. 'I was well into me teens, fourteen to be precise…'

Ruby had interrupted, 'Fourteen, hmm,' she said. 'Well, if you ask me, Frank Fanshaw, that's the very time a little lad needs his mam. Now you sit down and I'll make us a cup of tea and you can tell Ruby all about it.'

But Frank didn't want to tell Ruby Willoughby anything about anything. He was beginning to think it had been a big mistake coming to live in this lodging house with a nosey old bag of a landlady who had God knows how many of her own skeletons in the cupboard, of that he was in no doubt. From the start he'd thought Ruby Willoughby was a weird one, what with her herbs and her potions and her poisons and her calling up the dead on Wednesdays, regular as clockwork. And that daughter of hers, that Muriel – obsessed, she was, preserving all those dead things, down in that basement, and flaunting herself about outside the

Legion. And that creepy Stella kid, sullen, sulky and silent, always watching from the sidelines with those great big eyes, peering out from behind that straggly red hair, taking everything in, saying nowt. Aye, they were a queer lot alright.

And they went even more peculiar after the old man Worthy died. He'd been a herbalist, some kind of healer – not a proper doctor, more what you might call a quack, and Frank could never quite make him out either. Oh, he was nice enough, but a dark horse, like the rest of them. Then, when old Worthy passed away, you could have knocked Frank over with a feather when the old lady – she wasn't even qualified in herbs or medicine or owt of that sort – the brass neck of her, she just stepped into the old man's shoes, took over his practice and continued seeing to his 'clients', dispensing all them potions if you please, as though the old man hadn't actually died. The herbs and the chemicals and the all what-have-you, she kept the whole caboodle going, brazen as you like. Mind you, to be fair, she didn't do any of the laying on of hands that Worthy had done down in that basement, not as Frank ever saw, anyway. Old Ruby didn't have the Gift. And she drew the line at the Procedures – the women's doingses – none of those happened any more after Worthy turned up his toes. Frank doesn't know how Ruby got away with it, but she did, she kept on raking in the cash, carrying on as though she had every right. Bloody queer lot, those Willoughbys.

Then the baby Keating business. That was the day everything changed. For all of them. It makes Frank shrink even now to think of it. It was Stella that discovered the baby had 'vanished'. She wasn't much more than a kid herself, and they left her to find that the pram was empty. Frank redoubles his efforts to get the stopcock loose. To this day, Frank hasn't an earthly why he let himself get roped in to the baby Keating fiasco, and getting on for ten years now it's taken over his life. He's determined to be out if it, get it sorted, once and for all. Now Stella's out, Frank's got his chance. He'll make damn certain nobody's got anything on Frank Fanshaw. Then Frank might be able get on with his life. God knows, he's waited long enough.

At the time, the papers were full of it. Well, they would be, wouldn't they? Baby Keating this, baby Keating that, all sorts of insinuations, Frank's name on the front page of the *News of the World*. His mates at the shipyard, they couldn't credit it, Frank Fanshaw named in connection with the abduction of a baby from some seedy boarding house. And all the reporters flocking around, swarming into Hawthorn Leslie's like flies around a dung heap, wouldn't leave him alone. Even people who knew Frank were thinking there's never smoke without fire and looking at him in a different way, all suspicious like. All sorts of shite about his past misdemeanors had been dug up – half of it made up – and paraded in the papers for all to see. Most of it was lies – nasty, filthy lies. But mud sticks. He'd had to leave the work. His life had been a misery, an utter misery. He'd actually looked forward to Stella getting out, he'd actually dared hope that her getting out would be the end of it. How naïve he'd been. Stella Moon has a hell of a lot to answer for.

The first piece in the paper had also brought his mother – hawk-eye Hilda – scuttling out of the woodwork. She spotted it on the Sunday and by the Monday had ferreted Frank out. She came to the boarding house – Frank was on the backshift – and old Ma Willoughby had let her in. When Frank got in from work there they were, the two of them, sitting sipping tea, pally as you like. After that, Frank never saw his mother again, time passed and he very rarely thought of her. Old Ma Willoughby never mentioned her. Frank knew they kept in touch, though: he'd seen letters on the mantelpiece in his mother's spidery hand, he'd seen herbs packaged up with brown paper and string, ready to go off, Hilda's name and address on the packaging. He'd written down the address. Now Frank wonders if he can lay his hands on it. He might need some help in tracking down Ruby. If Hilda's still alive. If she's stayed in touch.

After Ruby realised Frank had told her lies about his mother, she didn't confront him or nothing: no, Ruby's ways were too subtle for that. She just gave Frank a look every time she wanted something done, and Frank had to live with that. Oh, Frank could tell Stella Moon a thing or two. It's not enough, when you've done a crime, that you do your time to pay for it. You think you've paid the price, you think that's the end of it? You're a fool, Stella Moon. Think again. If there's one thing Frank's learned in this life, it's that your past follows you around, it's always dragging along behind you, like a fucking bad smell. If Stella Moon thinks she can just come out of that jail and get a whole new life started, she's got another think coming.

The stopcock is completely stuck and Frank can't get it undone. He'll have to get a tool of some sort. He gets up and rummages about in the drawers till he finds something. He creeps back under the sink armed with a monkey wrench and a hammer with a broken handle. It takes him a good five minutes to get the monkey wrench fitted on top of all the rust. Frank nearly gives up, but if he's going to stay on here for a bit, he'll need water. Damn that bloody Stella.

He gives the monkey wrench a good clout with the hammer, and another, and another. The stop-cock suddenly gives way and Frank gets drenched in a gush of icy water that comes spurting from the pipe. He bangs his head on the underside of the sink trying to get away from it. In an instant he's lying in a freezing, filthy pool and water's still gushing out. Without being able to see anything of what he's doing, Frank fumbles, trying to tighten the stop-cock up again, but it's some while before he manages to shift it. He gets it closed up enough to stop the bigger gush, but it's still leaking quite badly and he's managed to get the whole thing cross-threaded, so there's no way he can stop it altogether. Frank stands up, soaked to the skin. The torch, still on the floor but now lying in water, has gone out. Frank kicks the back door open as water starts to flood the scullery. He curses Stella, he curses Ruby, he curses his mother, and he curses Muriel and Hedy and all the blasted bloody know-it-all women he's ever known.

Chapter Fifteen

Gareth isn't quite taking it in. And he's having trouble squaring how she seemed in real life, when he saw her, with what he's reading in this file. Stella Moon killed Muriel Moon. Was it deliberate? Did she plan it? Did she do it out of hatred? Had she always hated her mother? What's wrong with her? Has she killed anyone else? Gareth is fascinated and appalled, all at the same time. He wants to believe the best but he's ready to discover the worst. On and off he's squeamish at the memory of having come face-to-face with a killer. Yet now the panic's gone, he's doubly curiously drawn to the case. It fascinates him at least as much as it repels.

Stella was charged with Manslaughter, which suggests *prima facie* there was nothing intentional about the killing. Gareth can't tell the reasoning behind the charge. Yet to his mind, Stella's confession is ambiguous. It could be read as Murder. But there again, at a stretch, it could even be read as Self-Defence. Murder would seem the more likely interpretation, but the very fact that a defendant is prepared to confess to the lesser charge of Manslaughter... that saves the system a whole load of trouble having to have a full trial and prove Murder. Gareth has seen that kind of plea bargaining before, but never with a homicide. Gareth would like to have a better look among the police papers, see if a Murder charge was ever considered. And then of course there's the *mens rea* – the state of mind, the criminal intent – in relation to a charge of Murder. The law is complex. Gareth would be interested to see what the police had to say about that. He could look back at his Criminology notes. They'd been covering stuff like that in his Criminology MSc. And there'll be stuff about her state of mind in the file, psychiatric reports...

Bloody hell. Matricide. That's what it is. Matricide. Gareth says the word out loud, hearing it break the evening silence. Gareth knows nothing about matricide, but it's an interesting crime and he never thought it'd be like this.

Stella Moon killed her mother then gave herself up, confessed to the lot, cool as you please. She didn't even try to deny a thing. But who can tell whether she was telling the truth, the whole truth? Did she leave something out? Lying by omission. Telling the story in such a way that made it look like Manslaughter. Bloody cool customer, that Stella.

Gareth shakes his head, exhales sharply, sits forward in his chair and scratches his head. He pushes the file across the desk and looks at it from a distance, like it has suddenly become contaminated. He shakes his head. Who knows where the truth lies? There could be any number of truths, all of them true, or none of them. What the hell makes someone murder their own mother?

Bloody hell, what a mess. Thank God her 'rehabilitation' is down to Geoff and not to Gareth.

If she did do it on purpose, what a bloody dramatic way to do it. What must the mother have done to warrant that? And why did Stella give herself up? She could probably have got away with it, just acted like it was an accident, or better still, acted like she wasn't even there, like she'd been waiting at the Beach Hut the whole time for Muriel to come back. It doesn't make sense. None of it makes much sense to Gareth. You're always finding out things that surprise you in this job. Matricide, eh? The thought of it is fascinating and repulsive all at the same time. Gareth can't recall seeing anything about it in any of his textbooks. But he might just look it up. He needs to get a distance on it. The whole thing is making him feel nauseous again. Or maybe it's lack of food. It's late. Gareth suddenly feels very tired. He should get going.

Gareth pictures Stella, like she was this afternoon. Appearances are deceptive. She could have passed for normal, 'cept she doesn't say much, which could've been nerves, but Gareth suspects something deeper. In the Master's they'd had some lectures on syndromes, so he can look up his notes. But right now Gareth can't face much more. He should go home. But the whole thing's niggling. He definitely could do with a drink. He wonders how

Stella must feel, what it would be like to know you've murdered – he means killed – your own mother. What must it be like to have done that, then to have to go back to the house where you used to live with her? A hot flush passes over Gareth's face. He wishes he hadn't slipped up, that he'd got her some proper accommodation sorted. It's horrendous, her having to go back to that place. But Gareth can't go blaming himself, for Christ's sake.

This is what being professional is all about, the fine line between human empathy and detachment that enables you to appreciate the wider picture. Draw that line in the proper place, or it's impossible to help anybody. And that's exactly what he's come into this job for, to help people, to rescue unfortunates like Stella Moon. Some people need saving from themselves, it's not enough to feel sorry for them. A lot of these people are their own worst enemies, if only they could see it. In this job you actually can save them. You always have to keep in mind that it's the behaviour that's bad, not the person. It's the behaviour you change and the rest does itself. You have to put your own feelings to one side, not let them take over, or else you'll be no good to man nor beast.

Gareth gets up and pulls his jacket off the back of his chair. He's had enough of Stella Moon. This is a job. It's not his life. He'll go and get that drink. Just the one. He needs it. He deserves it.

Gareth hasn't quite got used to being a professional, to seeing himself as a representative of officialdom. Probation Officer Gareth Davies! If only his old Mamgu had been alive to see him: proud, she'd have been. Duw Duw, pleased as punch. You've done brilliantly, cariad bach. She'd have patted him on the shoulder: good as a hug, that was, from Mamgu. Gareth's wasn't one of those touchy-feely families. But you always knew where you stood. Gareth's choice of a career had been an issue.

'A career?' his Da had said. 'What d'you want a career for? What's wrong with a job?' No, Gareth's choice hadn't gone down well with his father. As far as Da was concerned, Gareth had defected, gone over to the enemy, let the whole working class down and turned his nose up and his back on his roots. But despite all that, Gareth has almost made it through his Master's at Cardiff University, only the Dissertation to do and, when that's done, the sky's the limit. There's nothing wrong with being proud of that achievement. Gareth's on the ladder now, and he's going all the way to the top.

Once he's fully qualified, Gareth will be able to make all the difference to people like Stella Moon, people who otherwise would fall by the wayside. His meeting with her this afternoon might have scared him a bit before, but it's a challenge, and now he's risen to it, and if he lets it, it will reinforce his commitment to his profession, give him a renewed enthusiasm, a new kind of vigour, add a whole new dimension to understanding the mind behind the crime. How crucial it is to know every little cranny, how significant the smallest thing can be, can make such a difference to the bigger picture. Gareth puts his jacket on, moves a few things round on his desk by way of tidying, and gets ready for going home.

Gareth is lucky. He's made it, or he's about to. There's not much to stand in the way now. Gareth Davies, BA, MSc, Criminology, University of Wales, Cardiff. Through sheer hard work, commitment and determination, Gareth is getting on in the world. But there's still an element of luck, of 'there but for the grace of God'. Take Stella Moon, for instance, look at her, not that different in age from Gareth, yet what a frigging mess she's made of her life so far. It's the function of the Probation Service to help her reintegrate into society, to rehabilitate her, to help her put the past behind her and not be defined solely by the fact of her – admittedly hideous – crime. She has done her sentence and now she has to put the past behind her and move on.

What will Gareth do if Geoff tries to palm the Moon case off on him? He's not sure how he'd handle that. But wait a minute – if he could use Stella Moon as a Case Study for the Dissertation, that could turn something unfortunate into more of an opportunity. There are plenty of 'unique angles' he could take to the case, and matricide is an interesting topic, not yet much discussed in the criminological literature, as far as Gareth has seen. There must be tons of theories about the motivation, mother-daughter conflict, something in the background that causes the dark side of the personality to erupt. Yes, it's a good idea, definitely worth thinking about. Gareth would have to clear it with Geoff, though. Seven years she did. She's lucky she didn't get mandatory Life, which she would have done for Murder. Matricide, eh? There's no specific crime of matricide, as far as Gareth knows. Not like infanticide, which is a special category of homicide, and makes reference to a deranged frame of mind. What about criminal 'responsibility' in matricide? Surely that's every bit as emotional a crime? Gareth exhales loudly. He's getting quite excited about getting his teeth into a matricide.

Gareth packs his briefcase. The fascinating thing is Stella Moon doesn't look the type, not at all the type. It just goes to show. She may be frail and innocent-looking, she may look more like a fragile little waif than a killer, but a killer she is. End of. Of course, Gareth knows that there isn't any one type of person who is capable of murder, just like there isn't only one type of murder. That's practically the first thing they tell you on the Master's. It may be convenient to put people into boxes, but people aren't pigeons. And there's a feisty streak to that Stella, if Gareth's not mistaken. Look at her, willing to go back to spend the night in that dingy, decrepit old boarding house. Yes, definitely a feisty streak, not far beneath the surface. She's 'unpredictable' – that's what they say. She could prove to be a handful. It could be best to stay well clear, forget about the Case Study and let Geoff keep her.

Stella Moon is, at the very least, impulsive, unpredictable, and more than a little weird. She's a mixture of feisty and fragile – Gareth's seen that already. He's seen it in those eyes. Dangerous mixture. Leave well alone, Gareth, if you know what's good for you. But Gareth's never been one to shy away from a challenge. You wouldn't see Dirty Harry Callahan backing off because something looks a bit difficult. On the contrary. Gareth has already surprised himself, going this far, coming into the office at night, reading other people's files. It's the first time he's ever done that. This is not going to become a habit. He's heard of people like that, with a morbid interest in the minds of criminals – it's not natural. Gareth claps the file shut and locks it away in the bottom drawer of Geoff's desk. He'll stop for a beer on the way home. He deserves one. He'll stop thinking about his Dissertation, and Stella Moon, who is not Gareth's problem. He'll get a carry out, go home and watch his *Dirty Harry* video with a chicken chow mein, a big Yorkie and a few cans of Carlsberg.

Gareth turns the lights off and leaves the office. He forgets to leave any note for Geoff. He also heads straight home and forgets to stop to get his beers, his chocolate and his Chinese carry-out.

Chapter Sixteen

Frank pulls off his wet clothes and shoes and wraps himself in some stinking old towels and a moth-eaten tartan blanket that smells of rat piss. Feeling around in the dark in the cupboard under the stairs – he's even past caring about that stinking cupboard – he pulls out enough bits and pieces to make a fire before jamming the door shut with a chair under the handle. He'll have to get his clothes dry before he can get out of this hellhole.

Frank has determined that the most crucial thing is to get rid of the evidence – that has to be the first thing. He's thinking more clearly now. Stella, Ruby, Hedy – they can all talk till they're hoarse, to the press, to the polis even, there's nothing anyone can do to Frank if there's no bloody body. So the first thing is to sort that, as soon as his clothes are dry. Then Stella, Ruby, Hedy, in no particular order. All that's belt and braces. The whole thing suddenly looks pretty straightforward, albeit he's a bit on the clock and he'll have to get his kit a bit dry. Frank doesn't want to draw undue attention to himself, just in case.

Frank gets the fire started then goes out the back to the coalhouse. Using the monkey wrench, he smashes open the padlock and drags open the door. Piles of old newspapers, a heap of old coal sacks, some cardboard boxes and some miserable crumbs of coal is all he finds. He scrapes up what he can of the slack with a shovel and tosses it onto the fire. It hisses. He's afraid for a moment that it has killed the flame altogether, which would be just his luck, but in a little while puffs of thick brown smoke break through and make their way up the chimney. Frank feels strangely cheered. He gets some of the old coal sacks and throws them on for good measure.

Now for his soaking clothes. He wrings them out onto the scullery floor. He has to leave the back door open so the flood of water from the broken pipe can pour over the back step and out into the yard. There's nothing he can do about that. He drapes his wet things over the old wooden clothes-horse and arranges it in front of the fire. Frank Fanshaw won't be going anywhere in a hurry, not before he's got this little lot dried off. Good job he had the foresight to get a couple of beers in.

Frank tiptoes barefoot through the flood in the scullery and fetches the axe from the coalhouse. He uses it to chop with heavy strikes through the chairs. Bit by bit, while his things are drying, he chops up the furniture and feeds it onto the fire. Watching it go up in flames, in the warmth of the fire, Frank begins to feel almost cheerful. He's got water now, and he's got a plan. Frank's clothes are still pretty damp, but he'll have to put them on. He hasn't got much choice, as a matter of fact. He'll have to go and get fags because that bloody Stella's nicked off with his and he's nearly finished the new packet.

The more Frank thinks about it, the more it seems likely that Stella isn't coming back to the boarding house. If Frank wants her, he's going to have to get out there and find her. Fuck knows where the crafty little bitch has got to. The trouble with Stella Moon is that you can never tell what she's thinking. She doesn't even know herself, half the time.

A touch of desperation is creeping into Frank's thoughts. He's finding it hard to keep his thoughts from spiralling, to keep the panic at bay. One minute he's OK and the next he's hearing things: sirens, footsteps in the hall, a key in the front door, something rattling at the back door. And Frank knows Stella could be anywhere: at this very minute, she could be talking to reporters or, God forbid, the polis. This very instant she could be telling them everything, for all Frank knows. She'll be passing the buck, saying the whole baby thing was his doing from start to finish, the sly little bitch. Frank wouldn't put anything past her. Tomorrow he could wake up to find his name blazed across the headlines once more. He couldn't live through that again. He'd have to top himself.

In an instant Frank decides it's best to get away from the boarding house, in case Stella does talk. It's not a good idea for

Frank to be found on this particular doorstep, or even at the Beach Hut, for that matter. Especially at the Beach Hut, now he comes to think of it.

But he has to go to the Beach Hut. If he can get the baby's body dug up, he can dispose of it properly, get rid of that important evidence – that at least will go part of the way to making sure they can't lay that particular crime on Frank Fanshaw. He'll go to the Beach Hut without Stella. He's got no choice. If he's in luck, he could find her there. Then the next step will be to track down old Ma Willoughby. Possibly catch up with Stella at that point.

Panic's setting in, causing Frank's thoughts to go careering all over the place. He needs to calm down, think logical. What if the polis are already after him? The crone next door knows he's been here, he's seen her curtains twitching. And the dentist, Mr Cohen. Frank's situation suddenly strikes him as urgent, possibly dangerous. Why hadn't he realised that before now? He's got to get away. He mustn't waste another second.

Frank pulls on the damp clothes and looks around to make sure he hasn't left anything. His fingerprints will be everywhere, if the polis do come. He rips a bit off the curtain and rushes round wiping door handles and surfaces, even the handle on the toilet chain. He stuffs the monkey wrench, the axe and the broken hammer into his duffle bag, runs upstairs again and grabs his bedside clock and his glasses and stuffs those into the bag as well. He pulls off the bedding and bundles it into the fire, holds it in with the poker till it goes up in flames. Then he's at the front door, ready to leave. He looks back along the hall, checks his pocket for the key and hears the water still pouring out in the scullery. Frank slams the front door shut: there's nowt he can do about that water. He should be going to sign on – no way is that a good idea at this point in time. If they're looking for him, the Social is the first place they'll go. He can't risk it. He'd better get away.

A car pulls up at the curb just as Frank is climbing over the front gate, causing all his innards to lurch. The dentist from across the way gets out. Frank puts his head down and starts to hurry away, but he's too late, Mr Cohen has spotted him.

'Mr Fanshaw!' the dentist shouts. 'Frank Fanshaw!' Mr Cohen comes rushing down the pavement after Frank and catches hold of his sleeve. 'Ah I thought it was you,' he says, puffing a bit.

'Ah, morning, Mr Cohen,' Frank says, 'afraid I'm in a bit of a hurry...'

'Won't take a minute, my man,' the dentist says. 'Only you were asking about old Mrs Willoughby. Well, I made a few inquiries on your behalf. Seems she was taken into a nursing home way back in 1970 or thereabouts. The goings on, you know, with the grand-daughter... Well, you can imagine, they'd be bound to take their toll on an old lady's health...'

'You mean she's still alive and kicking?'

'Oh, I don't know about that...' Mr Cohen says. 'I'm talking about after the court case. When the granddaughter went to prison. It was after that, apparently, they took her away.'

'Where did they take her?' Frank interrupts again.

'Somewhere down south. Brighton, I think.'

'Who told you that?'

'Fred Greenbank. Family doctor. Bumped into him at the Rotary. It was him that brought it up, actually, or I wouldn't have thought. He was saying the grand-daughter would be due to come out round about now.'

'Well, I suppose she would be, yes,' says Frank. 'Whereabouts in Brighton?'

'Now, I don't know that. I could ask old Greenbank...'

'Oh, no need to put yourself to that trouble.'

'No trouble, no trouble at all. What is it you want to know? The address of the nursing home?'

'No, really, it's alright. I just wondered what was happening to the house, that's all. It can't stay like this forever.' Frank gestures back at the boarding house. 'Can't be very nice for you, having a place so close by going to rack and ruin.'

'Well, no. As I say, it was way back in 1970 Mrs Willoughby went away. The old dear could have passed away between then and now, I suppose.'

'Would old Greenbank know?'

'Shouldn't think so. She'll have been off his books long since.'

'If she'd died, you'd think they'd have sold the house, under the will, whatever.'

The dentist shrugs and picks up his big black briefcase. 'Well, I'd better be off,' he says. 'Duty calls.' The dentist seemed to study Frank for a moment before looking at his watch, touching the brim of his hat and rushing off into the surgery. 'I'll say goodbye, then, Mr Fanshaw.'

The dentist gone, Frank looks down at himself. He looks a mess, and it's pretty obvious his clothes are more than a little on the damp side. Mr Cohen will be wondering what the hell, but Frank can't afford time to be thinking like that. He's got a lot to do, and the clock is ticking.

Brighton, eh? Maybe Frank will head off down to Brighton, have himself a little holiday, once he's been to the Beach Hut and got that business dealt with. First things first. He's got a bit of money put away in the Post Office. He'll get it out and keep it in cash, just in case. If old Ma Willoughby's still alive, it should be easy enough to find her down in Brighton. And if Frank can track her down, so can Stella. Get on with it, Frank. Get your wits about you.

Chapter Seventeen

Stella does not want to be alone in the boarding house tonight. The place gives her the creeps. She'd almost prefer it if hideous Frank Fanshaw were still there. But he appears to have gone. He's left a flood in the kitchen and chopped up half the furniture, by the looks of it. Stella sees as much in the dreary half-light that's coming through the grime on the window where Frank pulled the board off. Was that really only yesterday?

The waterlogged torch lies lifeless on the scullery floor, but Stella has the Zippo and she will find some candles. There'll be some in the front room – she doesn't want to go in there, not unless she has to. There'll be one on either side of the piano, in little saddle holders on the backs of two black elephants with real ivory tusks, sent from Africa years ago by some emigrated woman ever beholden to Grandpa Worthy. Better not to use those if she can help it. There's candles in the cupboard under the stairs, but Stella doesn't want to go in there either. Frank has left the door wedged shut with the one chair he hasn't taken the axe to. She lights the Zippo and searches in vain in the sideboard drawers and cupboards, but no candles. Stella needs candles. She can't hope to stay here tonight without them.

She's got it all planned. She'll drag a mattress from her grandmother's room, she'll open the porch door and sleep on the mattress in the doorway. She'll put the sneck on the front door. That way Frank Fanshaw, if he comes back, won't be able to get in the front with his key, and if by any chance – unlikely – he manages to scale the back wall and get in through the yard, Stella will be well placed to make a quick exit out the front. Sorted. But first she needs candles.

She can't think where there'll be any except in that cupboard under the stairs. And she's not even sure about firing the Zippo up in there in case the whole lot goes up. She'll have to take a chance.

Stella stands back and kicks the chair away from the door. She has to kick a few times with her heel before the chair falls away and the door swings open. The old familiar smell comes out straight away. Stella stands as far back as she can and flicks the Zippo a few times until it catches. The flame burns big and blue. She shrinks it and it settles. She holds the Zippo out at arm's length and looks into the cupboard from a distance. Nothing happens, apart from the smell. She takes a step or two forward, holds out the Zippo and scans the shelves.

All those chemicals. Still here. She can't resist looking. She looks from one fading label to another. *Diamorph. Hydroch. POISON. Dose 1/25 to 1/8 Grain.* Oh my God, Stella believes that's heroin. What did they want with heroin? She remembers Grandpa Worthy doling it out to ladies after their operations, instructing Stella to weigh the powder out on a little brass scale. She had no idea then what it was she was touching. My God. She moves the flame along the shelf, examines bottle after bottle. *Ethyl Morph. Hydrochloride POISON; Atropine pur POISON; Hydrag. Perchlor. POISON.* They're all bloody poisons. Frank was right, the poisons cupboard. Why did they need poisons? So many different ones? Grandpa Worthy must have known what he was doing, surely. Ladies came flocking for his laying on of hands and went away, pale, in taxis, clutching at their remedies, forever coming back for more, smiling and grateful: bottles of Brandy, sides of ham at Christmas. Stella remembers *atropine*, from the plant deadly nightshade. It causes convulsions then stops your heart.

Grandpa Worthy had discovered his Gift for healing after an accident down the pit put an end to his coal hewing days. He'd been three days down there, trapped, had been pulled out minus a bit of the back of his head and three of the fingers of his left hand.

The smell of fumes from the cupboard is making Stella light-headed. She can see the bottles of ether and chloroform are empty. She hasn't yet found any candles. She's about to give up and shut the door when she notices Grandpa Worthy's old leather medical bag, wedged into the back corner between two big green-glass carboys. Stella reaches into the corner and tugs at the old bag until she pulls it free in a cloud of dust and bits of straw and rodent shit. The familiar feel of the forbidden bag between her palms brings a rush of nausea and makes her heart go thump, thump, thump. She drops the bag down on the table and crams the cupboard door shut, wedges the chair and kicks it back into place before almost collapsing onto Grandma Willoughby's chair by the fireside. Stella leans forward and puts her head between her knees. Her head's swimming. It's the chemicals. They have that effect on you. She shouldn't have gone into the cupboard. *Curiosity killed the cat,* Grandma Willoughby says, waving a bony finger. Yesterday, when Stella was here with Frank, they'd had the cupboard open briefly; now it's like the smell's got stronger, more potent, the smell's more like it used to be.

Part of Stella belongs here. Part of her has never been away.

The old medical bag carries the same fascination: Stella was never allowed to touch it and she hardly dares touch it now. She wishes now she hadn't found it, or that she hadn't picked it up. Grandpa Worthy was certain Stella had the Gift, the same as he had. He said he'd teach her all he knew if she was willing, he promised she'd inherit his medical equipment, that he'd watch her from the other side to make sure she used her Gift wisely and correctly. Stella had had to promise not to breathe a word to her grandmother. Now Grandma Willoughby would turn in her grave if she knew Stella had been in that cupboard and had got her hands on the precious bag. Stella looks at the bag again. She could swear the clasps are more open than they were a minute ago. It can't do any harm to touch it, surely, not after all this time. Stella's a grown woman now and she's entitled to do what she wants, even including with her grandfather's bag, God rest his soul.

Stella stretches out her hand and brushes some dust off the bag. It's a kind of Gladstone bag, made of brown leather, covered in dust now after years of disuse on the floor of the cupboard. Two metal bars meet in the middle where the clasp is. She couldn't swear it, but it looks to Stella like the bag is opening of its own accord. The spring in the clasp is probably rusted away and cannot hold it closed. Stella tries not to breathe in the dust as she blows along the top where the rusty metal catches are now fully open. The leather is stiff, dull and cracked. In the weak light Stella can just make out some lettering embossed in the leather along one side of the bag: WW Willerby, it says. Which is the wrong spelling of her grandfather's name. And that middle W, that shouldn't be there either. His Christian name was Worthy and he didn't have a middle name.

Stella yanks hard on the metal bars and pulls the bag wide open, as wide as it will go. In her head, a baby is wailing.

A flashing sense of the passage of time, the completed shape of her grandfather's life, Grandma Willoughby sitting at the piano, the enduring sense of Muriel's longing. A smell of disinfectant. Ladies, murmuring into handkerchiefs, the clack, clack, clack of their heels disappearing down into the basement.

Then Stella is tipping the bag upside down, shaking it until its contents have fallen out, scattered, half onto the table, half across the floor. She bangs the bottom of it with the flat of her hand. Things clattering out all over the place, echoing in the silence. Stella watches as a dead rat falls out, bit by bit, the head only half disintegrated, the spindly little bones, its nest of straw, flakes of brown paper, bits of feathers. Stella shakes and bangs until the bag is completely empty. Little vials of liquid with silver caps and something else made of glass, smashing into pieces as they hit the floor.

Then something bigger falls with a softer thud, comes out last. A leather roll, tied round with a single thong, gone brittle with age. Stella tugs at the thong, it snaps, and the roll is spreading open on the table. It has a dark red velvet lining, worn shiny in places. Stella sees it's a pouch for instruments. There are long thick needles, rusted; a glass syringe with a metal plunger, the glass murky and clouded; pincers with sharp claw ends; rubber tubing, cracked and perished; a tiny hacksaw; hooks and spikes; a thing like an elongated corkscrew; flakes of rust leave stains on Stella's fingers. She picks up a small bottle marked 'Laudanum' and immediately pulls her hands away. She sees now what these horrible instruments are for.

Stella backs off, her hand clamped firmly against her mouth. She is going to be sick. She can't be here, in this house, alone, any more. Frank, horrible as he is, at least he is someone, alive and breathing. In this house there is nothing but death. Stella puts both hands to her face and tries not to breathe. In that cracked old bag were the hideous instruments of destruction. In that cupboard with its smells and its darkness and the terrible potions for desperate women, poisons all lined up along the dusty old shelves: Mugwort, Pennyroyal, Blue Cohosh, Laudanum, Chloral, Chloroform, death. Death has seeped into the walls of this house, it is in the air that Stella is breathing. She smells it, she tastes it, she feels it clasping at her throat, seeping its cold, malignant hyphae into her bones.

What a fool she is to have come back here, to have allowed herself to even think she could be free of all that happened in this house. She should have known better. Is it too late? Too late to get away?

Stella wretches with such force that vomit spurts out between her fingers and spatters down the wall and onto the floor, covering the instruments she's tipped out of the medical bag. She hasn't the will to stop the next lot from going all down her clothes.

She gropes her way to the chair by the fireside and tries to sit down, but she can hardly breathe for the thick smell of vomit and soot in the fireplace, the fumes from the cupboard. In the dim light she sees only shadows. Stella is sweating, dizzy and so very, very tired. She wants only to lie down, close her eyes, shut it away, blank it out.

It was easy, oh so easy, to hide things away from herself when she was young, but it comes harder now, so much harder. Stella can no longer block the memories from crowding in, one on top of the other, filling her up, taking her over.

It's all happening again, Stella knows it. She'd thought all that was behind her. Her heart thumps wildly like an animal trapped inside her, she can actually hear it scraping to get out. Something at her throat is trying to garrote her. The cloying taste of vomit is stuck to her teeth, waves of it well up inside her. She retches again and again, splattering vomit all over the fireside, all over the carpet. Exhausted, Stella wipes her mouth on her sleeve and sits back in her grandmother's chair, drenched with sweat.

This, Stella knows, is only the beginning.

Chapter Eighteen

Stella may have slept for moments, minutes, hours – she cannot tell. She has a strong desire to get up and go, get away from this house, be anywhere but here. But something is holding her down and won't let her get up. Her legs are weak, they won't let her stand. She can't fight any more. Stella is tired, so very tired. The house hasn't finished with her. She's drifting away again. It's too late.

In the front room, the sound of the piano playing.

> *Abide with me; fast falls the eventide;*
> *The darkness deepens; Lord with me abide.*
> *When other helpers fail and comforts flee,*
> *Help of the helpless, O abide with me.*

The start of the Sitting. Stella is being called. She'll have to go.

Stella stands up, still unsteady, and feels her way along the dark passageway, her footsteps slow, cold, deliberate, echo on the lino. She passes the door of her grandmother's room. It's tight shut, just as she left it. She walks as though pulled by an invisible rope towards where the piano is playing.

As she reaches the front room, the door swings open, it brushes across the carpet, lets her in, and then bangs shut behind her. Stella stands with her back to the door and breathes in familiar smells of candle wax, incense, soot and ashes. The bang of the door has set the chandelier in motion, made the windows rattle. The mirror over the fireplace swings from side to side. One by one, candles around the room flicker into light, their flames long and smoky, shivering shadows on the walls.

The lid of the piano has settled in the open position. It stops playing the hymn. The loud pedal is down, the melody's gone and the notes are all wrong, they're all discordant, running into each other, a clamorous noise. Stella jams her hands against her ears, but she's can't block the sound out. She's being carried away on the notes, pulled into another world. The lid of the piano bangs shut and the noise stops.

Here comes little Stella Moon, fourteen years old. Looks a lot younger, thin little thing. She sidles into the room, in her hand the special silver cross cloth she forgot to bring when she came in before. The child stands there, holding the silver cross cloth, trying to keep it neat, desperate not to crumple the edges. Stella stands there, wanting the Sitting to be over, wanting for the dried-up ladies with their crinkled faces, for creepy Mr Fanshaw, for fat Mrs Bradley with her bad breath, for them all to go away, for her mother Muriel to come back, to come back and take Stella away to the Beach Hut and never once let her come to the Sitting again.

Grandma Willoughby, all in black, sits at the piano, her face lit by candles in little elephant holders, one on either side, her thick feet working the pedals, her thick fingers moving across the keys.

> *Swift to its close ebbs out life's little day;*
> *Earth's joys grow dim; its glories pass away;*
> *Change and decay in all around I see;*
> *O Thou who changest not, abide with me.*

Grandmother Willoughby nods towards Stella. Stella walks to the piano and turns the pages of the hymnal as Grandma Willoughby plays.

Behind her, the assembled Ladies – not many today – are taking off their bristly black coats and their furry fox collars and hanging them on the coat-stand. Their neat hats, secured with fierce pins that glint in the candle light, remain perched on alabaster faces. The Ladies smell of lavender water and mothballs. They suck at indigestion tablets and shift their teeth about. They snap shut the little golden clasps of their stiff black handbags that they hold like shields with both hands in front of their hollowed bellies. Their knees are not visible and never have been. They are concealed in thick woollen stockings and hidden under heavy cotton undergarments and rough tweed skirts. Like the ones that hang on the Mary Jane in Grandma Willoughby's room.

Here comes Mrs Bradley. She's the last to arrive. She's the medium. She's got a new woman with her, that one from the Church. Grandma Willoughby looks round and nods as they come in. She continues to play.

I fear no foe, with Thee at hand to bless;
Ills have no weight, and tears no bitterness.
Where is death's sting? Where, grave, thy victory?
I triumph still, if Thou abide with me.

Mr Fanshaw is joining in this week. He's been away, in a big moody about something or other, Stella doesn't know what. But he's back now. He's in the good books because he's brought Grandma Willoughby's car back; she says he's got his tail between his legs. The ladies and Mr F take their places around the table. In a moment the Ladies will start to sing, their thin voices straining at the top notes, setting their sinewy necks vibrato. Mr Fanshaw doesn't sing, he never sings. He stands behind his chair, holding onto it as though it might float away. He's wearing a suit.

In the sweet by and by
We will meet on that beautiful shore...

Smoke sizzles up through the clinker, the fire coming to life. Grandma Willoughby looks up at Stella. Stella leaves the piano, unfolds the cloth with the silver cross and uses it to cover the mirror that hangs over the fireplace. She walks forward, takes her place at the table, hangs her head and closes her eyes. Like everyone else, Stella pulls on the white cotton gloves and lays her hands on the table, palms down flat, and breathes slowly.

The singing over, Grandma Willoughby closes the lid of the piano quietly. She sprinkles a small vial of holy water over the table, a few sage leaves newly crushed between her fingers. She too takes her place at the table, pulls on the gloves, hangs her head, and closes her eyes.

'Make the circle,' says Ruby Willoughby after a moment or two of silence.

White gloved thumbs are pressed together round the table, little fingers outstretched and touching, completing the round. 'Keep the circle,' Ruby says, her eyes still closed, 'you know the rules.'

Nods and murmurs of assent.

'Let us pray.'

Waiting, breathing calmly, eyes open now and focused on the flickering candles. Ruby nods to Mrs Bradley, who begins the Prayer of Protection in scarcely more than a whisper.

Divine white light of the Holy Ghost and all the Angels, surround our Circle; the love of God protect us; the light of God shine down among us; the power of God watch over us and keep us safe in His eternal glory. Lord, we come to you in peace and friendship. In the name of God the Father. Amen.

Amen. A pause, the sound of breathing.

Our beloved friends on the other side...

Mrs Bradley closes her eyes and speaks softly into the silence.

Commune with us dear friends departed. Commune with us...

Barely audible voices round the table repeat the invocation three more times.

Commune with us, dear friends departed, and move among us. Spirit friends, make your presence known...

Stella feels words clogging in her throat, tangible words, they're filling her mouth, starting to spill out. She can't swallow. She's biting down on the words but they won't go away, they're coming all the more, there's nothing she can do to stop them.

Spirits from other worlds and times long past, a voice that is at once Stella's and not Stella's comes spattering out of her mouth. *Spirit friends from the Other Side, come close to us... we welcome you in to move among us. Be guided by the lights of this room to visit upon us... Join our Circle, dear friends...*

The candles flicker, as though a draught has rushed through the room, their flames shrink small then grow taller.

The spirits of the past are moving among us. Friends departed, make us aware of your presence.

The room grows very cold. The sash window that was slightly open scrapes on its cord and crashes closed.

Ruby looks at Mrs Bradley.

'Shush, now,' Ruby says, closing her eyes more tightly, 'quiet now.' A tension runs through the white-gloved hands that rest around the table, reaching Stella.

'Keep the circle,' Mrs Bradley hisses, her mouth hardly opening.

Spirit friends, you are with us, Stella continues in a voice she does not recognise. *A spirit friend is joining our circle... Welcome, welcome to our circle, dear friend of the spirit. Your presence is felt. You are coming through to me now. What is it you wish to say to us?*

The room is icy. There is a strong smell of something decomposing. For a moment, Stella has a sense of something covering her face, a feeling of not being able to breathe.

'Stella!' Ruby begins to say, but Mrs Bradley interrupts.

'Keep the circle!'

'Our Stella...'

Stella continues to speak in short, breathless bursts, what comes out is only a rasping whisper.

Yes, yes we know that you are walking among us

Stella's eyes are wide open and staring.

We feel your presence

Tortured, incoherent noises are hissing out of Stella as though from the depths of her. The felt cloth with the silver cross on that Stella used to cover the mirror now falls and, as it falls, slides into the fire. A noisy gush of flame flies into the room as the cloth ignites and burns.

The room is pulsating, the smell of something decomposing is overwhelming, Stella can barely breathe. The rasping voice is still trying to get out of her with every laboured breath.

Ruby, alarmed, stands up, her hands still pressing on the table, the circle not yet broken.

'No, Ruby!' says Mrs Bradley. 'Let it take its course. To do anything at all is dangerous, we could lose her...'

Mrs Bradley looks around the table. The fear is palpable and visible in every tightened face.

'Please, everyone, keep calm. It's absolutely essential that we all stay calm. Keep the circle and this thing will pass.'

Mrs Bradley closes her eyes. As though speaking to someone inside her head, she nods and mumbles under her breath, 'Alright, yes, yes, I hear you...' She nods again, a look of intense concentration on her face. 'Spirit friend,' Mrs Bradley begins, 'you have come to us, and we ask now that you leave us.' Mrs Bradley breathes heavily. 'We ask now that you leave us,' she repeats, more firmly. 'Please leave us. Leave us now.' Mrs Bradley's hands are shaking and it is with obvious effort that she is keeping them on the table. 'You must leave us. You must leave us now.'

Stella is rasping out more words that make no sense, she's making strange noises she doesn't recognise as human. Her whole body is trembling, her consciousness wavering. She is going outside herself, she's leaving her own body... she can't get back...

Stella looks down and sees herself sitting at the table. She sees her mouth opening, her pale lips stretching back from her teeth. She hears the most terrible wailing coming from deep down inside her and echoing round the room.

'It's not working!' Ruby is shouting now to make herself heard above Stella's screaming. 'Mrs Bradley...do something! Stella! Stella! Stop it now! Stop that now!'

Stella's mouth is wide open, her wide eyes are staring, the scream has turned into a hoarse croaking sound that goes on and on, it sounds as though she is choking.

'Everyone keep calm, please keep calm. Don't break the circle. We could lose her,' Mrs Bradley shuts her eyes. 'I'll try again,' she says. 'Chant,' she commands, 'everyone, everyone together.'

The circle of white-gloved hands tenses once more around the table, as everyone begins to chant in phrases after Mrs Bradley.

Divine white light of the Holy Ghost and all the Angels, surround our Circle; the love of God protect us; the light of God shine down among us; the power of God keep us safe in His eternal glory.

Before they finish the prayer, the room fills with a stifling heat.

Stella's mouth is wide open, but she's really choking this time, she's gasping for breath.

Mrs Bradley begins to speak again, steadily and fast, in a monotone.

Most glorious God of the glorious Heavens, defend us in our battles against the rulers of the world of darkness, give us strength to defeat the spirits of wickedness, free us from the tyranny of the devil. May the Holy Church ever be our Guardian and our Protector. The God of Peace crush Satan that he may no longer hold us captive. The mercy of God's light shine down upon us and be with us. Cast out the devil into the wilderness that his power be removed and that he remain without power for time eternal. In the name of God the Father.

Amen, says everyone together. Amen, says Mrs Bradley again.

As she finishes, the mirror falls from its chain and smashes on the fireplace. The gasping fades. Stella begins to breathe again.

Then she begins to speak.

'Baby Keating has not gone missing,' she rasps, 'Baby Keating has not been abducted.' There is froth coming out of Stella's mouth as she struggles to get the words out. 'Baby Keating is dead.'

A sharp intake of breath around the room. Then silence. No-one moves.

'Don't you hear what I'm saying?' Stella is yelling now. She snatches her hands up from the table, breaking the circle. 'Did you hear what I said? The baby's dead.'

Still no-one moves. 'Is nobody listening to me?' Stella shouts, 'Baby Keating is dead. His body is buried at the back of the civvy.'

Stella slumps forward and lies motionless across the table.

Chapter Nineteen

Stella wakes up on the couch in the sitting room. She has no idea whether it's morning or night. The blackness is the same whether she opens her eyes or not. She lies still, her thoughts jumbled and disjointed. She tries to jam them together but they're bending and cracking like pieces of a jigsaw that refuse to fit together. Stella has woken up angry. Very angry. She lies still, her eyes closed, and counts back slowly in threes from 101, the way Marcia taught her. She listens to Marcia's rhythmic counting and feels the light pressure of Marcia's hands on her shoulders, Marcia's breath in her hair, the sound of Marcia's voice surrounding her.

But Marcia's not here. Marcia's not real, not any more. Here, Marcia's getting lost in the fear and the dark and the crowding in of memory. Marcia's lost, like Stella is lost.

Inside Stella, a scream is taking shape, a scream that begins somewhere deep inside, that wells up to strain against her vocal chords, that comes out as hardly more than a whimper. Stella knows that scream. It can fill her mouth till it's wide open for minutes on end, with no sound coming out, no sound at all.

Stella tries to get up, but her limbs no longer obey. She shifts on the couch, straightens her back and stretches her legs, aching all over. There's a nasty, sour taste in her mouth. Her clothes are covered in sick. The rancid smell of it brings on new waves of nausea. Stella knows now, she has to get up, she must get up and get out of this room, out of this room and out of this house. She throws herself from the couch and half stumbles, half crawls across the room and pulls the door behind her till it bangs tight shut. It's all she can do to make it to the passage. Her back slides down the wall and she slumps to the floor. Collapsed in the passageway, Stella drifting in and out of consciousness, floating among fragments of memory, blurred distorted images, the taste of chemicals, the smell of vomit, powerless to stop any of it.

Silence had fallen as the words left Stella's mouth. They were all looking at her, she could feel their penetrating eyes. She'd wanted to speak, but couldn't: she was drifting away. Then there was Frank, there were the Ladies round the table, standing up now. Stella's grandmother, Mrs Bradley, all staring at Stella, saying nothing. At that same moment, the door crashed open and Muriel burst into the room.

'What's all this hocus pocus bloody baloney?' she shouted. 'And you,' she shouted, prodding her finger at Ruby, 'how many times have I told you not to involve our Stella in your sinister goings on? She's only a kid, for Christ's sake.'

Muriel took Stella by the shoulders and tried to lift her up from the table. But as soon as she let go, Stella fell forward again, her body limp.

'What's the matter with her?' Muriel demanded. 'What have you done to her this time?' She bent down and looked into Stella's face. It was ashen, her eyes still wide and staring, her breathing fast and shallow. 'What in God's name have you done to her?' Muriel shook Stella's shoulder gently. 'Stella, can you hear me? It's me, Muriel, your mother...' Stella remained motionless. She could hear her mother, but she couldn't speak.

Muriel looked around at the assembled company. The Ladies were already fidgeting as if making to leave but unsure of the protocol.

'You're evil, the lot of you, that's what you are. You should be ashamed of yourselves, and her just a kid. Stella?' Muriel shook Stella by the shoulder again. Still Stella lay slumped across the table.

Muriel strode across the room and turned the main light on. She looked around and took in the burnt embers of the felt cloth about the fireside, the broken mirror in pieces on the floor.

'What the hell's been going on?'

Muriel bent down and touched Stella's arm. 'Stella, it's your mother, can you hear me?' She felt the pulse on Stella's wrist. 'It's racing. What have you done? Go and phone for an ambulance,' she said to Ruby, 'and be quick about it.'

'Muriel...'

'Get a doctor, I said. What's the matter with you? She's hardly breathing, she needs a bloody doctor.'

'Muriel. Get a hold of yourself,' said Ruby, smiling a weak smile at the Ladies before going on. 'Stella doesn't need a doctor. She's alright. She was in a trance, that's all. She'll be alright in a minute or two, isn't that right, Mrs Bradley? Best just to let her be.'

'Yes, yes, yes,' Mrs Bradley chimed in, 'There's really no need to worry, Muriel. She just needs to rest for a bit. This can happen before the... er... visitation leaves. I've seen this happen before. They really are best left alone...'

'You coming bursting in like that,' said Ruby to Muriel, 'breaking the circle...'

'I'll break your bloody circle!' Muriel yelled, 'I'll break your bloody necks. Get out, get out the lot of you. Get out of this house and never come back.'

'Now, now, Muriel,' said Ruby, 'this is my house, and I'll give the orders...'

The Ladies and Mrs Bradley were already on their feet, peeling off the white gloves and laying them down, gathering up their handbags and prayer books, saying they'd best be off and leave the family to sort out their own business. Frank stood up and made as if to leave with the rest of them.

'You'd better stay behind a bit, Mr Fanshaw,' said Ruby, 'if you don't mind helping to clear things up.'

Frank nodded, went to the fireplace and pushed at the bits of broken mirror with his foot. The Ladies congregated by the door, putting on coats and adjusting their hat-pins.

Ruby closed the front door and returned to the sitting room. 'That's them away,' she said to Frank.

Muriel and Frank had carried Stella to the sofa and covered her with the tartan blanket.

'I've given her some chloral,' Muriel said, edging herself onto the sofa beside Stella and putting her hand to Stella's brow. 'She should sleep.'

'Oh, Muriel,' Ruby said, 'you've no idea what trouble we're in.'

'Since when have your troubles been any concern of mine?'

'This does concern you, Muriel. It's baby Keating,' said Ruby. 'Somehow or other, our Stella knows . She knows the baby wasn't kidnapped… And now everyone knows.'

'What's baby Keating got to do with anything? ' said Muriel.

'Oh, our Muriel,' Ruby said. 'It was Stella who got the visitation. We couldn't stop her, it all happened so quick…' Ruby said. 'And, well, at the end, when you came in, Stella blurts out that the baby's dead and tells them where Frank buried his body.'

'You'll have to do something, Frank,' Muriel said. 'You're going to have to do something, Frank, and do it quick.'

'Do like what?'

Ruby was decisive. 'Go and get the baby. Take it somewhere else. Somewhere it won't be found. There's no other way. Otherwise, if they start making their mags go…'

'Christ all-bloody-mighty, not that again. Why have I got to do it?'

'There's no-one else,' Ruby said, 'You buried it in the first place. You know where it is.'

'Do it for Stella,' said Muriel, 'if you call yourself a man. It's Stella who'll suffer the most if this all comes out.'

'Stella?' said Frank, looking at the sleeping child on the sofa, her hair all over the place, her face very pale.

'Now, now,' Ruby said, 'that's enough. We've been through all that, and we none of us can be certain what happened, so let's leave it at that.'

'I know you like to think in your warped imagination that it was me who killed Baby Keating,' Muriel said, 'but let me remind you, Ruby Willoughby, it was *you* who made up the drink. It may have been our Stella who gave him the bottle. But it was *you* who made it up. I had nothing to do with any of that. The only thing I'm guilty of was trying to keep him breathing…'

'Don't be a fool, Muriel. It wasn't the chloretone that killed him.'

Stella stirred on the couch, pushing the blanket to the floor. Frank picked it up and covered her over again.

'Right,' he said, 'I'll go and get done what needs to be done… Muriel?'

'I'm having nothing more to do with it.'

'It's time you got off your high horse, our Muriel,' said Ruby, losing patience, 'you're going to help Frank whether you like it or not. Get the baby, take him to the Beach Hut and put him under where the new kitchen's going. It's the only way. Do as I say, or live to regret it.'

Muriel went over to the couch. Stella opened her eyes a little and looked up at her mother.

'I didn't mean to kill Baby Keating,' she said, 'really, I didn't.'

Those were the last words Stella Moon spoke for more than two years.

* * *

Is Stella having another breakdown? Is it the workings of the deranged imagination of strange precocious Stella Moon taking over? That's what they said the first time. That she'd brought it all on herself by an over-active imagination that amounted to hysterics, plain hysterics.

The séance had gone wrong and she'd wanted to scream, but the scream had got stuck somewhere deep inside her and Stella had closed her mouth and kept it there and hadn't uttered a single word for a full two years.

And now it's happening again. A re-run. An action replay, from half a lifetime ago.

Stella must get away from this house. Like Marcia says, she has to get back to now. But she can't even lift herself up off the floor. The house hasn't finished with her, not yet. It wants to tell its all to Stella Moon. The house will make her listen.

Chapter Twenty

All her life before now, in that rocking silence, Stella had found a peace, of sorts. But not any more. It's no longer working. And she starts to see now, that silence, it wasn't peace at all: it was just a way of going on living, a way of living with herself, with Grandma Willoughby, with Frank Fanshaw, without Muriel – a way to survive. Stella's silence had caused even Ruby and Muriel to set aside their differences in their joint efforts to get her well.

It was the shock, they said – she'd get over it. But Stella didn't get over whatever it was. They gave her chamomile tea and valerian, they talked kindly and brushed her hair, but still Stella had remained locked inside somewhere, where words no longer mattered. The shock, they said, had been too much for the child, a nervy child at the best of times. And there's no telling what a mischievous spirit will do, hell-bent on creating chaos and destruction, and see how it had gone and put all those silly ideas into her head about the baby, see how it made her tell all those lies, those terrible, terrible lies. Just give the poor child peace and quiet and she'll get over it, she'll soon be over it. Stella heard it all and registered not a flicker.

Time went by and they ran out of excuses and then they began to run out of hope. Ruby and Muriel started blaming each other openly, they each blamed themselves secretly, they alternately cursed Worthy for letting such a dreadful thing happen and begged and pleaded with him to come back from beyond his grave and put things right. They promised him such a thing would never happen again. They took turns, Ruby and Muriel, to watch Stella closely, watching and waiting for some sign, any sign, of change, however small. Ruby sat with her crochet and Stella rocked to the rhythm of it. Muriel paced the floor in stockinged feet and bit her nails and had to have false ones stuck on. But still Stella didn't speak.

Ruby determined out loud not to panic. She upped the doses and when that didn't work, she resorted to the laudanum and took a double dose herself. Stella shook and shivered, but still not a word passed her lips. Hot bottles, cold compresses, baths and inhalations, nothing made any difference. Then holy water and incantations and the laying on of hands by kind Father Headley – all had no effect. Still Stella rocked and rocked and no sounds came.

Then one night when Muriel was away, Ruby took the plunge and brought in the medium Mrs Bradley. But the very appearance of the woman at the bottom of the stairs, before she'd even removed her hat, had Stella hysterical, her arms flailing, her eyes staring and her mouth wide open a long, long time with nothing coming out but that terrible silent screaming. They'd had to slap her and slap her to make her stop and Mrs Bradley had hurried away before Muriel came back. As she left, Ruby had slammed Stella's door so hard bits of putty had fallen out the glass and Ruby announced as she thundered down the stairs that she couldn't stand it any more and she shouldn't be expected to cope and why was it always she who had to pick up the pieces, see to the mess of Muriel's damnable creation? Ruby Willoughby was washing her hands of the whole damn business, so help her God.

The temporary truce between Ruby and Muriel collapsed, as it was always going to, and Muriel went off to the Beach Hut with Frank. Ruby drove Stella to a sanitorium, a kind of convalescent place, somewhere on the Durham side, near Rowlands Gill. It was better for everyone, Ruby said. Stella hadn't protested. The poor girl was having a breakdown, she'd taken leave of her senses, was what Ruby told the sanitorium people. Despite all Ruby's efforts, Stella had turned out to be just like Muriel after all.

At first they'd come every other week to see her – sometimes Grandma Willoughby, sometimes Muriel, but never together. Mr Fanshaw might come with Muriel. They'd bring grapes and barley water and tell her everything was going to be alright. Stella had stared at them and studied their faces. Nothing made sense. Stella had no words, no tears, and no dreams, just silence. People tired of her and she of them.

The last time Muriel came she was all smiles and had brought a bunch of elderflowers, a box of Jaffa Cakes and a big bottle of Dandelion and Burdock. She'd talked excitedly about her plans for Stella to come to live with her at the Beach Hut. She'd been doing more of the taxidermy – it was going really well and she'd sold a couple of things and done a pet parrot for someone and was certain she'd soon be getting a lot more commissions. They'd be a lot better off. She'd been doing a lot less of the other thing and was trying to persuade Frank to be around a bit more. Stella had listened to Muriel's plans and promises, she'd looked into her mother's eyes, but she couldn't and wouldn't and didn't talk. Muriel lost patience. She'd taken hold of Stella's shoulders and shaken her, just a little bit, then harder, then out of control. She'd shaken Stella until Stella went limp, demanding that Stella agree to come away with her there and then, that very minute. She'd slapped Stella hard across the face and slapped her and slapped her, until Frank had pulled her off and Muriel had dropped to her knees and begged and begged for Stella to make even the smallest sound. Frank was standing by the door, telling Muriel they'd best get on and they'd see Stella in a week or two. Muriel dropped her hands, turned away and covered her face. She was crying as she left. Stella saw Frank put his arm around Muriel's heaving shoulders. He closed the door quietly behind them and they never came back.

Doctors, psychiatrists, nurses and social workers all came and went, all talking at Stella in voices that were too loud, voices that echoed and got all mixed up. They sedated her, they attached electrodes and passed currents until her body heaved and convulsed and then settled into a state even more inert than it was before. They took blood out of her veins. Stella watched impassively as it coursed along tubes and dripped into bottles. The medical people measured this and that. They peered into her face, shone sharp lights into her eyes and poked instruments in her ears. They put her on drips, they took her urine, they gave her tablets and capsules and liquids and barely warm weak tea. Nothing changed. After a while the doctors hardly came either.

Stella cannot heave herself up off the floor. She needs a drink, desperately. In the scullery water dribbles out under the sink where Frank broke the pipe. Stella imagines herself drinking it, lying under it, the cold water dripping into her open mouth. She imagines the feel of it, the smell of it, the taste of it, like graphite from a pencil, she wants to gulp and gulp and never stop. But she's too exhausted to do anything more than think of water. She hears it drip, drip, dripping in the scullery like a torture. She can't even crawl towards it. She has no strength left at all. Frank's not coming. It's no good, he's not coming back, he's given up on her. Stella closes her eyes and lets herself crumple to the floor.

Chapter Twenty-One

Stella was dead right. Frank Fanshaw was not coming back. He'd left the boarding house in a state of extreme agitation, desperate to get to the Beach Hut.

He had to get after Stella, but disposing of the body had to be the number one priority. Frank didn't know how he hadn't realised that before. He should have done it a long time ago. He'd had all those years when Stella was inside, and somehow it hadn't seemed important. Now it's different. Frank's agitation had only increased when he'd had to spend the night in the bus station in Newcastle. He'd hardly slept at all. Then even more anxiety as he tried to get from the town to the Beach Hut. He had to wait over an hour for the first bus, then the blasted thing had gone the longest possible route, round and round the houses, stopping at every damned godforsaken hole. Now it's taken him a good two and a half hours to get to bloody Alnwick, where Frank now has to wait another hour before he can get to Embleton. All the anxiety is doing his head in and rocketing his blood pressure, he can feel it thumping at his temples like a hammer.

At this rate, Stella will have blown the whistle a hundred times over, Old Ruby – if she's still alive – will have gone gaga, Hedy will have gone AWOL, the police will have dug up the baby's body and slapped a murder scene cordon round the Beach Hut and put out a warrant for the arrest of Frank Fanshaw before Frank even gets on the bloody bus. Frank can't help but wonder, in the light of everything, if it's sensible to keep on with the public transport. Embleton is only six miles from Alnwick, he could walk. He'd get there about five or six. He'd have plenty chance to stay incognito and stake the place out a bit, make sure it wasn't swarming with coppers before he approached too close... Frank's not sure what to do for the best. He decides to nip into the Tanner's Arms for a quick pie and a pint and a think about strategy.

But Frank doesn't get to think about anything. Neither does he get to enjoy the pie or the pint. In fact, he's only in the place thirty seconds before he makes a hasty exit. There, on the bar, an open copy of today's *Journal* shows a large picture of Stella Moon. The picture's enough to turn Frank hot and cold all at once. He doesn't even try to see what the article says. The landlord will think he's daft in the head. That can't be helped. Frank needs to make an excuse. He looks at his watch. The landlord's at the far end of the bar, pulling Frank's pint. He's looking over at Frank as he pulls. Frank taps his forefinger rapidly on the face of his watch, nods his head by way of an apology, says for the landlord to keep the drink and cancel the pie, he's mistimed himself, he has to run for the bus. The landlord shrugs, shakes his head, takes a swig of the half-pulled pint himself and tips the rest down the sink. Frank grabs his coat and his bag and dashes out into the street. His stomach can't cope with it. He has to nip over the road to the public toilets where his bowels turn themselves inside out.

The seriousness of his situation now weighs very heavy on Frank's mind. He has to calm down and think rational. At least it's not a new photograph of Stella: it's that old one from seven years ago. Conclusion: they're publishing this stuff without anyone having yet got close enough to get a newer pic of her. On the other hand, it's a big spread, not just a small one. Conclusion: it's not just a small, insignificant news item. Frank could buy his own copy of the paper and have a closer look. But no. What if it mentions him? There could be a picture of him on the next page for all he knows. Frank starts to sweat. He feels nauseous. He needs to know. But he daren't risk buying a paper. Not in Alnwick. The last thing he wants is to draw attention to himself when there's a cop shop just around the corner. But he needs to know what the papers are saying. They've got onto Stella quick enough. She hasn't been out two minutes. He could risk getting the paper. Get it in the supermarket beside the bus station. More anonymous. Decision made. Frank finishes in the toilet, puts his collar up and practically runs along the road.

The supermarket's sold out of the *Journal*, but Frank manages to get a four-pack of Brown Ales, two ham and egg sandwiches, a Twix, some fags, and a large bottle of Bell's. He pockets his change and gets onto the Embleton bus which, miracle of miracles, is now standing there empty and waiting in the bus station. Frank's not going to risk walking it, not with a stomach like he's got at the moment. He'll sit at the back and mind his own business.

Half an hour later, Frank's getting off at Embleton. He steels himself and walks into the village shop. There on the floor, piles of them, today's papers. Frank picks up a *Journal*, and a couple of the other papers, pays with the right money, says thank you very much and gets on his way.

So that was simple enough. He'll wait till he gets down the road a bit before he has a look. Frank's shaking as he heads down Sea Lane towards the golf course. All his insides are shuddering about in a state of terror. He takes a deep breath, several. Breathes in deep – sea air, which is supposed to be good for you – tries to calm down.

Frank wonders where Stella is. He needs to steel himself: she could have made her own way to the Beach Hut. Where else did she have to go? By the golf course there's a wooden bench. He needs to decide what to do with her if she is there, and if she won't see sense. Frank sits down, leans over and fiddles with his shoe till he's confident no-one's paying him any attention. There are a few people on the golf course, a couple over by the dunes with a border terrier and someone on a ride-on mower shaving the grass round the bunkers. No-one is taking any notice of Frank Fanshaw. He decides to chance looking at one of the papers. What could be more normal? A middle-aged man stopping for a minute or two to have a glance at the paper.

Frank opens *The Journal* and finds the page. Yes, there she is, it's Stella alright. He'd half begun to hope that his eyes in the Tanner's had deceived him, but no, it's her, staring out at him from the newspaper.

NORTH EAST KILLER RELEASED, the headline reads.

Stella Moon, who confessed to killing her mother Muriel Moon

*in 1970, has been released from Holloway Prison where she
served a full seven-year sentence for manslaughter. Many in
the area believed the young killer got off lightly and the police
should have done more to make a murder charge stick. It is
believed Miss Moon, who is now 25, has returned to the North
East. She grew up in Newcastle in the care of her grandmother,
Ruby Willoughby, now 82, who ran a lodging house and now
resides in a care home in the South of England. 'Matricide is an
extremely unusual crime,' a local expert told us, 'particularly
when committed by a female, and one so young.'*

*Miss Moon's name had appeared a few years earlier in
connection with another crime, the abduction of an infant, a
few weeks old, from the same lodging house. No-one was ever
charged with the abduction, and the whereabouts of the baby
has never been ascertained. But readers should rest assured the
Journal's intrepid reporter Daniel Macalinden is on the case. Mr
Macalinden reported on the abduction of Baby Keating in 1966
as well as following the Moon case to its inevitable conclusion in
1970. Our reporter believes he can make a convincing case for a
link between the two crimes and he is determined to get to the
bottom of it. Meanwhile red-headed killer Stella Moon is free to
go where she pleases in our county...*

Frank can't stand to read any more. He shuts the paper and
folds it up small enough to cram into his pocket. He looks around,
but still no-one appears to be paying him any mind.

Frank's having trouble thinking straight. His hands are shaking.
His stomach is gurgling, his bowels turning to water again. He
tries to tell himself that things aren't as bad as they could be, that
he probably still has time to do what he has to do. But anxiety
is hurting his chest, making it hard to get his breath. There's a
terrible tightness, he can't seem to get enough air in.

All Frank can think of is getting to the Beach Hut and disposing
of the evidence. Getting rid of the bloody baby. Finally rid of the
sodding baby that has been the bain of his life for the last ten
years. It's only a matter of a time till the polis starts looking into

the baby business again, till the papers start hounding Frank Fanshaw like they did when the baby went missing, like they did when Stella killed Muriel. Only a matter of time till Macalinden gets a proper handle on the story. Frank has to act fast. He feels exhausted and ill but forces himself to get up and get onto the dune path, heading for the Beach Hut. He's got to get there quick, before he shits his pants.

How the hell he'd managed to get himself so mixed up with Stella Moon's crimes, Frank still cannot fathom.

He'd read somewhere that burying a body makes you some kind of accessory even if you've got nothing to do with the actual death. Add to that the fact that it's the body of a baby you're talking about, and that makes it all the more serious for Frank, given what he's already done time for. Plus, what Stella Moon could accuse him of if she chose to open her mouth – if she hasn't already shopped him for God knows what. Frank's chest hurts, it's burning from the exertion and breathing in cold damp air. He could be going to have heart attack for all he knows. That could be a blessing. Anything would be better than the way Frank feels at this moment.

Slow down, Frank. Slow down. There's no point in getting yourself all worked up. Think about it logically. You've been alright for getting on ten years. The only thing that's changed is Stella has come out. OK, the press have reported it, but if Stella was going to squeal, she'd have done so by now. Ditto Ruby Willoughby. Ditto Hedy Keating. None of them have uttered a squeak in getting on for a decade. And for a very good reason. So calm yourself down.

Nevertheless, Frank knows he will feel an awful lot safer once he's obliterated all trace of the baby's body, once he knows for certain Stella Moon – whatever she does or does not remember – can't go dropping him in it. Meanwhile, he'll have to concentrate on not getting himself seen or, at least not recognised, in case the papers do get the bit between their teeth and start printing pictures of him. Those old pictures they had, they looked nothing like him in the first place. He'll be alright. He'll be alright, Frank tells himself. He. Will. Be. Alright.

Frank arrives at the Beach Hut calmer than he was ten minutes ago. He's had a few slugs from the bottle of Bell's on the way.

Looking over from a distance, Frank can see the place looks deserted. There's no cops or anyone about. All quiet on the Western Front. Still, Frank can't help being anxious as he lets himself in with his key. He's surprised it still works, the lock being as rusty as it is with all the sea salt. He pushes the door open with his foot. It's quite dark and he can't see that much. The place smells bad – in fact, it stinks. And what a mess! Frank picks his way across the floor. That smell, it's Muriel's chemicals. And damp. An unlived-in smell. Mould. Frank lights a couple of candles and his eyes soon acclimatise. He looks more closely. He sees several of Muriel's bottles and jars and specimens lying about on the floor. There could have been intruders. Frank glances around. The windows look intact enough. He takes a candle and goes through to the kitchen.

Frank stops dead at the kitchen door and dares not take a further step. He hold the flickering candle out at arm's length, but even in that bad light he can see the very thing he didn't want to see, the very last thing he thought he would see. A fucking dirty, great hole in the floor, exactly where the baby's body should be.

So where the hell has that gone? Who the fuck has taken it?

Frank realises after a few moments that he has stopped breathing. He has to consciously start again. Breath in, Frank, breath out. The pain in his chest is back. The panic welling. Frank feels like an utter bloody idiot. He's going to be sick. Up comes the whisky, burns his gullet, nearly chokes him. Get a grip, Frank, get a bloody grip.

The baby's been dug up. Somebody's took it. Which means Frank is in the shit. Somebody knows there's a dead baby, a dead baby that was buried under the kitchen floor. Which means that somebody, whoever they are, could be watching Frank Fanshaw, watching him right now, right this minute. There could be cameras. Somebody watching. Collecting evidence. Frank is afraid to turn round, afraid to move. He stands there, staring into the hole, staring into the ruddy gaping hole. What a frigging mess.

How the hell is he going to get out of this? Who the fuck's got the baby? And what the fuck for?

Maybe it's Frank that's going gaga. Ten years have passed since Stella killed the kid. Frank may have forgot a lot of things, but he wouldn't forget something like burying a dead body and he'd swear on his life he and Muriel buried it there, right there, under that kitchen floor. Frank distinctly remembers. Muriel taxidermied it. She was queer like that. He shouldn't have let her. He'd tried to stop her, but trying to stop Muriel was always going to be a losing battle. So he'd told himself the kid was dead, so what harm was there in letting Muriel have her way? There was no real way Frank could have persuaded her otherwise.

But look. The chickens have come home to roost. Whoever's got that baby has a taxidermied corpse: grotesque, hideous, yes, to Frank's mind, but more or less intact, recognisable as Hedy Keating's little 'un that disappeared from the boarding house. Christ. Frank is sweating. Trying to think things through. A rush of memories and panic all jumbled up, what the fuck, how the fuck, where the fuck? He looks some more into the gaping bloody great hole. He pokes around the sandy earth with his foot. No, definitely nothing in there. It's gone. But when? Who? Why? The hole looks like it's been dug a canny long time, the sandy earth completely dried out. Who would do that? Nobody but Frank and Muriel knew it was there. And Ruby. They'd told Ruby.

Frank's plans are all to cock. He hadn't factored in for this. And fear is making him irrational. He can't think logical while his mind is whirling off in all directions and he's listening for the cops to arrive at any moment. He takes a few more slugs from the whisky bottle. Get a grip, Frank, get a bloody grip.

Whoever took the body – whoever's got the body. The polis? Have they been and got it? They couldn't have. It said in the paper the baby's abduction was a crime still waiting to be solved. It can't be the polis. Oh, God. OK. Think through it Frank. Three possibilities, no, four; Ruby, Hedy, and Stella. Or some random unknown person. Which includes the polis. Because the press can tell lies on purpose. To put criminals off the scent. What is most likely? Frank can't tell. It could be any. Or two of them, acting in cahoots. Someone setting a trap for him. Another long slug from the bottle. Christ almighty.

Frank steps outside onto the veranda, stands and listens. It's still out there, and quiet. He can't see nowt except the lighthouse on the Farnes doing its periodic sweep. He can't hear a thing, nothing except the rush, rush, rush of the sea all mixed up with the rush, rush, rush of his own blood going past his ears. Fuck you, Stella Moon. Fuck you, fuck you, fuck you. What the fuck is he going to do?

Chapter Twenty-Two

Gareth's incompetence – there's no other word for it, he's been obliged to admit to himself – Gareth's stupid, distracted bungling meant Stella Moon, fresh out of jail and therefore in the category 'vulnerable' had had to spend last night by herself in the derelict Boarding House or – even worse scenario – not alone, but with that creep (whose name Gareth can't immediately recall, Frank some-body) who was there, or came back, whatever. Upshot is Gareth's had a very bad night. His conscience pricked him into the small hours, then wide awake at five thirty. Now the anxiety's spread and he's worrying about everything under the sun. He hopes to God she shows up this morning at the housing place. Gareth curses himself, he can't even remember what he told her about that, he can't believe he can't remember. Gareth can hear Mamgu's voice in his head telling him he'd better pull his socks up. Gareth knows he'll never get anywhere if he keeps on making mistakes like that. He cannot think how the hell he got so distracted.

Gareth's rushed in early to work. He's rung the housing place, left an urgent message for them to get Geoff on the case. Hopefully they'll catch him before he leaves for the office, and then Geoff can go straight there and get the accommodation sorted. That done, Gareth feels a bit lighter. Then temptation gets the better of him and, no-one about, he goes to Geoff's desk and retrieves the Moon file from where he locked it last night. Gareth tells himself if he's going to use it for a Case Study in his MSc Dissertation – some-thing he'd been thinking about in the night and decided it wasn't a bad idea: both he and Stella, as well as the wider knowledge base, would benefit. He's going to have to familiarise himself with all aspects of the case. What Geoff will have to say about the idea, whether he'll have ethical issues – he usually does – well, Gareth will cross that bridge when he comes to it. Geoff may want to hang onto the case. Strictly speaking, Gareth's not senior enough to be taking it over entirely, but Geoff could supervise him. Whatever, Gareth needs to get himself on top of it, show Geoff he's on top of it, that he's been prepared to put his own time in on it, etc.

Gareth knows there has to be a professional distance between Probation Officer and client. It's a very basic rule. And it's for the good of everyone. But the reality is a little more complex. Not with every client. It's only her. There's something about Stella Moon, she haunts you, you can't easily step away. Gareth could never explain that to Geoff, so maybe he just has to wait and Geoff will find out for himself. Anyone would be fascinated by the fact that Stella Moon looks so ruddy normal … He'd better put the file away, before the others come. He's not quite sure how to go about discussing things with Geoff.

In Gareth's head, Stella is standing bedraggled in the rain, in those silly, old-fashioned clothes way too big for her and those daft golden slippers. She's standing there, thin and pale with the little blue suitcase she hardly dares part with, a self-confessed killer, yet strangely innocent and vulnerable, crying out with need. There's something else too, something else about her – she's tough, self-contained, invincible. Those wide eyes, the determined set of the mouth, the way she stands straight and defiant, like she's prepared to take on the world if need be. And that weird silence, how she shrinks inside herself and to all intents and purposes disappears, for no apparent reason. Gareth should stop thinking about her. He doesn't want her taking him over. Get on with your own work, Gareth Davies, before Clara and Geoff get in.

* * *

Back at the boarding house, Stella is lying crumpled on the hallway floor, slipping in and out of consciousness, knowing she has to get away from the house but unable to summon up enough strength to stand, let alone walk. She's lost all track of time, so many memories have come crowding in, it's like they've been soaked all this time in the mortar of these walls and now she's back they're flooding out to claim her. Voices, all yammering at once – Muriel, her grandmother,

Frank. Struggle as she might, Stella cannot keep them at bay. She tries to focus on Marcia, tries to calm herself by bringing Marcia's face into view, tries to conjure up Marcia's warmth and Marcia's smell, the feel of her hand on Stella's wrist, the way her uniformed breasts had pressed against Stella as Marcia lifted her up and carried her back to the Infirmary wing. How much Marcia had risked for her. There's no-one to do that now, not here... And the house, determined to reclaim her. Stella wonders if she can crawl on her belly to the front door, or at least a bit closer to it.

* * *

Last night, Gareth had watched his *Dirty Harry* video for the umpteenth time. He practically knows the dialogue off by heart. Harry Callahan made mistakes, but deliberate ones. Harry Callahan got involved in cases, emotionally, more often than not. He never bothered about keeping his nose clean or 'satisfying his superiors,' – far from it. Harry would scoff at Gareth's scruples. He gets where he wants to be, because everything comes from the heart. Gareth can't honestly say his heart is in probation work. He wishes it were. But it's not. Maybe Stella Moon can help him. He *is* interested in her case, in matricide. A bit of graft and Gareth could become an expert. Gareth *could* get passionate over a case like Stella Moon's.

Gareth is engrossed in his own work when, quite a while later, Geoff comes in looking flustered.

'You look like you've come through a hedge backwards,' says Gareth.

Geoff takes off his jacket, hangs it on the back of his chair, tucks his shirt in and smoothes his hair down.

'Wretched Stella Moon woman,' he says, 'has gone and done a runner. I've been to the housing place, and all the way across to the Spinney Flats with the bloody housing officer. No sight nor sound of our Miss Moon. And then the sodding car breaks down right in the middle of the effing estate, can you believe it? Talk about stress. I've had to come back on the blasted bus.'

'D'you mean for the emergency accommodation? She didn't show?' Gareth says, a wave of heat passing through him. The housing place must have got the message he left, surely. Gareth daren't ask. He wishes yet again that he hadn't let her go back to the boarding house on her own.

'Damn right,' Geoff says, 'and I waited an hour for the bloody AA to come for the car and missed the Murray case conference. Walked miles before I found a sodding phone box that wasn't vandalised.'

'Why didn't Stella Moon show up, then?' Gareth asks. He'll blame himself if anything's happened to her.

'And how the hell am I supposed to know that?' Geoff says. 'I'm not a bloody mind reader.' Geoff is pacing about in the room.

'Keep your hair on,' says Gareth. 'I was only asking. You need to sit down, Geoff.' This was not a good time to mention case studies for Dissertations.

Geoff plonks himself down in his chair, flicks through the pile of post on his desk. Clara comes in and neglects to apologise for her own lateness, and Geoff's starting to have a go at her when he stops himself mid-sentence.

'Sorry,' says Geoff. 'I'm stressed out. Totally stressed out. This bloody job gets to you sometimes.'

'Don't let it,' says Gareth in his calmest voice.

Geoff has slit open an envelope and is reading a letter closely. He bangs his palm against his forehead. 'That's all I bloody need!'

'What's up, mate?' asks Gareth.

'Jamie bloody Benson's trial's been brought forward. I might have known that would happen. As if I didn't have enough on...'

'I've just about finished the Charlton report,' says Gareth, 'I can give you a hand.'

'Thanks Gareth, but you don't know Benson. It's a really shite one. I'll have to get the stuff ready for Friday. Shit. It's going to have to be all-nighters. Bloody damn and hell. What a disaster.'

Geoff picks up the phone, dials a number, listens for a while then bangs the phone back down.

'And that sodding psychiatrist is never bloody there.' Geoff leans back in his chair and runs both hands through his hair.

'Tell you what, Geoff. I'll be finished this Charlton thing by this afternoon. I'll help you out. You do Benson, I'll take one of your other ones. What else have you got on? And what about your car?'

'Oh, shit and double shit!' says Geoff, jumping up. 'I forgot, I'm meant to pick it up at half past. Be a mate and get me a taxi, will you?' Geoff grabs his jacket and runs down the stairs three at a time.

So Stella Moon didn't show up at the housing thing. Queer: she seemed pretty desperate for somewhere to stay. Gareth hopes it's not his fault. He can't exactly remember what instructions he left her with. He should have made a note, put it on the file. More than likely she'll come back shivering cold and homeless, pleading some pathetic mitigating circumstance, the way they do. All the same, Gareth hopes nothing bad has happened. This Frank she mentioned, he sounded dodgy, reading between the lines. But the girl's a survivor. He could take her case over to help Geoff out, just while Geoff's doing Benson. Gareth could offer anyway, he won't mention the Case Study. A killer. It'd look good on his CV even without the actual Case Study.

If he's going to take the case over, Gareth had better have a proper look at the file again, legit now. He puts the Charlton report to one side, clears his desk, puts his pens and his pencil in the mug with the broken handle, his rubber and his stapler in the top right hand drawer, and adjusts his Anglepoise. He brushes a few biscuit crumbs off with the side of his hand and goes to get the file. He's been in the office since six thirty this morning, so he could leave the office early, he could take the file home and read it in comfort. Gareth doesn't usually take files home, in fact he never does, but this is an exception. This is a favour he's doing for Geoff. This is beyond the call of duty. He could leave Geoff a note, though it's unlikely that Geoff will be back tonight. Gareth rings the housing officer, but there's no answer. He looks at the clock. It's nearly 6.30pm, so they'll have closed long ago. He hadn't realised it was that late. He's been at work more than twelve hours. Gareth bundles the Moon file into his briefcase, writes Geoff a quick note, turns the lights off and leaves the office. He takes the bus home, the briefcase held tightly between his feet. He could just have another little look in that file, kill some time whilst he's on the bus.

Chapter Twenty-Three

Night has long since closed in and Frank still doesn't know how to handle the whole situation. The baby is gone, it's thrown him into a panic. Realistically, he tells himself, he can't do anything till the morning, so he might as well go to bed and try and get some sleep since he got precious little last night in that frigging bus station. But he'll not get any sleep, not in this particular place, not with thoughts of that Macalinden plaguing him. He could be snooping anywhere. He was the kind of bloke who'd stop at nothing, once he's got the scent.

Frank remembers him from before, from when the baby was 'abducted'. That's what they'd led Stella to believe, that Baby Keating been taken from his pram outside the boarding house. Ruby Willoughby, with her wily ways, even set it up so it was Stella – not much more than a bit bairn herself at the time – who was the one who found the pram empty on her way to school. Frank remembers the shocked look on Stella's little face as she came running back through that morning to tell Hedy her baby's pram was empty.

Macalinden – sly, he was – had quizzed Stella on more than one occasion, though by rights he wasn't supposed to speak to her, Stella being not only a minor but one of the main witnesses to the baby's disappearance. Macalinden had been relentless, hanging about in the back lane at all hours on the off chance of seeing Stella. He hadn't given the kid a minute's peace. And Ruby'd been reluctant to bend Macalinden's ear in case he smelled a rat. But in the end it hadn't been that difficult, feeding Stella the bones of the story of how poor Baby Keating had disappeared, been stolen from his pram, right under their noses, breaking his mother's heart and such, and Stella in turn had fed the story to Macalinden with the innocent conviction of which only children are capable.

The polis had swallowed the same story, then they'd gone straight after the estranged Mr Jim Keating when Stella suggested maybe she'd caught a glimpse of someone who looked a bit like him that very morning. But they'd never found anything and Baby Keating's disappearance remains, to this day, one of Newcastle Constabulary's unsolved crimes. Frank's got a good right to be dismayed to find the Macalinden man has rekindled his interest.

It wasn't until the séance went wrong a while later that Stella discovered the truth – the baby wasn't abducted, he'd been killed, and it was Stella herself who'd administered the fateful dose. That anyway was Muriel's story, and Frank had come to believe it. At the time, Frank was prepared to believe the killing had been done unwittingly. But Frank no longer believes it was innocent, not given what Stella went on to do to Muriel.

The shock of it all had caused Stella to have some kind of breakdown. Whether the whole sorry episode was forgotten or wiped out, or what happened to Stella's memory, was anyone's guess.

So meandered Frank's thoughts that night as he lay on the damp bed with all his clothes on, boots included, the front door locked and wedged, the back door locked and the key in his trouser pocket in case he has to make a quick getaway. For a second night, he can't sleep. The place stinks of memories, and Frank's now living a whole new episode of the horrible saga that goes on and on.

It seems to Frank now that he had loved Muriel. He'd loved her in his own stupid, selfish, clumsy, inadequate way. He'd never told her. He'd never realised it himself until tonight, not really. Now, lying in this bed, remembering how things were, thinking how they might have been.

Frank had even loved Stella. No-one would believe that he'd actually cared about her, not with his history, but it's true – he had. He'd loved Stella, he's just always gone about those sorts of things in the wrong way.

He can't face another stint in prison, no way. He'll top himself first.

Towards dawn, Frank drops into that strange place between

waking and sleeping, his head still in turmoil. The thought of filling that bloody hole in has put his memories on action replay.

'Bury the baby?' Frank had said. 'What? Without a funeral? What are you talking about? That's not right, Mrs Willoughby, it's not right, and you know it.'

Yes, Frank had been against it from the start.

'Look at it this way,' Ruby said, 'there's been a death in this house, the death of a baby, in circumstances we don't want going into. We'd all be under suspicion…'

'I don't believe what I'm hearing,' Frank interrupted. 'Bury the bairn, and him not even christened.'

Ruby was desperate to conceal the baby's death from the authorities, who hadn't yet even been informed of his birth. Ruby's line was that they'd all – everyone in the boarding house – be under suspicion, so the simplest thing was to bury his little body and be done with it.

'What the hell are you talking about, woman, under suspicion?' Frank had challenged her, 'How can we possibly be under suspicion? The baby's died of some illness. We should just get the doctor.'

'With respect, Mr Fanshaw, it's not for us to be deciding what the little mite's died of. As far as that goes, the least said, soonest mended.'

Frank was beginning to understand what Ruby Willoughby was made of. Tough as old boots. You couldn't argue with her.

'The point is, we're all suspects,' Ruby was saying. Frank's attention had wandered. 'All of us. Including Muriel. Including Hedy – she wouldn't be the first mother to act in desperation. Yes, we'll all be investigated. Including your good self, if I might say so. Especially your good self, Mr Fanshaw.'

Good God. Frank was beginning to get the picture, and a pretty ugly picture it was. He'd never laid a finger on that baby, and Ruby knew it. She must have found out about his conviction. Or about Stella. Or both. Jesus Christ.

Frank was beginning to get the gist of it. There really was no stopping Ruby Willoughby once she got started.

'We need to bury the body – *you* need to bury the body, Mr Fanshaw. And that's all there is to it.'

Frank hadn't stood an earthly against Ruby's manipulations. He'd allowed himself to be cajoled – it was a kind of blackmail – into doing something he knew was on the far wrong side of wrong. But there it was, his past had caught up with him. She'd found out, there seemed no way out. So Frank had taken the baby the very next morning and buried him behind the civvy. The place, a bit of waste ground where people dumped stuff – rubble, old prams, mangles, bikes, – was only ever used by the street girls. Frank had carried Baby Keating to the furthest corner, laid him on the ground wrapped in his blankets and started to dig.

But he couldn't dig. The ground had been frozen and was chokka with hardcore: he couldn't get the spade in, and the gravity, the momentousness, the sheer damn idiotic stupidity of what he was doing kept crowding out his mind. He couldn't think, he couldn't breathe. What the hell did he think he was doing? Digging a bloody grave in the middle of the night for a baby that had nowt to do with him? And God only knew exactly how and why the poor little beggar had met his untimely end. Poor little bastard. Frank knew deep down he'd never get away with it. Even all the years he hasn't been caught, he's tormented himself, he's punished himself ten times over, more than if he'd been found out, locked up and the key chucked down the sewer.

After his earlier stint at Her Majesty's Pleasure, Frank had sworn he'd keep on the straight and narrow, and he'd been doing not too badly. Until he'd gone to that bloody boarding house. Until that little bitch Stella Moon came along. Sly little madam, knocked him right off track, coming in from school in that little uniform, climbing onto his lap, wiggling herself about and looking at him with those eyes, whispering how she loved him and did he want to play with her? It was Stella who had been his undoing. Frank rues the day he ever clapped eyes on her. And Ruby Willoughby would never be satisfied until she made Frank pay the full cost of everything and more.

Frank had been trying very hard to go straight, to behave like proper men are supposed to behave. The very night before he buried poor Baby Keating, he'd felt himself footloose and fancy free. He'd been with Nina, paid her, and been determined to keep his focus on the women, exclusively, nothing, no-one else.

Where was the proper man now, then? Frank was no more than a cowering loser, still at the behest of Ruby Willoughby. Frank didn't feel like a proper man now any more than he had that night he'd stabbed at the solid earth with the spade again and again, trying to dig a frigging hole that wouldn't be dug. Frank Fanshaw couldn't even dig a hole in the godforsaken waste ground. He'd had to conceal the body though, hole or no hole. Mrs W was right, if the death came to light, they'd all have their necks on the line, like a load of frigging chickens, Frank more than anyone. He cursed the day he'd had relations with Hedy Keating. He'd give his right arm never to have set eyes on her. He didn't even like her: he'd felt sorry for her, he'd only gone with her to wind Muriel up. It had taken him weeks of cajoling to get Hedy to do anything in the first place, and he'd never even enjoyed it. It was just a convenience, pure convenience – an act of charity. Mind you, after Baby Keating arrived, Frank had rather liked lying there, sucking at those milk-filled tits. That'd been a new one on Frank. Very enjoyable. You couldn't get none of that from Nina's kind. That lot wouldn't even kiss a bloke. Anything but. Everything but. Those milk-filled tits had been something else. Now look at where they've landed him.

Frank curses the thoughts of women – Muriel, and bloody Hedy Keating – crowding out his head. They're making him go hard and right now he can't be bothered with all that rigmarole. He shouldn't be wasting his time thinking about bloody women who want everything and give you sweet fuck all. They're all the bloody same. Suck every last drop out of you and then what? Leave you with their dead fucking babies to get rid of. In the end, Frank had just covered the baby up with rubble, bit by bit with his bare hands, he'd piled it all on top and got away before the light came properly up. The poor little bastard.

The burial place now being common knowledge, Frank had to shift it double quick, so the next thing was he and Muriel were speeding off up the road with the exhumed body of little Baby Keating in the back of old Ruby's Austin. Under strict instructions from Ruby to get rid of it, dispose of it good and proper, they'd gone straight to the Beach Hut, where Frank had been pulling down the old lean-to with a view to putting a kitchen on.

He'd wanted to do as Ruby said, get it over and done with. But no, Muriel had never been one for doing what she was told, especially when she was told by Ruby. The only reason she'd agree to anything was to protect Stella. But she'd have it her way, or nothing. Instead of burying the baby, Muriel taxidermied it, she got all her instruments out and she skinned the little body, and she boned it and wired it up. She stuffed it, she preserved it and she dressed it, washed its blankets and all its clothes and put them all back on, nappy and everything.

Frank had looked on in disgusted fascination, not at the body itself, which he couldn't even bear to look at – no, it was the meticulous care Muriel lavished on that little stuffed baby that was beyond anything he'd ever imagined could happen: so much care she'd lavished. Frank had feared she'd keep it, that she wouldn't let it go. He'd dug a good hole under what would become the new kitchen floor, and he'd backed off, just hoping that Muriel would let go and see sense. It took a while, but in the end she wrapped it in the crotchet shawl Ruby'd made long ago for Stella, and she allowed Frank to bury it under the kitchen floor.

No wonder Frank can't sleep properly. The shock of arriving at the Beach Hut to find that gaping bloody great hole in the kitchen floor, being surrounded now by the stink of those same chemicals in every particle of poisonous air he is breathing. And Christ knows where Stella's gone or where Ruby is. And that Macalinden, sniffing round every corner.

Frank gets up. He's going to fill that hole back in for starters. Put the floorboards back. Eliminate all trace.

Then make himself scarce. To Brighton. Find Ruby.

Chapter Twenty-Four

Gareth's sitting on his couch, his brain boggled with Stella Moon. He's been reading the file ever since he got in. He puts it down on the coffee table and takes another sip of whisky, followed by a gulp of Carlsberg. He's probably doing this the wrong way round, but what the hell. He leans back on the sofa and looks at his watch. He should make himself something to eat. It's not a good idea to be drinking on an empty stomach. Too late to worry about that now, though. Gareth is finding it hard to rouse himself. He needs a nap. He's been overworking, all this not sleeping right, going to work before it's even light, bringing work home. He'll go out and get a fish supper. But first a bit of shut-eye.

It's exhausting when you get engrossed in other folks' traumas. They get under your skin, some of them. You feel sorry for them. Some of them you develop an understanding for and, when that happens, you just know you're the first person, the very first person ever to take the trouble even to try to understand. And as that person, that's where the possibility lies of making a difference. On the other hand, Gareth, that's where you yourself can get lost. Gareth drains a third can of Carlsberg, shoves a cushion under his head and stretches his legs out on the couch. His eyes shut of their own accord. He pulls his coat from the back of the sofa, half covers himself up and falls immediately to sleep.

He sleeps uneasily. He's half aware of tossing and turning: the sofa's no good. He wakes up more tired with a crick in his neck and starving hungry. Thirsty as hell. And he's woken up angry with Stella Moon. All his life Gareth has had it drummed into him that anger is rarely an appropriate response to anything, but there he is, waking up angry about someone he hardly knows. Well, he does know her. He knows her better than she knows him. He's read her file, or most of the important bits. The kid's had a tough time of it, he can see that. Gareth is angry because he feels badly that he let her down over the accommodation thing. Gareth opens another Carlsberg, takes a few gulps and remembers he was going to get fish and chips. He finishes off the can, grabs his coat and he goes out. Evil night, he'll go in the Zodiac. He shouldn't have drunk so much, but no matter, it'll be alright, he can risk it. Gareth runs back into his flat, grabs the car keys and rushes off down the stairs again. He meets old Mr Dickinson from the second floor on his way up.

'Evening, Mr Dickinson,' says Gareth as he hurries by.

'And a very good evening to you too, my lad.' Mr Dickinson seems glad of an excuse to stop for a moment, rest his weight on the banister and get his breath. 'You off to meet your lass, then?' Mr Dickinson chuckles. He knows full well Gareth isn't courting.

'Fish and chips.' says Gareth. 'Haven't had my tea yet. Been working late.'

'Smells like it. I didn't know you was working down the brewery, lad,' the old man chuckles. 'Better get a move on, they stop frying at half past.'

Gareth hurries on down the stairs. The chip shop is closed when he gets there, but the lights are still on. He pushes at the door but it's locked. Through the window he can see Carlos in his grubby apron wiping down the stainless steel fryers. Gareth uses his car keys to tap on the window. Carlos looks over and gestures with his hand.

'*Tutto finito*,' he mouths, shaking his head. He turns back and continues wiping. Gareth taps again, louder this time. Drying his hands on the towel that hangs over his shoulder, Carlos comes over to the door. He's shaking his head and gesturing to indicate that work time, for him, is over. He turns the sign that says 'Open' to the side that says 'Closed' and pulls the blind down behind it.

Gareth will have to try the other chippy on Chillingham Road. That could still be open. He gets into the Zodiac again and speeds off, hardly checking what's behind him. But there's not much traffic at this time of night. With any luck, the Chilly Road place will still be open. Gareth gets there just in time. He gets his cod and chips with salt and vinegar and mushy peas and extra batter, and has opened the paper and started cramming chips into his mouth before he gets back to the car. He winds the window down a bit so it doesn't get all steamed up and turns the radio on. 'You're the One That I Want', John Travolta and Olivia Newton-John singing in unison. Gareth hadn't liked that song at all before this night, but somehow now he thinks it's not so bad and he's humming along with it through a mouthful of half-chewed fish supper. Every now and again, he wipes his greasy mouth on an old shammy leather he finds in the glove compartment. Then it's Abba, 'Take a Chance on Me'. He listens for a moment then turns the radio off. What the hell are all these pop songs on about? They're all making him think of Stella Moon. What the fuck's going on there? He's got the killer on the brain. Gareth finishes his fish supper in silence.

Quite nice to come out in the old Zodiac instead of having it standing doing nothing. Gareth had picked that model even though it was well out of date by the time he got it. A Zodiac is the closest thing you can get in the UK to Dirty Harry Callahan's Cadillac. With the eye of faith, they look very similar. And driving it makes Gareth feel good. A little trip in the Zodiac is preferable to sitting in his flat by himself, spending the entire evening reading about the weird world of Stella Moon. Talking of which, the boarding house she talks about is round here, somewhere in Chilly Road. She could still be there, given that she failed to turn up at the housing place this morning. Gareth could do a drive-by. No harm in that.

He screws up the fish and chip paper and throws it onto the floor on the passenger side. He wipes his mouth on the back of his hand and starts up the engine. He's only a little drunk, he can take a chance and cruise along Chillingham Road. He's not sure where the place actually is. Gareth peers at all the houses as he drives north. The length of the long, straight road – mostly terraced houses, a long parade of shops, St Gabriel's church hall, more houses, only a few with lights on, though it's hardly eleven. Gareth's keeping his eyes peeled for one with boarded up windows, and he's almost at the end, almost at the flyover, when he spots one that could be it. That must be it. At the last moment, he swings the Zodiac round into the side street and stops.

No harm in having a little shufty. Gareth gets out, locks up and looks around. There's nobody about. A dark, clear night for a change, with a few stars, though you can never see that many – the city gives off too much light, not like Risca in the South Wales valleys, where Gareth comes from. It can be pitch black there, the heavens starry. Gareth leaves the Zodiac and walks along the main road, past the dentist on the corner and along in front of the boarding house. If he's not mistaken, the front door looks like it's standing open. What's the harm in going in? There'll be nobody about. He could just have a quick look, nothing more. Gareth hurries back to the Zodiac and gets his torch, flicks it on and off a few times to make sure it's working and locks up again.

The front door of the house is indeed open, but the porch door just inside is locked. Gareth tries to see through the glass, and shines his torch through.

'Oh my God,' Gareth gasps. He can see a body, lying on the floor. He has to strain and twist to make it out, but oh, God, it's Stella. The stupid little cow. What's she gone and done?

Gareth rattles the handle on the porch door frantically. It's not budging. It's locked from the inside. He can see Stella lying there, still as death. Oh, God help her. Pressing his forehead against the glass, Gareth shines the torch down at an angle towards the lock on the inside and squints through, but he can't see if there's a key in there or not. He rattles at the door, very hard this time, but it's firmly locked, possibly bolted as well, he can't see. He kicks the door at the bottom, twice – futile, he knows. He bangs on the glass with the flats of his hands, shouts Stella's name, banging at the same time, bang, bang, banging, kicking at the door. There's no point trying to break the glass, there's a metal mesh on the other side. But Gareth can see Stella lying there, not moving. Oh, God. It's all Gareth's fault. He shouldn't have left her.

Chapter Twenty-Five

Through the dimpled glass of the porch door, Stella vaguely registers a light – torchlight, flickering across her face. Frank. Frank. It must be Frank. He's come back. He's hammering on the glass. The light again. Stella opens her mouth to shout but her voice is gone or her will is gone and only a small mewing sound comes out. More banging. Kicking. He's trying to kick the door in. He can't get in.

Go away, Frank. Just go away, just go away.

Stella drifts in and out of consciousness. She's so thirsty. So very thirsty. But she has no strength to get to where the water is.

Water, she hears water.

It's the sea lashing up onto the Saddle Rock, the sea lashing against the cliffs, the sea smashing Muriel against the rocks.

They said she had no face left. Muriel washed up broken. Broken by the sea broken against the rocks.

Water gurgling out from the broken pipe in the scullery, dripping down the back step, drips like a torture. A magnified, thundering waterfall.

Stella's head swimming with water, so much water, drowning.

Muriel drowning, bobbing in the water, face down.

'Charles Darwin,' says Marcia, standing at a blackboard, a long cane in her left hand that traces a wiggly chalk line round and round the garden. 'Charles Darwin,' she repeats, 'had a path. A path he used for walking and thinking. Every day at 11am precisely, he'd get up from his desk. It's the rhythm we're interested in. The rhythm of walking, the steady plod, plod, plod. It helps the thoughts to find their place. Try it, Stella.'

Stella cannot walk. She cannot even stand up.

Picture a place – it has to be a good place. Imagine you're walking. Feel the rhythm of your tread, feel it smooth and even, everything, smooth and even.

Marcia's strong, black hand spreads butter onto crumpets. Stella watches her fingers flex, the miracle of Marcia's fingers flexing.

The warmth of Marcia's hand between her shoulder blades, the steadying flat of Marcia's hand.

Walk, Stella. You can walk.

Stella is walking the dune path, soft sand underfoot, soft salty breeze coming in off the sea. Stella follows the soft sand path. It's Marcia up ahead. It's Marcia she's following, not Muriel.

Marcia, wait, wait, wait for me.

Stella, sitting alone on the Saddle Rock, looking out across the smooth, silver sea.

In the little blue suitcase there's a letter from Marcia. Addressed to Stella. She still hasn't opened it. Marcia said not to open it. That was the very last thing she said.

'Don't open the letter, Stella, not until you've written every-thing down in the blue silk book. I would like to know your story. I would like *you* to know your story. Then you open the letter. Have you got that?'

Stella is suddenly desperate to touch the suitcase. She wants the suitcase, she needs the reassurance of her hand on the soft worn leather. She feels around her but touches nothing but the wall. Her hand reaches out and touches nothing but the cold lino floor. Pressing both her hands to the floor, Stella tries to push herself up. She has to get the case. She has to get water.

Then there are legs in front of her, two strong legs, standing square in front of her, thick blue serge trousers and a big bunch of keys dangles from the leather belt. Then an arm, two arms, reaching down to her. *Marcia.* Stella stretches out to grasp the open hands, but they're not there, there's nothing there. Stella grasps at the air. There's nothing there.

The banging goes on, the boom bang boom of the big bass drum, in a big brass band – the Salvation Army band – marching. Navy blue uniforms, stout black boots trampling all over her. She must get up and get away from here. Stella twists her body and tries to curl her body up, curl it up against the wall. There's yelling and panic and yelling and someone screaming out her name.

'Stella! Stella!' *Marcia, Marcia.* The banging stops. The marching feet are splashing through water.

Marcia, help me.

Maybe Stella doesn't want help. Maybe she wants to lie here and fade away in this hellhole where she belongs. She's never really left this place, not really. Here is where she'll stay until she fades away. No point in calling for Marcia. Marcia's miles away. Another place, always was, always will be. Stella has been foolish. Worse than foolish to think anything else was possible.

In the letter it will say 'sorry, Stella' and that Marcia has her own life, her own job and her own home in London. Shall we just stay friends, though? I'd like that.

Why would Marcia want Stella or anyone like Stella hanging like a millstone?

And Marcia would be right.

Stella knows now she is someone who has killed not once, but twice. What does that make her, eh?

Marcia will wash her hands of her. Stella deserves it. Everything that happened between them was nothing. It meant nothing. It was meaningless. It was nothing

Everyone, washing their hands, holding them under the broken pipe, wringing their hands. Washing, washing, washing.

Chapter Twenty-Six

Gareth is sweating with desperation to get to Stella who is lying, apparently unconscious, on the hallway floor. He is suddenly more sober than sober, but wishes to God anyway he hadn't had all that drink. He'll have to get the police, get the ambulance, break the glass – do something – but he must be well over the limit, which could be extremely embarrassing. Then he remembers Stella saying how she'd climbed in at the back, that boards had been pulled off and the window smashed. He'll try that. The glass won't break, so it's the only way. Gareth rushes round the back. For a moment he can't imagine how he can scale a wall as high as that. But he's got to – he's got no choice. He has to get to her. He could already be too late. Dirty Harry Callahan, spurring him on.

The torchlight glints on the broken glass embedded along the top. God only knows what Stella's done to herself. Or had done to her. That Frank Fanshaw? Gareth curses himself for letting Stella come back on her own.

There's no way he can climb that wall, but Gareth has an idea. He brings the Zodiac round into the back lane and bumps it up the curb onto the narrow pavement as close to the wall as he can get it, so close he hears the front wing mirror scrape along the wall. No matter. Gareth is about to save someone's life. He uses the car to stand on so he can heave himself up and over the wall. He catches his hand on the broken glass but doesn't even look at it before he drops down on the other side, wipes his hands down his trousers and looks about in the yellowish light from the streetlamp. Stella said she'd got in through a window at the back. He runs through the lean-to and out the other side. There it is, the broken window, the boards off. Gareth climbs in.

What a stink. Vomit. Gareth shines the torch down. It's all over the place. He's treading in it and he's treading on a load of other stuff as well: metal things, tools of some sort, scientific instruments. He shouts Stella's name, but there's no reply. Gareth stumbles over the debris, rushes along the passage, and there she is, collapsed on the floor.

Gareth grabs hold of Stella by the tops of her arms, pulls her upright, shakes her, shouts her name. Her head flops forwards. She's still warm. Is she breathing? Sickly hair is dried up and stuck to her face. With an extended middle finger, his hand shaking, Gareth fumbles at her neck. She's got a pulse. Thank the Lord, she's got a pulse, she's still alive. Thank God she's alive. Gareth gets down on his knees beside her. Please, God, he's got to her in time.

Stella is very drowsy. She seems to be trying to open her eyes, but they keep on closing. She must have taken something, or been given something.

'It's me,' Gareth says. 'It's me, Gareth. Wake up, Stella. You have to wake up.' He's trying to hold her upright, gripping her tightly round the upper arms. 'You have to stay awake, Stella.' He shakes her lightly.

She can't seem to open her eyes. Gareth shakes her again, gently.

'It's me, Gareth. Gareth Davies. From probation,' he says. 'Stella? Speak to me, Stella. If you can hear me, say something.'

Stella's eyes flicker open, but Gareth is not sure they've focused.

'Tell me what you've taken,' he says, authority taking over, tiredness and drink leaving him.

Stella closes her eyes again. If she's taken something he has to keep her awake, he has to find out what she's taken and get her to a hospital. Gareth is suddenly more sober than he's ever been in his life.

'Stay awake, Stella,' he says, 'you've got to stay awake.' Holding her upper arms tight, Gareth heaves her up and tries to prop her upright against the wall. Her limp body falls sideways.

'No,' Stella mumbles through lips parched and cracked. She shakes her head and lifts an arm as if to push him away, but there's no strength in it. She flops back again. 'No,' she curls away from him and hunches up against the wall.

Gareth has to keep her awake. He checks her pulse again: it's steady – fast, but steady – and she's breathing. He should get an ambulance, but he would have to leave her to get to a phone and God knows where the nearest call box is. Gareth puts his arms under Stella's armpits and tries again to haul her up into a sitting position. She's a dead weight and stinks of sick. He can see now that she's covered in the stuff. He pushes her back so she is almost sitting up against the wall. Now there's sick all over Gareth's hands. Stella's head flops forward onto her chest. Her breathing's shallow. Amphetamine?

'Stella, answer me – what have you taken?' Gareth is insistent, talking like's she's deaf. 'Open your eyes and tell me. I've got to know what it was.' He'd noticed a strong chemical smell when he came through the back kitchen, but it wasn't a smell he was familiar with. He shines the beam of the torch around the floor but can't see any sign of tablets or bottles or syringes or anything. He's going to have to get an ambulance, and Christ knows what they'll think when they get here and smell the drink on him.

Stella tries again to shake herself free, but hasn't got the strength. 'Let me alone,' she mumbles, her head lolling.

'For God's sake,' says Gareth, 'I'm trying to help you. But you've got to help yourself. Stop being so pathetic.'

Stella remains inert. Gareth is surprised at the anger in his own voice.

'Have you taken something? Stella! I need to know.' Gareth looks around on the floor again, but there's no sign. 'Look,' he says more gently, crouching down in front of Stella and taking her hand in his, 'just tell me what it is you've taken and I'll get you to the hospital. I'll go and phone for an ambulance as soon as I know if it's safe to leave you.'

Stella shakes her head. 'I haven't taken anything,' she says, pulling her hand out of Gareth's grasp. 'Water. Get water.'

'Well, you're getting an ambulance whether you want one or not,' says Gareth. 'But you'll be a lot better off if I can tell them what you've taken.'

'Just get water.'

Gareth can hardly make out what she's saying.

'What's that smell, then? You wouldn't be in this state if you hadn't taken something. Are you a druggie? Is that it?' Gareth grabs hold of Stella's wrist, yanks up her sleeve and examines the inside of one arm, then the other. No sign of drug use, but there are scars on the insides of both arms, old scars, healed, but Gareth sees them. She's a cutter.

'Get off!' Stella wrenches her arm free and tugs her sleeves back down. 'I've not taken anything. Either get water or fuck off.'

Gareth stands back. Then he sees Stella's got blood on her, it looks like fresh blood, smeared all over her arms and her front, her neck and the side of her face. It takes Gareth a few moments to realise the blood is his. In those few moments he goes to hell and back. He looks at his hand where he caught it on the glass on the wall. It's cut quite badly.

'It's me who needs the ambulance,' he laughs and holds up his bleeding hand. Stella smiles weakly.

'That's better,' says Gareth. 'That's more like it. Now, you sure you haven't taken anything, hand on heart?'

Stella nods wearily. 'Just get water.'

'Well, if it's not drugs, what's happened to you then? You looked like you were at death's door a few minutes ago.'

Had that Frank been back?

'I don't understand what's got you into this state. And what's that smell…sort of like ether, or chloroform?'

Stella shuts her eyes and shakes her head. She shakes it and shakes it and then rests it back against the wall and sighs. 'Water, please, get water … so thirsty…'

'What's got you into this state? You're covered in sick. It's all over the floor in there.' Gareth nods in the direction of the scullery. 'You'd passed out. Are you ill? What's the matter with you?'

Stella shakes her head. 'Fuck's sake, get some fucking water.'

Gareth jumps up and rushes through to the scullery, looking at the vomit mess on the floor and more of it on the fireside. He can't imagine what Stella's been up to, puking up all over the shop. She says she hasn't taken anything, but he's not sure he believes her. Why else is she in that state? But at least she's not dead and it's

149

now clear to him that she's not going to die. And thank God he's probably not going to have to call the ambulance. If he can just get her hydrated…

Gareth gets his trousers soaking trying to get a beaker of water from the leaking pipe. He steadies Stella's head and puts the beaker to her mouth, but she takes it out of his hand and drinks it herself, slopping it all about, her hand's that shaky.

'I'm not a fucking invalid.' She hands the beaker back to him. 'Get some more.'

Stella drains the second beaker and lets it drop. It rolls across the lino. Gareth picks it up.

She's exhausted. What the hell has she been doing? Her face is the wrong colour and it's not just the bad light.

'See to your hand,' she says, 'in the cupboard, in the back kitchen.'

'Let's get you cleaned up first, eh? You stink of sick, if you don't mind me saying. How come you were sick? Promise me you never took anything?'

Stella shakes her head. 'Think what you like.' She tries once again to get to her feet, but she's too weak. 'It's none of your business.'

She seems to be breathing more steadily.

'None of my business? Eh? Ha! Now that's where you're wrong, my girl,' says Gareth. 'The Stella Moon case is mine from now on, I'll have you know.'

A twinge of doubt: Gareth hasn't actually quite taken the case over yet. Geoff hasn't actually passed it over, not quite. Gareth brushes his misgivings aside. If it weren't for Gareth coming here tonight, God knows what could have happened.

'I'm not a *case*,' Stella says, defiant. 'And I'm not your girl, either,' she adds. 'Help me up, would you? Then you can get on your way.'

'I didn't mean…'

If you're thinking Stella for your MSc Case Study, Gareth, you're not really going about it the right way.

'I know what you meant,' Stella says, pulling herself up now. 'Just stop talking about me like that, that's all.'

'What?' says Gareth. 'Where did that come from?'

'I'm only saying,' says Stella, almost standing up.

'Well, blow me down! I find you here, collapsed in a heap, covered in vomit. I'm helping you the best I can, in the middle of the night, out of nothing more than the goodness of my heart, and here you are, giving me a lecture.'

She's a handful, this one. What his MSc tutor might refer to as a personal challenge.

'Just shine the torch, Gareth,' Stella says, 'so's I can see.'

Gareth helps Stella stagger down the passage. She stops beside the back kitchen door and leans her back against the wall.

'God,' she says, breathing deep.

'What?'

'Shite. I feel absolutely shite.'

Gareth helps Stella down the step and into the chair. He gets her settled, then lays the torch on the table so it lights up some of the room.

'You stood up too quick,' he says, 'It can make you light-headed. You've been under a lot of stress, you're dehydrated. No wonder you feel shite. I'll get you some more water. You put your head down, that's it, between to your knees, that's the way...'

Gareth rests his hand on Stella's back as she leans forward. He can feel her skinny backbone, the individual vertebrae, like the bones of a little bird. He takes his hand away.

'It's cold in here. I'll light the fire. Shall I light the fire?' Gareth kneels down by the fireplace, splattered with vomit. There was nothing in the file about her being a druggie.

Stella straightens up again and pushes her hair from her face.

'Bit better?' Gareth says.

'Bit,' says Stella.

She sits there in silence, sipping the water as Gareth pokes about in the fireplace for something to get the fire started.

'What are you doing here in the middle of the night? Plus you stink of drink. It's making me feel sick again, the smell.'

Gareth hasn't yet worked out himself what the hell he's doing.

'I came out for fish and chips and found myself wondering why you never showed up at the housing place. Geoff told me. He was mightily pissed off. He waited for hours, then his car broke down.'

'Whoever he is he can stuff himself,' Stella says, 'if he thinks I'm going to some mangy...'

'There's grateful.'

Stella shrugs.

'Well, you can hardly stay here, can you?' says Gareth. 'I mean, look at the place. Vomit City. Talk about mangy...'

'I wasn't planning on staying here. If you remember,' Stella says, 'I didn't exactly have a damn deal of choice though.'

Time to change the subject, Gareth.

'What's all that water pouring out?'

Stella shrugs again. 'Dunno. Frank Fanshaw must have done it. It wasn't like that yesterday.'

'Where's he now? Is he living here?'

Stella shrugs. 'No idea. Look, you haven't got a cigarette, have you? I don't know where mine have gone.'

Gareth shakes his head. 'I gave up. Frank Fanshaw. What did he want you for? I'll get you some water in a bowl or something. You can get yourself cleaned up.'

'Find my case first. Where is it? A little blue suitcase. I need my case. Oh my God, don't tell me I've lost it.'

'How could you have lost it? Don't be dull. You're getting into a panic over nothing.' Gareth shines the beam around the room. 'There it is, by the door. Don't panic.' Gareth fetches the case and puts it down beside Stella. 'Are there any candles in here or something? This battery's not going to last forever.' Gareth shakes the torch. The beam flickers, visibly weaker.

Stella doesn't answer. She's holding the suitcase upended in both hands but hasn't opened it.

'Hello? Candles?' says Gareth. 'I'd offer to go and buy some, but it's the middle of the night.'

Stella stands up, still unsteady, and pads through to the scullery. She comes back with another beaker of water. Her hand's shaking badly, and it looks as though her legs won't hold her up for long. She must have been well dehydrated. Half an hour ago Gareth was

152

convinced she was at death's door. Now she may be alive but she seems to keep getting lost in some kind of reverie.

'Candles?' Gareth tries again.

'Front room,' Stella says, 'the candles are in the front room.'

'I'll take the torch, OK? I'll come straight back.' Gareth is not half way along the passage when Stella screams at him to stop. Then she's got up and is staggering along the corridor after him, grabbing hold of his jumper.

'Gareth! No!' she shouts. 'Don't go into that room! I shouldn't have told you to go. It was a joke. But it's not funny. Really, it's not funny. Come back. We'll manage in the dark. We'll get out of here. I want to get out of here. Come on, let's get out of here.'

Gareth's voice is kind. 'It's OK, it's OK.' He's holding the tops of her arms as if to steady her. 'I'll just get the candles. I told you, I'll come straight back. You need some light to get yourself cleaned up. You can't go anywhere in that state, look at you…'

In the failing light of the torch, Gareth sees Stella as she is: filthy, stinking, disheveled and tormented. She's scary, this girl is – a proper shape-shifter. How could he have felt that stupid tenderness towards her only a moment ago?

'Don't go in that room! Do not go into that room!' Stella is yelling now, commanding, giving out orders, wild-eyed and mad.

Gareth is starting to get that claustrophobic feeling again, like yesterday. The desire to be a million miles away. Gareth can't imagine what it was that pulled him towards Stella Moon, if anything did, anything beyond his stupid drunkenness. Or duty – that's all it was – an over-developed sense of duty. One of the crosses he has to bear, that's all she is. Gareth sighs. It's remarkably easy to switch back into Probation Officer mode, the effect of the drink now a distant memory. God only knows what she's hiding in that room. He's going to have to get the police. He can see it coming. Damnation. He's getting a bit sick of her stupid games.

'Why can't I go into that room? What's in there I'm not supposed to see?'

Stella shakes her head. She is still blocking the passage. He'll have to physically remove her if he wants to get by.

'Come on, Stella. What – or who – have you got in there? Stop playing your stupid games.' Gareth looks at her, but she turns her face away. 'Is it Frank? Is he in there? What have you done to him? There's not much that can shock me, Stella, so you might as well just tell me what's going on. I wish you'd realise I'm supposed to be here to help you. I'm on your side, for fuck's sake.'

Stella still doesn't budge. He's going to have to manhandle her to get her out of the way. Maybe he should just give up, bugger off home and let her get on with her stupid, sad little life. She's really nothing to do with him anyway. Let Geoff keep her. Sod to the Case Study and the whole fucking MSc. Sod to the whole fucking lot of it.

OK. One more go.

'If you'll let me past, I'll just get the candles. I won't look at anything else in there. I promise.' Gareth draws his hand across his throat. 'Hope to die.'

But Stella won't be cajoled. She's a stubborn little bitch, but Gareth can be stubborn as well. Never in his life has he bitten off more than he can chew. And this is not going to be the first time. Certainly not with this skinny, carrot-headed little misfit. Dirty Harry Callahan wouldn't let himself be defeated, not at this stage.

'Come on now, Stella, you're being ridiculous.' Gareth pushes at her gently by the shoulder, but her resistance is firm.

'It's not. Please, Gareth, it's not ridiculous. You're really not to go in there.'

Stella sounds pathetic now, another change of personality. She's manipulating Gareth – that's what she's doing. He'll get the better of her, for certain, he's got her sussed. He'll do whatever it takes to achieve what he wants and he'll have no regrets. Gareth's mission is to rescue Stella Moon, even if she doesn't want to be rescued. Victims often resist being rescued. It's a common phenomenon. Stella Moon really would make a cracking Case Study.

Stella's still talking. 'You're not to even open the door. Believe me, Gareth, you do not want to open that door.'

Then she's withering, she's starting to cry, she's collapsing to the floor again. She must be serious. This is for real. She's not just acting. What the hell is going on?

'OK, OK,' says Gareth, crouching down beside her and taking her trembling hands in his. She's getting into a state again, breathing fast and shallow, almost back to where they were an hour ago. 'It's OK,' he says again, 'I'm not going in there, alright, if it means that much to you. Now, come on – tell me what's all this about. Have you got that Frank in there? Have you done something to him?'

Stella shakes her head.

'Well, what then? Tell me.'

'I can't,' says Stella, 'I really can't. Not while we're in this house.'

'Right, we'll go somewhere else.' Gareth will be more than glad to get out of here, anyway. The place is starting to give him the heebie jeebies. He definitely doesn't want to be here when the torch runs out. 'We'll get out of here and then you can tell me what's going on, OK?' he continues. Stella lets him pull her to her feet. 'You're a strange girl, Stella Moon, no mistaking.' At least she's stopped crying. Gareth lets go of her hands. 'Now, where are we gonna go?'

Stella shrugs. 'I don't know. Anywhere away from here. Can't we go back to your place? Or have you got a wife or something?'

'No, I haven't got a wife,' Gareth says, a little too quickly. This Stella girl is a bit weird about boundaries. He'll have to watch out. He definitely can't take her back to his place: first of all, look at the state she's in. If old man Dickinson saw her... it doesn't bear thinking about. And second, it's not professional. It's not what you do, taking clients – offenders, murderers – into your flat. They're not even supposed to know where you live. They're only supposed to see the professional exterior. And Gareth is well aware he's already stretched his professionalism with Stella Moon well beyond normal limits.

'I can't take you to my place,' he says. 'It's neither convenient nor appropriate.'

'Well, what then?' says Stella, as though the responsibility of finding her somewhere to go were entirely Gareth's. She's dodgy about boundaries alright.

'You get yourself cleaned up and we'll think of something. Here, you have the torch and I'll wait right here until you shout, OK?'

Stella takes the torch and leaves Gareth in the passage. 'You won't go in there, will you? Promise me you won't open that door? Cross your heart.'

Gareth holds up a finger and draws it across his chest, making a cross. 'On my life,' he says, 'I won't go anywhere near that door. I'll wait right here until you shout, OK?'

Gareth has no intention of going into that room, none at all of digging himself in more deeply than he already is. If there's something nasty in that particular woodshed, Gareth really doesn't want to see it.

When Stella comes out some ten minutes later, she looks a different person – almost normal. That wild hair of hers is pulled tight into a pony-tail and tied back with an elastic band. She's wearing normal black jeans and a black sweater. On her feet, normal black and white baseball boots, though she doesn't seem to have socks. In her hand, the little blue suitcase. Only the eyes haven't changed – those wide, staring eyes. So much trust in them, so much fear, so much anger. Gareth can hardly stop looking at them.

'How do I look?' Stella says, putting out her arms, spinning around. 'I feel a whole lot better for drinking some water. And getting those smelly things off. They were covered in yuck.'

'You don't have to tell me,' says Gareth. He laughs. Maybe Stella's not so bad after all. She's like a kid really. 'Come on, let's make a move.'

When he goes back into the back kitchen to fetch the torch, Gareth sees the thin silk dress and the lacy cardigan and the gold lamé slippers lying in the fireplace among all the sick.

'Don't you want these things?' he asks. 'They could easily be washed.'

Stella hesitates for a moment. 'OK. Can you bring them, Gareth? I don't think I can touch them.'

Gareth bundles the clothes up in an old towel he finds on the back of the scullery door and ties them up. 'The Zodiac's just round the back,' Gareth says, pulling the keys from his pocket. Without looking back, he follows Stella out and closes the front door behind them.

Chapter Twenty-Seven

Stella scrambles into the back seat of the Zodiac without even commenting on the type of car it is, which indicates to Gareth she's far too wrapped up in herself by half. Next she's shoving Gareth's things along to make room for herself and doing it with a carelessness that indicates to Gareth a distinct lack of respect. She's dragging the suitcase in after her.

'Give me the bag,' Gareth says, reaching across her and taking hold of the suitcase. 'I'll put it in the boot.'

But Stella snatches it away from him and holds on to it, out of Gareth's reach.

'No, it's alright,' she says, her voice calmer than her actions indicate. 'I'll keep hold of it, if that's OK.'

'It's up to you.' She's like a kid, refusing to part with a new toy. 'Sorry about all the paperwork,' Gareth says, 'Work stuff.' He comes round the other side and gathers up the papers Stella's shoved aside. 'I'll put this little lot in the boot, then. You got enough room by there?'

'Yeah, thanks.' She's sitting there, the suitcase on her lap. 'Yeah, thanks a lot.'

Stella wriggles in her seat. She's like a kid, going on an outing.

'It smells in here,' she says.

'That's because it's not a brand-new car.' Gareth tries not to sound exasperated. 'It'll be a classic though, one day – just you watch. Did you ever see *Dirty Harry*?'

'A stinking old classic,' Stella laughs. Then, 'What are we waiting for? Why aren't we going?'

Yep. Totally wrapped up in herself.

'We can't exactly get going until we know where we're going to,' says Gareth, adjusting the rear mirror. God help him if he gets stopped driving about in the middle of the night. He feels alright, but he must still be well over the limit.

'There's not exactly that many places you can go in the middle of the night now, is there?' Gareth starts the engine and leaves it running, puts the fan on to demist the windscreen. He looks at Stella in the rear-view mirror, but looks away almost straight away. Eye contact with her is disturbing, even via a mirror. Especially via a mirror.

'Well?' Gareth says, 'where do you suggest we go?'

'D'you mind if I have a cigarette?' Stella says. 'Only I haven't had one since I was sick before, and I'm gasping.'

Gareth has long since given up on the nicotine and he can't stand people smoking in the car. Plus she's already complained of it being smelly. 'Go ahead,' he hears himself say, 'do what you like.'

'You want one?' Stella lights one and is handing him the packet and the box of matches. 'Sorry, they've got a bit bashed.'

'Might as well,' says Gareth. What the hell? Having a drunken fag with a murderer in the car in the middle of the night suddenly seems all in a day's work. He lights one, inhales and tries unsuccessfully to stifle a cough. What the fuck? Gareth is smoking when he doesn't smoke any more. He's driving when he's had an excess of drink. He's parading about in the middle of the night with a client that's not even his. A murderer. What the fuck is going on?

But she has that effect on him, he realises. She shifts the boundaries. She puts them where she wants them. She makes him act against his will. She definitely would make an excellent Case Study. Gareth needs to rethink that one. He's supposed to have his proposal in by the end of term, so there's still a bit of time. Gareth winds his window down and the two of them sit smoking, inhaling and blowing smoke out into the cold night air. Smoking is a bonding activity, it occurs to Gareth, mutually supportive doing-yourselves-in. Crazy. He throws the half-smoked fag out.

It's stopped raining, but it's still cold and wet. Nobody about. Just the occasional car swishes past on the main road. He waits for Stella to finish her cigarette.

'The Beach Hut,' Stella says suddenly, flicking her fag end out the window and winding it up. 'We can go to the Beach Hut. I've got the keys. They're in here somewhere…'

She's suddenly come to life. She opens the suitcase and feels around for the keys.

'Yeah. Got them.' She holds the keys up and dangles them by Gareth's ear.

Gareth has read about the Beach Hut in the file and feels completely disinclined to go anywhere near the place. It's isolated. It's miles away. Not to mention that it might not still be standing. He's heard of places like that getting buried in sand blown up by the wind, or the wood simply rotting and collapsing and blowing away.

'Doesn't that place have a lot of…er…memories? I would've thought you'd had a guts-full of that type of thing for one night.'

Stella is shaking her hair free from its band. Her eyes are brighter than Gareth has seen them, shining out at him from the dark of the mirror. Her hair is like snakes.

'No need to be s-c-a-r-e-d, Mr Social Worker,' she mocks, animated. 'Just take me as far as the road. You don't have to come in.'

Gareth, trapped between the living, breathing Stella – he can feel and smell the heat and the damp of her – and the cold likeness in the mirror, whose bright stare seems to be looking straight through him. That stare's making him choose between being a man or a mouse.

'Believe me, Gareth,' she's saying, 'the Beach Hut has nothing, and I mean *nothing*, on what is in there,' Stella nods towards the boarding house. Gareth watches her reflection in the mirror. 'Thank God we've got out of it. I'll tell you one day. Let's just go now. I want to get away from here. Please, Gareth.'

'I'd rather find you one of those all-night hostel things. Or a hotel.'

'I can't afford a hotel, Gareth.'

'I know you can't, but I can lend you. I'll pay. You don't have to pay me back…'

'I'm not taking money off you. I'm not a fucking charity case. Just take me to the Beach Hut. I'll be fine.'

She's evidently not going to budge from that opinion.

'Anyway,' she adds, in that smaller, little-girl voice, 'let's face it,

Gareth, I've nowhere else to go.'

'Alright, if that's what you want.' Gareth is going against his own better judgment. 'If you're certain. It's just, you were in a terrible state back there. I don't want to make things worse than they already are.'

'I know. You've rescued me. And I'm grateful, but you don't have to rub it in. Just take me to the Beach Hut, and your job's done. Then you can wash your hands of me.'

The fact is, she does have to go somewhere, and Gareth actually doesn't want to shoulder the responsibility of Stella Moon a moment longer than he has to. What the fuck? His brain can't think straight.

'I'm game for anything,' he says, putting the Zodiac into gear. Listen to yourself, Gareth. 'I can't wait to see the Beach Hut, after everything you've told me,' he says, driving off.

'What are you talking about?' Stella says. 'I never told you anything.'

Slightly panicked, Stella suddenly remembers Marcia's letter. Please, God, it's still in the bag. She's terrified of losing it before she's even read it. She flips open the case and rummages around in the dark. It's there. Thank God for that. She keeps her fingers on it for a few moments, then slips it into the cover of the blue silk notebook and closes the case quietly. Panic over.

'Did you want something?' Gareth asks.

He's heard her fiddling about in the case.

'It's alright,' Stella says. 'I was just checking something. I keep having a panic in case I lose it. I keep imagining I've lost it.'

'It must be something precious?'

'It's just a letter,' Stella says. 'Only I haven't read it yet.'

'Put the light on if you like – it's just there, to the right of your head.'

'No, no. I don't want to read it. Not just yet.'

Gareth keeps on driving. He's not even going to ask what the fuck's going on there. The lights change and Gareth turns right onto the Great North Road at Gosforth High Street. It's going to be nearly an hour till they get to the Beach Hut. Gareth hopes Stella will fall asleep and stay asleep. Right now, that's all he asks.

Chapter Twenty-Eight

Stella's never going to be able to open Marcia's letter because she's never going to be able to write anything in the lovely blue silk notebook. She's never going to sully those lovely clean pages with her grim little story. She might as well open the letter now and find out the worst. Find out it was all a big mistake and Marcia's sorry, but she actually doesn't want to know.

What if the whole thing is a figment of Stella's deranged imagination? Marcia just believing – really, really believing – in the Sisterhood thing, and putting her beliefs in Sisterhood into action. Stella should look at the letter. What's written in there is more reliable than Stella's memory, which anyway is full of crap and always has been.

But part of Stella doesn't want to know the truth, doesn't anyway trust the truth, or that which masquerades as truth. Memory may be fallible, but so is everything else. Truth is personal to each of us and is not to be equated with facts. There are things that happen inside of us which are real and true, yet cannot be seen and cannot be told and possibly – probably – will not be remembered. This doesn't mean they're not true. Of that much, Stella is certain.

What Stella remembers most is the feel of Marcia's hands, and how she could feel the touch of them before they actually made contact with Stella's skin. She could feel Marcia's touch with her eyes closed, her skin felt it before Stella did which, granted, makes no sense at all, but that's how it was. That was real. There's no way that kind of skin-knowing isn't real.

As Stella's key worker, Marcia was the person who once a week drove Stella through the prison gates and into the outside world. In the unmarked Transit, Marcia drove Stella through the streets of North London to her therapy sessions at the Tavistock Clinic in Belsize Park. Stella was considered to be some kind of special case and had dispensation to go to the Tavistock, where a Dr Porpora was an expert on Matricide. Stella could never tell him very much because she couldn't remember very much. They'd even tried hypnosis, but that just made her go mute and shake.

Marcia would always wait outside, and she'd be there when Stella came out, waiting, and she'd step forward, no words, just put her arms around Stella and would hold her – just stand there holding her – for as long as it took. No questions, no answers. Marcia just held her, that's all. Now Stella remembers the feel of Marcia's large breasts pressing up against her, how she felt the strength of Marcia seeping into her, how she breathed in the essence of the strength of Marcia, deep into her lungs and held it there. In those moments, Stella had felt something pass silently and surely between them: an exchange – yes, it was two-way, Stella was convinced of that – an exchange of something deep and strong and thick and sweet, like the soul of her was being tugged free of its bearings.

All of which now sounds delusional. Things like that don't happen in real life. But at the time, Stella had believed – and Marcia had believed. Marcia too, hadn't she? She believed that there was a reciprocal exchange of...what? Stella didn't know what it was, but maybe, surely... Was it the beginnings of... Was it love she'd felt for Marcia? Marcia had felt for her?

Stella won't think about the letter, not for a long time. Respect for what she'd promised Marcia must take priority over Stella's desire for instant gratification, her need for truth – whatever truth was. Marcia's conditions will be fulfilled before the letter will be opened.

From the start, Marcia had encouraged Stella to write things down. She was always counselling against 'dwelling' on things, against gazing at your navel instead of doing something about whatever it was that was getting to you. Marcia was a great one for Action. She said the best and the quickest way to get over stuff was to write it down. Writing was a form of Action of which Marcia thoroughly approved. It helped you see the wood for the trees. It helped you find out what you thought about something, helped you see what was and was not important. And as for memories, you didn't have to let them imprison you. Put them on the page, Marcia said, write them down, set them free: it's up to you to put the past behind you.

Stella had tried, but found that writing anything – let alone anything about yourself or your life story – was nowhere near as easy as Marcia seemed to think. No way at all. In fact, it was impossible. It wasn't that Stella was afraid of the blank page. She wasn't afraid of it. It wasn't that she couldn't think of anything to write. She could think of plenty. It wasn't that she didn't have time. She had plenty of time. No, it was something else, something worse, much worse: something deep, incomprehensible and inaccessible, something that wanted to stay hidden away. It caused a horror at the very thought of putting words on paper. Phrases, sentences, whole paragraphs would form themselves inside Stella's head, they'd repeat themselves over and over with the greatest insistence till Stella thought her brain would explode, but she couldn't write them down. The antagonism she felt to writing was visceral, it came from the depths not of her mind but of her body, it was a loathing, it was palpable disgust.

So no, Stella was not going to be writing anything down, not just yet, not for Marcia, not for herself, not for anyone.

Chapter Twenty-Nine

Stella doesn't wake when Gareth stops for petrol half way up the A1. He buys milk, coffee, biscuits and Wine Gums in the 24-hour services. She doesn't move when he gets back into the car, bangs the door shut and starts the engine. She's motionless until he's passed the Alnwick turn and he shouts to wake up because he doesn't know where he's going.

'Where are we?' Stella says, her voice coarse with sleep.

'We just passed Alnwick.'

Stella pushes herself up into a half sitting position and strains to look out of the window.

'Turn off the next one. It'll say Seahouses or Beadnell or something.' Stella rubs her eyes and pushes her hair back from her face, but it only flops forward again.

Gareth watches in the rear-view mirror, as though he's checking for traffic. Wild hair snaking all over the place from behind those pale little hands. She's like the Medusa. But the smallness, the whiteness, those fragile little hands. Unbelievable to think that those thin, little hands killed a full-grown woman – pushed her over the cliff to her death. Gareth is in the car in the middle of nowhere, in the middle of the night with a tiny-handed killer with bright, staring eyes. Careful of the mirror, Gareth. Gaze directly upon her and you'll turn to stone. Gareth looks away. What on earth is he thinking of? He feels his life tipping sideways.

'Your hair's escaping,' he hears himself say, realising a moment too late the intimacy of the comment. Her repeated gestures to keep the snake hair back from her face are futile. Then she's leaning forward, resting her right hand on his shoulder. For a brief moment, her hair is brushing against his face, her fingers digging into his flesh. He can smell her musky smell.

'This is it,' she's saying, 'this is the turn.'

If he breathes in now, he'll breathe in her breath. She's lifting her hand from his shoulder. She's perched on the edge of the back seat, her left hand gripping the back of Gareth's seat now as he steers left off the main road, taking the corner a little too fast, a little too wide. Nearly came off the road there. He needs to concentrate.

They leave the main road and they're bumping along on a smaller lane, the headlamps picking out potholes, hedges and trees, bare now, racing by on either side with Stella directing the way. She keeps leaning forward to look over Gareth's shoulder, her hand pressing into his shoulder, her breath on his neck. Away from the boarding house, she's come alive, giving off an energy that wasn't there before. She smells different. Then she's scrambling over into the front seat, arms and legs everywhere, nearly knocking them off course again.

'Oops, sorry...' Stella says, laughing, as she plumps down into the front seat.

'Hey, steady on,' Gareth says, 'you'll have us in the ditch in a minute,' knowing as he says it he doesn't mean a word of it. Stella Moon can scramble where she likes. It feels right to have her sitting up front beside him. Gareth and Stella.

What the hell is he thinking of? The sooner he drops her off, the better. She's too weird for words. She's lighting a cigarette but doesn't offer Gareth one. She winds down her window to half way, sucks in the air, inhales the smell of the sea.

'I love the sea,' Stella says, inhaling deeply again. 'I love the sound of it and the smell of it and the taste of it and the power of it, and...'

She stops abruptly, takes another drag on her cigarette. Somehow Gareth knows what she's thinking. She's thinking of Muriel, the night she died, the sea at the Saddle Rock, the sea at the foot of the cliffs. The sea. The sea, it's reminding her, how it swallowed her mother up.

Gareth winds his window down as well and breathes in the freshness of the night air. He speeds up: he wants to enjoy the feel of the rushing wind in his hair, the way the noise of it drowns out everything. He wants to share something with Stella. But the moment's passed. Stella has thrown her cigarette out and is winding up her window.

'At least it's not raining,' she says, sitting back in her seat.

Gareth can't fathom this girl. She's a mystery. One thing one minute, something else the next. He can't read her moods from her face. He turns to look at her. She returns his gaze, smiles, looks ahead again.

Her teeth are a little crooked. Gareth imagines her wearing a brace to straighten them up when she was a girl. How little he knows about her. He wants to know about her, things that aren't written in the file.

'Not far now,' she says as they continue along the uneven road, her hands gripping the dashboard.

Gareth keeps looking at those little killer hands.

* * *

It's three in the morning when Gareth pulls in behind The Fisherman's Arms at Low Newton. He'd meant to leave Stella at the top of the road and get back to Newcastle. But it's cold. And it's pitch black. And she'd been really ill only a couple of hours ago. And what the hell if Gareth does set foot inside the Beach Hut – is he a man or a mouse? Dirty Harry Callahan would relish every minute of this, not be wanting to back off like a chicken. Gareth will walk as far as the Beach Hut with her, make sure she gets there and make sure she gets in, if the place is still standing.

Gareth offers Stella the old Barbour jacket he keeps in the boot of the Zodiac. It's miles big, but she doesn't seem to mind. He sort of admires that. Bit different from Clara. Gareth had taken Clara out a couple of times, and she wouldn't be caught dead in Gareth's musty old coat. Gareth imagines Clara, tottering her way up the dune path in her high heels as he follows Stella in her baseball boots by the light of the torch. He should have got some batteries when they stopped for petrol – too late now. Uncannily, Stella says, 'There should be some paraffin lamps, for when the torch runs out. At least stay for a coffee, Gareth. God, I hope there's some Calor Gas.'

Gareth follows Stella along the steep, winding, narrow path up into the dunes, his feet slipping about and half sinking in the sand. She's got the torch and she's leading the way, so he has no idea where he is, where he's heading or whether he'll be able to find his way back. He's ended up having to trust her. He must be mad. He's pulled two ways. Sense tells him just leave her at the door and go. Duty requires nothing more than that.

Stella has stopped outside one of the little wooden huts close to the top of the dune ridge. Gareth had imagined something a bit more grandiose, but this thing, it really is hardly more than an overgrown shed – and a dilapidated one at that. He can't see much in the dark, but its roofing felt is flapping, and the wood of the veranda is obviously rotted and dropping to bits.

Stella is shining the torch into the suitcase and rummaging about in the bottom. At least the hut's still here. God knows what it's like inside. Gareth should go back now, but he might as well have a look inside since he's come all this way. It's wild up here with the wind and the sea crashing. Gareth can hardly hear himself think. It must have been a bit like this on That Night.

'The keys are here somewhere,' Stella shouts against the sound of the wind.

'Your life in a bag,' Gareth says. He doesn't know why he is making these inane remarks.

Stella looks at him. 'Actually, Gareth, I do have my whole life in this bag.'

He shouldn't be making fun of her. He didn't mean it that way. It just came out. She takes things the wrong way.

Stella starts rummaging again. She's pulled some stuff out of the suitcase and is holding it under her chin. Gareth waits, looks out across the sea, can't see much, just a vast expanse of black. The bright beam of a lighthouse scoops every now and then around the bay. Must be the one on the Farnes. Gareth's eyes drift to the south end of the bay. He can't help looking over there to where It happened. The ruin of Dunstanburgh Castle, visible in the moonlight like a rotten old tooth, the long high cliff where the ruin sits. He must be an idiot, bringing Stella here. How can he expect her to stay in this place by herself? How can he expect her to get better here?

'Ah, at last,' Stella says, fishing out the bunch of keys from the suitcase. 'I knew I had them somewhere. Shine the light on the lock, will you, Gareth?'

She hands him the torch, unlocks the door and it creaks wonkily open.

'After you,' Gareth says, shining the torch in front of her.

'Can you go first?' Stella stands aside.

'Alright. I can go first. I don't mind.'

She's making him do that man or mouse thing again. But Gareth's got no problem with that, he's just doing his job. He steps inside, Stella following with both hands clasping onto the back of his jacket. She's almost breathing onto his neck like she did in the car. Gareth flashes the torchlight around the room. It looks just like she'd described it in the Statement: all mess and chaos – even the smell's still there.

'God, talk about a stink,' Gareth says, taking a further step inside.

Still holding onto his jacket, Stella wedges the door open with an old newspaper.

'Nobody's been here for…em…for seven years,' Stella says, 'or I don't think they have. This is how it was, the last time.'

Gareth wishes she'd stop hanging on to his jacket like that. It's making him feel trapped. That, and the smell. Those stuffed creatures. Their goggly glass eyes dropped everywhere and rolling around on the filthy floor. Those nameless specimens in jars. No wonder the girl's weird.

'That smell's in the rugs. Soaked into the floorboards. You'd think after all that time it'd be gone.'

She's got hold of Gareth's sleeve now. She's physical, this one, too physical. She keeps peering into his face. Gareth takes a step away from her so she has to let go of his arm.

'Oh, sorry,' he says, 'I'm just trying to take it all in. Place smells damp to me, like you'd expect a closed-up place to smell – damp, dust, cobwebs. And chemicals. I'd open the windows if I were you, if you're gonna stay here. Can't be good for you, breathing that stuff in.'

168

'The paraffin lamps should be in the kitchen. Let's get them. Have some light. Cheer the place up? Eh, Gareth?'

She's acting like a kid on a camping holiday. If she lights a match, the whole place will probably go up.

Gareth shrugs. 'If I were you, I'd air the place a bit first,' he says. 'Anyway, I'd better be off. I've got work tomorrow. Today, rather. It's tomorrow already!'

Gareth watches Stella stepping over broken glass, picking her way among the mess towards the kitchen. He stays put. But before long she's shrieking, shouting for him to come. When he gets to the kitchen she is standing, staring at the middle of the kitchen floor.

'What's up?' says Gareth, 'What's wrong?'

Stella is shining the torch around on the floor.

'Someone's been here,' she says. 'There should be a hole there. In the kitchen floor. There was a hole there, the day Muriel died. It was there. Somebody's been here and filled it all in.'

Gareth doesn't understand the significance of what she is saying. There was a hole in the kitchen floor. Someone's filled it in. So what? It's time Gareth was making tracks. He wants to get away from here. Stella Moon is giving him that claustrophobia thing again. Get back to Newcastle, Gareth. Get back to your nice normal flat. Get back to your nice normal life. Try to get a bit of kip in before you have to get up for work. This is not a normal place. Neither was the boarding house. Stella Moon is not a normal person.

'Don't go. Not just yet,' Stella says in that silly little voice she can put on.

She's a killer, she's a defenceless little waif. So skinny she could snap in two. She wants him to stay. He half wants to stay. She needs taking care of. He wants to take care of her. Knight in shining armour. Gareth to the rescue. He's done his job already, done more than his job – way beyond already – way beyond the boundary, beyond the limits of duty.

Now she's confusing him more by changing her mind. 'I'm sorry,' she's saying. 'It's getting light. You'd better be getting back.

Sort your cases out.'

'You'll be alright by yourself?' he asks. Stella nods. 'No more repeats of last night's antics?'

'That's hardly likely to happen here now, is it?'

Gareth shrugs. 'If you say so.'

With Stella Moon, Gareth has no idea what's likely to happen and what's not likely to happen. She has a thick wall around her, this girl, harbouring hell knows what. It's not Gareth's place to pry. Here's his chance to be free of her. Take it, Gareth, take it while you still can.

'I'll be alright,' she says.

He believes it. He wants to believe it. She will be alright. He has to believe it. She wants him to leave. He'll go. She's a client, not a friend.

'Thanks, Gareth,' Stella says. She kisses him lightly on the cheek at the door. Gareth feels the coarseness of her hair against his face, the musky smell of her, the warmth of her body close to his. She does mean for him to go. 'I'm really grateful for what you've done.'

She's grateful, that's it.

'Just doing my job,' Gareth smiles.

'Sure you can you find your way back?' Stella has already sat back down by the paraffin stove. She's leaning forward towards it, warming her hands, talking over her shoulder to Gareth without turning round.

Gareth nods. 'I'll find it. But I'd better have the torch.'

'It's there. By the door.'

'You won't need it?'

'You take it.'

'Bye, Stella.'

'Bye, Gareth.'

Chapter Thirty

So that was the second time that Gareth had been itching to get away from Stella, and she could hardly blame him.

Stella looks around at the terrible mess of the place and goes round, banging all the windows open, trying to get rid of the stink. She's more glad than not glad that Gareth's gone: he's not a calming influence with the way he stands in judgement – probably saying the opposite of what's going on in his head, and the annoying way he trots out platitudes. Marcia had warned Stella about social-work speak, which she knew from her own training. The difference with Marcia was she could see behind the slogans. Marcia, unlike Gareth seemingly, could see the person as separate from the crime. Anyway, Gareth's gone now and Stella's glad because she needs to think and she can't think when he's there. He takes up too much space.

Nothing's working out like it was supposed to. Marcia did warn Stella about that also – the precariousness of plans. But, as with many bits of Marcia's good advice, Stella has failed to take much notice. She's never been very good at taking things in when terror blurs the edges.

Learning curve, Stella. Blundering forth into the unknown is not a strategy that works in all, or even any, circumstances.

Mistakes and challenges aside, Stella feels strangely light-hearted now she's away from the Boarding House, now Gareth's gone, now she's alone in the Beach Hut. She feels strangely unburdened, even though it's the middle of the night, in the middle of nowhere and winter is setting in. Muriel and her weird obsessions with preserving things are more present than they ever were when she was alive, but Stella doesn't even mind that: in fact, all that is an odd kind of comfort, even as Stella knows she is facing difficulties. Nothing can be as bad as those things she has already survived. She's scarred, yes, but her spirit is not broken.

That hole in the floor, and the fact that it's been filled in – evidently recently, judging by the dampness of the sandy earth round the edges of the kitchen – what does all that mean? The hole was there the day Muriel died, Stella remembers it.

The day Muriel died. Which was the last time Stella – or anyone? – was at the Beach Hut. Which means, not Grandma Willoughby, surely. She'd have found the climb up the dune path impossible now. So that only leaves Frank Fanshaw, with whatever agenda he's pursuing. It's Frank who must have been here and, for whatever reason, he's filled the hole in. Which means, if he's been here so recently, he could still be close by.

Stella looks about for some sign of Frank, but sees nothing immediately. Certainly he hasn't cleared up anything on the main room floor. Then Stella notices the newspapers, a small pile of them by the stove. She picks one up. And another. They are dated the day before. So he was here yesterday. So possibly still here today. The papers are all folded in such a way that the pictures of Stella are showing. For a moment her heart drops into the pit of her stomach, then it starts to thump with a hard, irregular thump. Stella feels heat and nausea spreading through her body.

She sits down beside the paraffin lamp and tries to see what the papers are saying. There are various versions of her photograph and various versions of her story, all a bit different but all quoting the same source, the intrepid reporter, Daniel Macalinden.

Macalinden. Yes, Stella remembers him. She remembers him trying to get to the bottom of the abduction of Baby Keating. Then it was him again, when Muriel died – he took up Muriel's story. He knew nothing about Muriel, but he saw fit to write her story, like she was some unfortunate victim of a vicious, evil, devil daughter. Macalinden knew nothing about Stella, but he saw fit to comment on every aspect of her life. So all that was about to start again.

Stella poured over the papers until the paraffin light flickered too dim to see anything. She didn't know how long she'd sat there, trying to make sense of what she was reading, trying to remember, trying to fit the pieces together. And there, in the loneliness of the Beach Hut, as the orange ball of autumn sun appeared on the eastern horizon, the full horror of her situation began to dawn on Stella.

The whole sad business that had been her life, the horrible reality of the killings, it all returns to Stella, it rises up and punches her in the gut.

Stella has killed before.

The baby. Hedy Keating's baby.

Stella killed Hedy Keating's baby.

Stella has killed not once, but twice.

And Frank Fanshaw knows. And he knows the newspaper man is, right this moment, determined to dig out the truth. Macalinden must be searching right now for Stella, and for Frank, for Grandma Willoughby and Hedy Keating.

Stella resolves there and then to turn herself in. She has no choice. She'd thought she'd paid her dues, she'd believed she could put the past behind her and restart her life. But no, she sees now, that's not possible. Instead, a closely-guarded family secret has caught Stella up. What a fool she was to think all that was past and gone. It's cracked open the world as Stella knew it, and revealed a reality, a darker and more horrible one than she ever could have thought possible. No wonder she'd buried the memory all this time.

Stella will turn herself in. It's the only way. She'll face up once and for all to the crimes she has committed.

But Frank won't want her to do that, Stella realises. Because he buried the baby's body. Which makes him an accessory. That's why he wants to stop her. Self protection will be Frank Fanshaw's priority, as it always was. Frank will stop at nothing. Stella is in danger. Frank could walk through that door at any moment, determined to silence her.

Chapter Thirty-One

He'd been a bit funny to start with but, in the end, Geoff had been alright about Gareth taking over the Moon file, said he trusted him and all that. Gareth hadn't actually mentioned the Case Study plan. He would do that later, once he's proved himself by getting Stella back on track. Gareth wants to present it – obviously – as a case study of success. He's been thinking a successful MSc could lead on to a PhD and, in point of fact, he quite fancies his career taking an academic turn. He can't see himself being forever fulfilled in probation. It's nice to think that Stella's going to have a place in helping Gareth with his career, a sort of payback for all he's doing for her. And, to be honest, Geoff had said he was glad to be shot of the case: the psychological ones weren't Geoff's forte. Give him Benson any day, bad as he was. It wasn't often, Geoff had added, clapping Gareth on the shoulder, that you found a good solid colleague like Gareth willing to help you out. Willing and more than able.

Clara was perched at her desk, peering into the mirror of a powder compact and plucking out stray eyebrows. She only had the thinnest of lines as it was.

'Can't wait to start my new job,' she was saying. 'I'll be so glad to get out of this place! All those weird people, locked away in that filing cabinet.' She plucked at a few more hairs, ran her forefinger over her eyebrow and peered into the mirror again to examine her work. 'Most of them have got a screw loose, if you ask me,' she went on, still squinting at her face in the mirror. 'They should be put away, the lot of them – not running loose and causing a menace to the public.' She licked her finger and smoothed her eyebrows again. 'Talking of which,' she said, snapping her compact closed and dropping it into her handbag, 'did you know Stella Moon was in the loony bin for two years, or maybe it was even three, before she even went to prison? That one must have spent half her life behind bars. Think of it. Half your entire life.'

'For your information, Clara, that's not actually true. You shouldn't believe everything you read in the gutter press. And you should have a bit more respect. It wasn't even a psychiatric hospital, it was a sanitorium, and then a children's home where she was,' Geoff said. 'There but for the… Clara.'

'How did you hear that about Stella… Stella Moon, Clara?' Gareth interrupted. 'Has it been in the papers?'

Gareth should have been keeping an eye on the press, but somehow it's slipped his mind. Has he missed a crucial development?

'If it hasn't,' said Clara, 'it soon will be.' She replaced her tweezers in the pencil tin on her desk.

'And how do you know that bit of information?' Gareth asked. He should really keep on top of things: in this job you have to. He though he'd been keeping up with the papers. 'How d'you know that, Clara?'

'The man from the paper.'

'What man from what paper? When was that, Clara?' Geoff was concerned. He'd stopped in the middle of what he was doing and was looking across at Clara. 'How come you never mentioned this before now?'

'It was only yesterday,' said Clara. 'You two weren't even here. And I'm mentioning it now, aren't I? What d'you think I'm doing now?'

'You know you don't to talk to the press, Clara. It's a condition of the job.' Geoff's voice was stern and authoritative.

'Well, I didn't talk to them, if you must know – not really. It was him who talked to me. He was very nice. I didn't tell him anything he didn't already know.'

'Good God!' said Geoff. 'As if I didn't have enough on my plate, and now you throw out that little bombshell! What exactly did you say to him?'

'Mr Macalinden,' Clara interjected.

'You can be sued, you know,' Geoff continued, 'breach of confidentiality is a breach of contract. Confidentiality is the number one rule in this game, Clara.'

'Well, what was I supposed to do?'

'You're supposed to keep your stupid mouth shut, that's what.' Geoff had stood up and was pacing about in the room.

'I don't see why you're blaming me,' Clara said. 'I haven't done anything wrong. I told you, he knew everything anyway, I don't even know why he came, when he already knew all there was to know...'

'Clara,' Geoff sounded exasperated, 'don't be so naïve. That's how they do it, journalists – they talk like they know it all, they wait to see if you contradict them. It's a strategy. Oh my God, what a bloody mess. I'll have to sort this out.'

'Hey, steady on, Geoff,' Gareth said. 'It might not be as bad as you think. We don't even know who he was or what Clara told him. What did you say, Clara, exactly?'

'How come you even know anything about the Moon case anyway, Clara?' Geoff interrupted, 'Stella Moon's only just come out. You're peddling fiction just like the rest of them. Getting off on it. You can't have known any more about it than what was in the papers at the time, and it's unlikely, given your age, that you'd remember it.'

Clara looked over at Gareth.

'She looked at the file,' Gareth said.

'She what? She looked at the file? And you knew about it?' Geoff shook his head. 'This is incredible. Is there anything else I need to know?'

'He let me look at it,' said Clara. 'Or he didn't stop me. He saw me doing it. He discussed it with me the other day.'

Geoff wrenched his tie loose and undid the top buttons of his shirt. 'Hell's bloody teeth,' he said.

'Well, you're never even here...' Clara's voice was small.

'Never here! Never bloody here! That's because my time is all taken up sorting out the messes that you're always causing.'

'Don't be too hard on her, Geoff,' said Gareth. 'It's my fault if it's anyone's. To be fair, the Moon girl did come in here to register with us while you and I were out, and Clara had to see what was

176

going on. It was the day I went to get her signed on and filled out her accommodation forms. I left you a note.'

'You never left me any note.'

'I'm sorry, I thought I did. I meant to. It was me who dropped off her housing forms. Then you went to meet her and she didn't show...'

'Be all that as it may,' said Geoff, 'I need to know what Clara said to that journalist so I can see if I can do any damage limitation. What did you say his name was?'

'Macalinden.'

'We need to check the papers, that's the first thing, eh, Geoff?' said Gareth.

'Well, Gareth,' Geoff said, 'it's your problem now, not mine. As of five minutes ago, the file's yours, remember? You sort it out.'

'He said there'd be psychiatric reports in the file,' continued Clara. 'He asked if he could have a look at them, just to verify...'

'Please, please, *please* don't tell me you let him look at the file, Clara?'

'No. of course I didn't. I'm not that stupid. Anyways, the file wasn't even there.'

Geoff wrenched open the drawer of the filing cabinet and made a cursory search for the Moon file.

'That's all we need,' he said, beyond exasperation. 'Someone's nicked the fucking file.'

'It's in my flat,' said Gareth, as calmly as he could, as though having someone else's file in your flat was a normal occurrence. He felt hot under Geoff's gaze. In all the confusion of last night, Gareth had come straight to the office from the Beach Hut and had forgotten to call in at the flat to fetch the file. He had yet to tell Geoff anything of his trip out last night. This was not the right moment for such confessions.

'What the hell is the effing file doing in your effing flat, Gareth? My God, this gets worse by the minute. That file is highly confidential. It's got confidential written all over it. In large, red capital letters. It's not supposed to go out of the office. Jesus Christ, I don't believe this. What the fuck is going on?'

'I'll go and fetch it now,' said Gareth getting up. He pulls on his coat. 'I'll bring some of today's papers back with me. Won't be a minute.'

Thirty-five minutes later, Gareth is back in the office and a bit out of breath.

'There's a bit here,' says Geoff, shaking the *Echo* and folding it back, 'but you'd hardly call it a feature. Nothing about her until you get to page four, so they're hardly treating it as a scoop.'

'Read it out,' says Gareth, lighting himself a cigarette. He's hooked again. Thanks, Stella.

Geoff reads from page four of the *Echo*. 'Child Killer Freed is the headline. God, the way they've put that,' Geoff says, 'designed to maximise sensation.'

'It sounds like she killed a child, the way they've put it.' Gareth takes a deep drag on his cigarette. 'What else does it say?'

'"Child killer Stella Moon is back in the community. After only seven years in prison for the brutal killing of her mother, Muriel Moon, flame-haired Miss Moon, now 25, has been released and is believed to have returned to the North East to start a normal life. Reliable sources have informed us that Miss Moon's release is unconditional, but that she has agreed to co-operate with the Probation Service on a rehabilitation programme. Yesterday, a spokesman for the Service told our reporter that the rehab programme is yet to be finalised. This paper hopes, along with the majority of its right-minded readers, that the proposed rehabilitation will take full account of Miss Moon's long-standing unstable mental condition and her unpredictable character, and that every necessary step will be taken to ensure that this cold-blooded killer does not pose any danger to other innocent human beings. Miss Moon is believed to be staying in emergency accommodation in the Byker area."'

'Then there's another bit', Geoff continues, 'that says reporter Daniel Macalinden was on the case ten years ago when a baby was abducted from the boarding house where Stella Moon lived. He also covered the matricide, he's still trying to get to the bottom of it all, apparently. That's it,' says Geoff, 'but that was only the early edition.' He folds the paper in half and lays it down on his desk.

'It's enough to have all and sundry high-tailing after her,' says Gareth. 'They'll be crawling all over, Geoff.'

Geoff shrugs. 'Like I said, Gareth, she's yours now, not mine.'

'I'll have to warn her,' Gareth says, 'she could be facing a lynch mob if the papers are going to be stirring stuff up with that kind of language.'

'She will have to be warned,' says Geoff, 'but we've no way of knowing where she is. We'd best get the police on to it.'

'It's going to be a free-for-all. She'll be hounded,' Gareth says.

It seems to Gareth that the issue of warning Stella the press has got wind of her release is now pretty acute. Judging by the state she was in when he'd found her last night (was that only last night? It seems like eons ago), Stella's mental health could be in jeopardy if the press starts revealing all the nasty details. According to what he's seen in the file, the experts didn't agree on any diagnosis for her, but each of them was satisfied that there was something wrong. Since the press hadn't been allowed to print any of that at the time, Stella having been a Ward of Court, they'd be having a field day now.

'What is it?' Geoff says.

'The Stella Moon thing,' Gareth says. 'I do think we have to warn her. About the press, I mean. I'd say she could be in a fragile psychological state. The psychiatric reports. They don't agree what's wrong with her, but they all say there's something. The newspapers could rip her into shreds. Christ knows what they'll dig up, but this file's full of shit you wouldn't want going public...'

'I don't know what we can do about any of that,' says Geoff, 'first, since there appears to be no injunction against reporting and secondly, she's gone AWOL. And thirdly,' he adds, 'we can hardly get the police involved if there's no injunction. They'll just tell us to bog off and they've got proper crimes to solve etc.'

'I didn't mean the police,' says Gareth 'They'd probably freak her out anyway. I mean find her, tell her what's in store. Then she can go elsewhere, if need be; a safe house, police protection if there's any threat to her, change her identity...'

'Well, we know she's not where she's supposed to be. But, Gareth, mate, that leaves a hell of a lot of places where she could be.'

'There's that boarding house in Heaton, and the Beach Hut up at Embleton, both mentioned in the statements.'

'Bit of a long shot, isn't it? She'd have to be mental to go back to either of those places.'

'But she is mental, Geoff,' Gareth says, 'that's the whole point.' Gareth stands up, closes the file and pulls his jacket from the back of his chair.

Minutes later, he is speeding up the A1 towards the Beach Hut, through torrential, sleety rain. Stella's file slides about on the back seat of the Zodiac, papers falling about everywhere, but Gareth's got his foot down and doesn't intend to stop for anything.

Chapter Thirty-Two

For once in his life, Frank Fanshaw has had a bit of luck. He's managed to track down Ruby Willoughby and now he waits in the foyer of the Warrender Place Nursing Home, Brighton, wishing he'd given his boots a bit of spit and polish. He'd clean forgot about smartening himself up in his haste to grab his chance to get to old Ma Willoughby. The Sister has gone to check which room she's in: she's recently been moved, apparently, owing to what the Sister refers to as 'inevitable deterioration', and is now, it appears, on the second floor – the floor reserved for 'the old folk who need special attention'.

'You'll see what I mean,' the Sister adds, 'when we get there. How long d'you say it is since you've seen your aunt?'

Frank is very aware of his grubby attire and stumbles to reply convincingly. He's seen the Sister giving him one of those looks. No doubt she'll think him a gold-digger, estranged for the old lady's lifetime and only moving in for the kill. If only she knew.

'I'm afraid old Mrs Willoughby hasn't been herself at all lately,' the Sister is saying. 'She took a bad turn, just a few days ago…'

'Oh,' says Frank, aware that he's going to have to do better than that, 'Oh, I'm sorry to hear that.'

'Anyway,' the Sister continues, 'you'll see for yourself in a minute. She'll be pleased as punch to see you, I think. It's not often old Ruby gets a visitor.'

'Oh,' says Frank again.

They're going up in the lift, and Frank's beginning to be very anxious about how Ruby is going to react to him. He wouldn't put it past her to start yelling and shouting all kinds of blue murder the minute she claps eyes on him.

'Only glad to be of service,' Frank says. He follows the Sister along the echoing corridor.

The Sister stops outside one of the doors on the second floor.

She wipes her hands down her starched white apron before crooking her forefinger and knocking lightly on the door, drawing her ear towards it. She opens the door, leans forward and puts her head round. She seems to Frank very business-like, not at all like the nurses he likes to think about. He smiles to himself at the thought of the 'nurses' whose services he's benefitted from over the years. The Sister's uniform is not right for a start: skirt right down to her knees, stocking tops well hidden. And the shoes are much too clumpy. And a beam end to match. Frank moves to the side so he is no longer standing directly behind the Sister.

'Ruby, are you decent?' the Sister asks as she steps into the room, one hand still on the door handle. She turns and nods to Frank to wait where he is. 'You've got a visitor today, Mrs Willoughby. Your nephew come to see you. Now, isn't that nice for you?' The Sister laughs a little and beckons Frank in with a small nod.

Frank follows the Sister into a high room with big Georgian windows, hung with thick brocade curtains – it's the middle of the day and Ruby's got them closed. Not like Ruby to shut the light out. The room has a serious air and is full of dark, old-fashioned furniture, some of which Frank recognises. She must have had it brought down. She's not doing too badly, old Ma Willoughby, bit more up-market here than that stinking old boarding house. Frank thinks about the flood he left in the scullery, the chairs chopped up and burnt.

And there she is, there's Ruby Willoughby, sitting in a wing-back chair beside a gas fire, dwarfed by the grand marble fireplace. Slipped down low in the chair, Ruby looks tiny, much smaller than Frank remembers her, but it's only been eight years or so since he saw her. Ruby doesn't look up. For a moment, Frank isn't entirely sure he's got the right Ruby Willoughby. He could have entirely the wrong person. He tries to fit the frail little figure to the memory of his formidable former landlady. The Sister strides across to the window, pulls back the curtains and fixes them behind their tasseled tie-backs. Ruby watches her, then moves her eyes to look across at Frank. Has she recognised him? Frank can see it's Ruby Willoughby alright, there's no mistaking that look on her face. She knows it's him.

'Your nephew Frank to see you, Ruby.' The Sister nods in Frank's direction.

Is Ruby going to let on? His face is in full view now. Ruby must know it's him. But she's not reacting. Maybe she has gone gaga after all.

'There, now,' the Sister says. 'And what do you say, Ruby?'

Ruby looks at Frank as though seeing him for the first time. He's sunk. She's lost her marbles. She doesn't recognise him. He's got there too late. He's missed his chance. Damn. Damn. Damn and blast.

'Come now, Ruby, have you lost your manners?' The Sister turns to Frank. 'Don't mind her, Mr Fanshaw. They're all a bit slow on the uptake, they get like that. You mustn't take it personally.'

Then Ruby comes alive. She starts flustering and fidgeting with a large, grubby-looking handkerchief on her lap.

'Bad penny,' Ruby mutters, looking away and continuing to twist at the handkerchief. 'Bad bloody penny…that's what he is…' Ruby goes on mumbling and fidgeting.

'Now, now, Ruby,' says the Sister, 'that's not how we welcome our visitors.' She goes over and plumps up the cushions behind Ruby. 'Let's see if we can get you a bit comfier, see if we can put you in a better humour. Do sit down, Mr Fanshaw. Make yourself at home.' The Sister gestures to a chair on the other side of the fire.

'Well, if you're sure…' Frank sits down.

Ruby continues to mutter and twist at the hanky.

'Now,' says the Sister, 'it must be nearly time for elevenses. If I can leave you two to get re-acquainted, I'll go and see where the tray's got to.'

'If it's not too much trouble…' says Frank, taking his cap off and shuffling a bit in his seat. He's made it, he's just about made it.

But no – Ruby starts shouting. 'I don't want him in here! Get him out! Take him away!' She tries to stand up, but it seems her legs won't hold her. 'Nothing but a bad bloody penny,' Ruby shrieks. 'Take him away, take him away!'

Frank stands up as if to leave. This could be too risky, too bloody risky, in front of that Sister, if old Ma W loses it. His hand goes to his jacket pocket where he's stuffed his cap.

183

'Here, here,' the Sister says, 'we'll have less of that, if you don't mind. Now you sit back down, Mr Fanshaw.' She pushes Frank in the chest so he's obliged to sit back down. 'And you, Ruby Willoughby,' she says, wagging her finger, 'you've got to learn to be a bit more polite. It's not often you get a visitor now, is it? You should be making the most of it. Now, I'm going to fetch that coffee. When I come back, I expect to find you two the best of friends.'

The Sister gives Frank a wink.

'If you're sure,' says Frank, 'I don't want to cause no upset...'

Ruby has gone silent and is staring tightlipped at the hanky she's gripping in both hands. The Sister winks at Frank again and swishes out of the room, leaving the door wide open.

'Shut that door.' Ruby says as soon as the Sister is out of the room. Her voice is firm, just like old times. Frank looks at her and hesitates. 'Shut the bloody door, I said,' Ruby repeats. 'Are you deaf, man?'

There's not much wrong with her, then. That frail old lady stuff – it's all an act. Frank gets up and pushes the door closed. Ruby hasn't changed, evidently: still dishing out orders. Frank is not altogether sure how to gauge her – probably best to let her speak first. He's not sure how to play it. A minute ago she looked like a frail old lady, totally benign. So much so, Frank couldn't imagine how one time she'd scared the living daylights out of him. But Ruby Willoughby worked her powers in a quiet way, silently. She wasn't an obvious bully. She had a way of wheedling round, of getting you to do exactly what she wanted. Oh, she had a way with her alright.

Frank will have to get the conversation going with old Mother Willoughby before the Sister comes back. What if she smells a rat? What if there's some late edition of some paper with his picture in it? What if that Sister's phoning the polis this very second? Frank hasn't got much longer to make sure the old lady doesn't shop him, but he doesn't know where to start. He'll have to say something. Here goes:

'You know who I am, don't you?' Frank's voice sounds a little thin. He clears his throat, wipes his mouth on the back of his hand. 'You remember me?'

'I know a bad bloody penny when I see one,' says Ruby. Her fingers are starting to twist at the handkerchief again. 'You always were turning up, like a bad penny. Now you're following me about like a bad bloody smell. I've a mind to...' Ruby's voice trails off as she stuffs the hanky into her cardigan pocket and sits up straight, hands now resting firmly on the arms of her chair.

Frank knows that pose. The old stick sounds perfectly alright now: there's nothing frail or gaga about her. He registers that tone of voice, the hallmark of Ruby Willoughby. And he's surprised to discover it has the same old effect on him. Frank too sits up straighter and plants his two feet parallel and flat on the floor. Muriel had that same capacity for condemnation, for making you feel shame when there was nothing for you actually to be ashamed about. Just like Ruby, Muriel only had to look at you and you were six again, waiting for a clip around the ear. Now, sitting watching Ruby, Frank realises Stella's got it too, that same air of devious authority, that penetrating stare, that same accusatory way of looking – looking through you as though they knew some terrible truth about you that you don't even know about yourself. Yes, Stella's got that same trait. An image of the three of them – Ruby, Muriel and Stella – springs to Frank's mind. Three generations, sitting in a line, the three bloody monkeys. Ruby is staring at him in that way of hers.

'Out with it, man!' she shouts, breaking the silence. Her shrill voice jolts Frank. He should have planned a strategy, known what to say and in what order. He's going to come across like a bumbling fool. 'What is it you're after? What is it you want? Money? If it's more money you're after, you can go and whistle.'

'I'm not after your money,' Frank manages to say.

'What then, if it's not money?'

'Your Stella's out. Of prison. I've seen her...'

'What's that got to do with me, may I ask? I've washed my hands of Stella long since. Why else d'you think I'm in here, in this hellhole? Stella Moon can rot in hell, as far as I'm concerned. She's no granddaughter of mine.'

'And the papers know she's out. They won't stop there. They're onto the Baby Keating business.'

'Get out! Get out, before I press the bell for...'

'Come on, now,' Frank is pleasantly surprised to find he's got the upper hand so quickly. He didn't imagine he'd get Ruby Willoughby rattled quite so easily. 'Now, you know you're not going to do that. You're in this up to the neck, Ruby Willoughby. Just as much as I am. More so, in fact.'

'I'm an old lady,' Ruby says. 'I live in a care home. None of that matters to me any more. If you think it does, you're mistaken.'

'Oh, but it will,' Frank says. 'It'll matter to you a great deal when the papers catch up with you, when they get their hands on your Stella, when they start sniffing about the place and find out about the dead baby. Somebody's dug up the body, and it sure as hell wasn't me.'

'I don't know what you're talking about,' Ruby says.

'The baby's body,' Frank explains, 'that we buried at the Beach Hut. After Stella told everyone it was at the back of the civvy. Remember? Well, it's gone. I've been up to the Beach Hut and it's not there. I was going to get rid of it once and for all, but I can't because it's not there. Somebody's already took it. All there is is a great big hole in the kitchen floor.'

'What do you mean, the body's gone? Don't be stupid, man. It'll have dropped to bits long since. It's getting on ten years, man. There'll be nothing left of it. You can't pull the wool over my eyes that easy.'

'I'm telling you it's not there,' Frank says. 'I don't mean disintegrated. I mean stolen. Someone's dug it up and taken it away it. If you would listen, woman.'

'How much is it you're after?'

'You're not listening. The body of Baby Keating is gone. Which means trouble. For you, for me, for all us. Don't ask me how or why or when or where it's been taken to, because I've no idea. I just know it's not there where me and Muriel put it.'

Just then, the Sister comes back into the room carrying the tray. Did she come straight in, or has she been hovering outside the door, listening?

186

'Ah, I knew you two'd get along like a house on fire,' she says as she puts the tray down onto the coffee table. 'Now, who wants what?'

After the sister leaves, Frank produces a picture of Stella he's torn out of the paper. He shoves it right in front of Ruby's face and tells her the Macalinden reporter is determined to ferret out the truth about baby Keating.

'Go away,' Ruby says, calm as you like. She bats the newspaper cutting to the floor with the back of her hand. 'I'm not interested in anything you have to say. Now or at any other time.' Ruby picks up her walking stick and waves it at Frank. 'Get out. Get out of here. Crawl back into the woodwork where you belong. Cockroach.'

The walking stick catches her cup and saucer on the table, sends it flying across the room, tea splashing everywhere.

'Now look what you've done!' Ruby is fumbling at the side of the fireplace for the buzzer to summon a nurse, but Frank snatches the red cord out of her grasp.

'Not so fast, lady,' Frank says, holding the cord just out of her reach. 'We're in deep shit, you and me both. Have you any idea where the body is? Are you still in touch with Hedy?'

'Get out!' Ruby shouts, 'This is your last chance, Frank Fanshaw. Before I summons the Sister and tell her who you really are.'

'Oh, come on. You know you're not going to do that.' Frank drops the emergency cord, but Ruby doesn't make a grab for it. 'That Sister'll be far more interested to know who you are.'

Frank's about to get the upper hand here and he knows it.

'Now,' he says, picking up the china from the floor and setting it back on the little table beside Ruby. 'Now, there's no sense in the two of us fighting, is there? We're on the same side, you and me. We're both in it up to our necks and it's only a matter of time till the whole ruddy can of worms cracks open. We've got to make sure that doesn't happen, don't we? The both of us, we've got to work together.'

Ruby says nothing, just fidgets with the edge of the blanket that's over her knees.

'I'll do the leg work, but you'll have to supply the intelligence.'

Frank continues. 'One: we need to find Stella. Two: we need to find Hedy. And we need to find them before that reporter finds them. Before anyone starts digging about in the dirt behind what Stella did to Muriel. Before all the nasty business about the dead baby comes out. Because make no mistake, that's what'll happen. The body's gone, like I told you. It could be the police who've got it. They could be setting a trap. We could be too late already.'

Ruby blows her nose and mops her upper lip with the handkerchief.

'Do you see what I am saying?' Frank says. He can't seem to get through to her that the clock is ticking.

'It can't have been dug up,' Ruby says. 'Ten year ago the baby died. It'll have rotted away by now.'

Frank shakes his head. He can hardly bring himself to tell Ruby what he knows. The shock of what Muriel did could kill an old woman, and much as he resents Ruby and the hold she's had on him for so long, he doesn't want to do that. But he'll have to come clean. Or she won't appreciate what's at stake. He's got no choice.

'What are you looking like that for, man?' Ruby says.

'Muriel…she…well, she…'

'She what? What did Muriel do?'

'I'm sorry… She decided she wanted the baby preserved… Baby Keating, he wasn't buried in a normal way.'

Ruby brings both hands to her face.

'She what? Oh my God, what are you saying? Oh, may the Good Lord forgive her,' Ruby crosses herself. 'Oh Mr Fanshaw… and you let her? You let her do such a wicked thing?'

'I didn't have any say, not with Muriel. You know what she was like. The same as I didn't have any say with you when you conned me into burying it. Like mother, like daughter.'

Frank can hear the clatter of dishes in the corridor. They could be bringing Ruby's lunch in any minute. But he can't afford to back off now he's got this far.

'If you'll just tell me the truth…'

'It wasn't our Stella who killed the baby,' Ruby interrupts. 'It was Muriel. There. Now you know.'

It takes Frank a moment or two to absorb exactly what Ruby is saying.

'You mean…you mean…all this time? All these years and you let your Stella go on thinking that she'd done it?'

'Our Stella won't have remembered a thing. She was too young to understand, and too far gone…'

Frank stands up and paces the floor, shaking his head. Ruby seems shrunk into her chair, only half the size she was a few moments ago. Yet Frank can't bring himself to feel sorry for her. Is there no end to the lies and deception – the evil – that this woman is capable of? Why in God's name?

'You let your Stella – a kid, a fourteen-year-old kid she was, when you roped her into that séance… You're telling me you let your Stella think – no, you led her to believe – she'd killed a baby? You let her carry on thinking she'd done something she didn't actually do? That she'd killed a baby…' Frank exhales loudly, puts his fist to his face, bangs it against his mouth. 'And all for what? To let Muriel off the hook?'

Why the hell would Ruby want to let Muriel off the hook? They were always at loggerheads about everything. Ruby remains sunk in her chair. Frank sits down again in the other chair, runs both hands through his hair, and stands up again.

'I don't know why you did that,' he shakes his head again. 'I really can't see why you did that.'

'I didn't lead Stella into anything. That was Muriel. Covering her own back.'

'Why haven't you told Stella the truth long before now, then? If you'd told her the truth, you might have saved your own daughter's life. If Stella had known the truth, your Muriel might still be alive.'

It's clear to Frank that Ruby's not concerned with the truth – she never has been. She's only ever wanted to paper over the cracks, get herself off the hook and make everything appear to be normal. Ruby couldn't give a toss about the truth, she can't face it, hasn't got the foggiest about the havoc she's wreaked in other people's lives. She's sitting there sniveling into her hanky, but Frank'll be buggered if he feels sorry for her.

'She wasn't my Muriel,' Ruby snivels. 'Muriel wasn't my daughter.'

What is she saying now? Frank snorts. How many more lies has she got stored up?

'Muriel wasn't mine.' Ruby is saying. 'She was Worthy's. She wasn't anything to do with me. She did her level best from day one to come between me and Worthy. Believe me, Frank Fanshaw, you don't know the half of it.'

Frank's no longer sure he wants to know the half of it. He's tired of this woman and all her grim secrets. But he has a mission to accomplish. His own self-preservation will keep him there until it's clear what next step he has to take.

'This beggars belief, the lot of it. I must say, you and Muriel acted like mother and daughter, always at each other's throats.'

The clattering of crockery outside in the corridor is getting louder. Time's short.

'And how come you know about your Muriel and Baby Keating? How do you know Muriel did that? She never let on a word of it to me, and she told me some queer things. Muriel always maintained it was Stella, trying to shut the baby up to stop the mother going mad with all the screaming. Muriel always said it was Stella that plied the baby with stuff out of your cupboard, stuff you'd made up in actual fact, for the express purpose of keeping him quiet. You're as guilty as the rest of them, Ruby Willoughby, more than.'

'Tch,' Ruby says, 'I knew Muriel. I knew what she was capable of. Worthy wouldn't have her left alone with Stella. And for good reason. Why d'you think I went through that court case to keep Stella away from her mother? On his deathbed, he made me swear I'd protect Stella. But I never imagined Baby Keating, not until… until it was too late. Then I put two and two together.' Ruby put her hanky to her face.

Her voice has gone thin. But Frank's not going to give her no sympathy. Let her weep. She'll rot in hell for what she's done. She could have told the truth to Stella, but no, she chose to lie, she chose to shield Muriel, even though she hated her. And at the end of the day, Ruby Willoughby chose to shield herself. It's all far worse than Frank had imagined. It's sick.

'It's Stella I feel sorry for,' Frank says. 'No wonder she's like she is. No wonder she did what she did. You and Muriel, the pair of you, you never gave the kid a chance.'

'Well, I can't say as I noticed you being slow to cash in, Frank Fanshaw.' The old woman's claws are full out now. 'Don't think I didn't know what was going on the minute my back was turned. Oh, no, I saw it. I saw it all.'

'There was nothing that ever occurred without full consent. I can put my hand on my heart and say that. May God strike me dead.'

Ruby is scathing. 'Don't talk rot! What a load of phooey. A child can't consent. How can a child consent? Don't talk ridiculous.'

'Stella wasn't a child, as you put it. Or if she was, she knew what she was doing. And she accepted the cash.'

'Sex. Barely a teenager. With a man of forty-five.' Ruby's voice is shaking with anger. 'You think that's alright, do you? Well, I don't. You didn't think about Stella, did you? You didn't stop for a single minute and think about her, what you were doing, the effect it might have on her. Oh, no. All Frank Fanshaw thought about was himself, being led around by what's down his trousers, and sod the consequences for everybody else. Don't you dare judge me, Frank Fanshaw. You're in no position to judge anybody.' Ruby sits back in her chair, puts her hand to her chest, takes deep breaths.

'You've no idea, have you, of the harm it causes?' Ruby says when she gets her breath back. 'It's was Muriel's undoing, way back. Yes, that was the start of it.' Ruby's mopping at her eyes with the hanky again. 'Oh, yes. Things'd be very different if it was the male sex who got in the family way.'

'Stella was never in danger of being in the family way.'

'No, but Muriel was. Fourteen years old she was, until Worthy got it took away.'

'Good God, woman. What are you saying?'

'Worthy – he had no other option. Oh, God forgive him! He regretted it to the end. But he did it for me, he did it to bring me

191

some peace of mind. He did it for Muriel, so she could have a future. Oh, Mr Fanshaw, have some pity on an old woman, show some mercy.'

'The Lord in heaven, what am I hearing? Worthy Willoughby did an abortion on his own daughter. Fourteen years old. And you let him do it, for your own convenience.'

'I had no say, I tell you. Muriel was not my daughter. She was Worthy's. She wouldn't listen to anyone but her precious father.'

'Who was the father of her baby, then?'

'Muriel was nothing but a liar, an evil little twister. I'm glad Stella killed her. I hope she rots in hell.'

'Who got her pregnant?'

'I've no idea. And I don't think she had either. You know better than most people what Muriel was like, Mr Fanshaw. Well, I can tell you she was like that from being knee high to a grasshopper. She couldn't keep her hands off men, couldn't have cared less who or what they were. The father could have been any Tom, Dick or Harry,' Ruby shrugs. 'Muriel, she liked to stir up trouble, though, didn't she? She claimed it was our Billy,' Ruby snorts. 'Our Billy. Can you imagine? Said he'd "interfered" with her. And once the story was told, there was no changing it. Story stuck. Nasty little liar. Worthy, he had no option but to step in, or the police would have got involved. It was for the best, Mr Fanshaw,' Ruby nods her head, 'for the best, believe me, whatever you might think from this distance.'

'How d'you know Muriel was lying? Did you ever even ask her brother what had happened?'

'I told you, Billy was not Muriel's brother. He was my son, my only son. I didn't need to ask him. Billy wasn't like that. I knew for a fact he would never do such a thing, never on God's earth would he have done a thing like that. It was the shock of it all that killed him. It was Muriel that sent him to an early grave,' Ruby says. 'He took his own life when was only twenty-seven. The only thing I ever loved, and Muriel destroyed him with her lies. And Worthy, well, things could never be the same after that, could they?'

Frank sighs. He'd known Muriel had a troubled past, but had

no idea of the extent of it.

'You never loved Muriel. You never cared enough about her to believe her. What if she was telling the truth?'

'Muriel deserved to be destroyed like a rabid dog deserves to be destroyed, when it's nothing but a danger to itself and everybody and everything it comes in contact with. After what she did to Billy, I hated her – I tell you, I hated her. She took him away from me, and she tried her damnedest to take Worthy. Don't you go judging me, Frank Fanshaw, I tell you, you don't know the half of it.'

'Oh my God.' Frank rests his head in his hands and keeps it there. He'd had no idea.

Ruby blows her nose hard into her handkerchief. She sounds satisfied. Frank's opened a hornets' nest, and his own problems are nowhere near solved.

One of the care staff nudges the door open with her shoulder and comes in carrying a tray with hot lunch for Ruby. She looks askance at Frank, but makes no comment. Frank really should have gone before now. His presence will almost certainly be remarked upon, but he's past caring. His position here has served its purpose and very soon he'll be going and never coming back. Ruby waves her arm at the food, tells the girl to take it away, she's not hungry. The girl carries it back out of the room, comes back in with a sandwich in a plastic wrapper and puts it on Ruby's lap. She clears the uneaten breakfast things off the little table. She smiles at Frank as she leaves, pulling the door closed behind her.

Going back through the gates of the Warrender Park Nursing Home that day, Frank had more than achieved his mission. And it pleased him to know he was going through those gates for the very last time. Next stop, find Stella. If she's not at the boarding house, chances are she'll be at the Beach Hut. He'll check both. It was obvious to both Frank and Ruby that Stella did remember more than she'd ever let on. The crucial thing was to make sure she didn't spill the beans. Then after Frank had sorted Stella out, it would be Hedy Keating's turn.

Chapter Thirty-Three

The snow came early that year. Freakishly, in the night, in early November. Fat white flakes from a thick leaden sky, falling softly, all along the coast, whiting out everything from Berwick to Tynemouth. The dunes disappeared and not a blade of marram was left protruding. The corrugated roofs of the beach huts bowed under the weight of snow, the sand was white with it, the sea stilled.

Stella, sleepless and alone at the Beach Hut, had lain awake listening to the strange encroaching silence, trying to realise this was likely to be her last night of freedom for a very long time, the last chance she'd have to do the writing for Marcia. The big snow-fall in the night had put paid to her plans to head straight back to Newcastle and, for the time being anyway, she was strangely grateful. The snow also meant it was unlikely that either Frank Fanshaw or the Macalinden bloke would show up on her door-step. She could make the most of the short time she had left, try to calm down a bit and write something to explain herself to Marcia. It wouldn't be the sort of thing Marcia was hoping for, but at least it would go some way to explaining. And saying sorry.

Just before sunrise, when the night was at its coldest, Stella hauled one of Muriel's old fisherman's sweaters out of the trunk. It stank like a wet dog and was full of moth holes, but at least it would keep her warm. Then Stella tipped and banged the dust and the cobwebs out of the perished wellies, also belonging to Muriel. She shoved her bare feet into them so she could go and bring some wood in. There was a strange half-comfort to be had from being in Muriel's shoes again, in the fact that Stella was now mistress of this territory, in knowing that she was free and alone to make the most of her time here until the snow'd melted enough to travel and make her second confession possible. Stella tugged open the door and looked out from the iced-up veranda across the slab of steel-grey sea. On the other side of the bay, she could see flurries rushing in from the Arctic on a sharp north-easterly, coating the headland, blurring the castle ruin and blotting out the cliffs, the cliffs where Muriel died.

As Stella looked out across the sea, the cliffs transformed: a thick white blind came down and the world was made that bit smaller. Stella stepped back inside and pushed and kicked at the swollen door to jam it shut again. She'd managed, after years of soul-searching and struggle, somehow to come to terms with the killing of her mother. Now she had to start again. Now there was another one. Now Stella had dues to pay for the baby. She knew it wasn't going to be easy: she knew what happened in prison to people who'd harmed a child.

And there was part of Stella that almost wanted to run away and hide, to forget about it all again, turn the clock backwards, stay in denial. Another part of her knew that would never again be possible. And even if it were possible, Stella knew that was not the road she would now choose to take. She'd killed the baby. She was willing to face up to it. She would pay the price.

Back inside the Beach Hut, Stella turned the Chubb key in the deadlock, wedged a wicker chair underneath the handle, dragged the old wooden trunk across and pushed it up against the chair.

Stella wrote and wrote in the blue silk notebook. She wrote for Marcia. She wrote until her hand could no longer grasp the pen. The need to sleep – when it came – came heavy. She stumbled to the bed, curled herself up under the damp covers and closed herself inside the silence.

Stella had tried, face to face, to tell Marcia everything, all the small things she remembered. But there hadn't been much. There were gaps she didn't know how to fill, had never known how to fill. Marcia had laughed, disbelieving. Then, more serious.

'That's peculiar,' Marcia said, 'to have such fat chunks of your life totally missing.' Stella knew what Marcia was thinking, that there could be *anything* in those gaps. Anything. 'Or nothing,' Marcia said, 'maybe there's nothing.' So Stella had convinced herself there was nothing – there seemed nothing to remember, so maybe there was nothing. How wrong she'd been.

Now Stella knows what was missing. Now she will have to do what has to be done, which includes telling Marcia. Marcia had always said how important it is to know your own story. That's the route to knowing who you are. So, yes, Stella had wanted to remember, wanted to be able to tell the whole story.

Then all the horrible stuff had landed on her at the Boarding House, and Stella no longer believed that remembering it all did anyone any good. Nobody had advised her that the price of remembering might be too high; nobody said to watch it, it might shrink you to the size of a lentil. No, nobody said anything about how remembering can take away everything from under you and leave you with nothing, leave you not knowing what you've done or not done, or why or when or where. A memory that rips the ground from under you, so not a single thing makes any sense any more. You're left grabbing after certainties that slip away as soon as you get anywhere near them. You're left grasping and desperate and you still don't know who the fuck you are, because you haven't got a past, because you haven't got a story, you haven't got a future because you haven't got a story. All you've got are the gaping holes in someone else's script – Muriel's, your grandmother's, and yours, Marcia. Yes, yours, every fucker else's fucking script but your own, Stella Moon.

So, Marcia, memories are just little stories you tell yourself, are they? Is that what they are? Do you really think that's what they are? Well, do you?

Killing a baby! That's a nice little story for you, Marcia. Fuck you, Marcia, fuck your know-all stupid mantras. What the fuck did Marcia ever know about Stella's life? About anyone's life but her own? How could Marcia have known anything when Stella herself had been blind to it, when so much had been buried, hidden away, distorted, destroyed?

Tell Stella this, Marcia: why do people do anything, anything at all? Why don't they just lay down and die, before the absolute futility of this shitheap we call life collapses all around them?

Little fucking stories, they can practically kill you.

Baby Keating, dead and buried.

Your fault, Stella – nasty, vicious Stella Moon.

Now look what she's done. Capable of anything, red-haired devil. Keep right away from her.

You should be ashamed of yourself, Stella Moon.

The burden of knowing – Stella can no longer push it away.

Stella huddles tighter in the damp bed. The cold has seeped right into her bones and frozen them. Her body aches with the effort of keeping warm. She's too cold even to shiver. Soon there'll be no paraffin left and that will be that. She would drag the mattress into the main room, lie down in front of the stove, if she had the strength.

Rehabilitation and therapy. Connect up your memories into a nice little storyline. Give it a happy ending. Here's your life, here's a story, here's a timeline. Come on, Stella. A beginning, a middle and an end. Where you came from, where you are, where you're going to. Take responsibility for what you've done. Tell it how it was. Own it. Then draw a line under your crime. Draw a line and move on. Come on, Stella.

That was the theory.

Stella hadn't been able to do any of it. There had only been gaps and confusion.

I don't have a story, Stella had wanted to scream into their stupid, concerned faces. *I don't have any fucking story.*

Stella preferred endless games of Battleships, Hangman and Noughts and Crosses, with Marcia. Sharing bags of Mint Imperials. Chanting games like *I went to Paris and I took with me*…a feather boa, a pair of purple pyjamas, a pink monkey with a hat on. A turquoise-blue Indian silk notebook with handmade paper. A letter from Marcia, not yet opened. Muriel's little blue suitcase. Her small grey haversack. The empty Kilner jar.

In any case, Stella had never had any problem whatsoever 'owning' – as they put it – her crime. From the start, she'd taken full and proper responsibility. Straight away she'd admitted what she'd done to Muriel. Dialled 999 – apparently – and asked for the coastguard with a steady voice. At the police station, she'd replied to every question, she'd made a confession, signed it and dated it. Stella did not need to make any personal acknowledgement of her crime, the final, triumphant line of any therapeutic story.

Stella is going to have to get up to put more wood on the fire. She hauls herself out of bed, pulls the blanket around her and shuffles into the other room. She clears one pane with her sleeve. It's still snowing. She brings some wood in and keeps the fire going. Stella wraps herself in the damp blanket and lies down on the rug in front of the stove.

They wanted a motive, a motive for matricide, like they couldn't complete their picture if she couldn't give them a motive. But if there was a motive, Stella could never have put it into words. There are some things that can't be put into words, things there are no words for, things you know but hardly know, and somewhere deep down, somewhere beyond words, a whole different life is lived continually, a life before and beyond the words for telling it. Prison, they said, hardly out of earshot, could well be quite the wrong place for this one: she'd be better off up the road. Have you seen her eyes?

There were four reviews of Stella's case. Her medical records were shared out, thumbed, annotated. No-one agreed with anyone else. Report after report, no-one was any the wiser. Stella shrugged and said again she was sorry for what she'd done, she was sorry she couldn't help them any further, if anything did come to her, she'd let them know. The last case conference looked from one person to the next and told Stella that was all, thank you very much, she could go.

Marcia was waiting to escort her back through all the locked gates and echoing corridors. She looked at Stella and smiled. Marcia, the only one who wasn't trying to wring words out of her, the only one Stella wanted to tell anything to. Marcia's big bunch of keys jangled against her hip. She said not to worry, you can write it down in your own time. When the time was right, the words would come. Then she'd be lucky if she could keep them away.

All Stella had wanted was to get out of Holloway and for the seven years to pass so she could get the hell out, put it all behind her and start her life again. How she'd longed for the day those gates clanked shut behind her, how she'd itched for it. And then, when it came, it was like it had sneaked up on her and taken her unawares. It came too suddenly and it came too soon. Stella wasn't ready. The day of her release landed on her like the meteor landed on the dinosaurs. It landed on her the very moment she no longer wanted it. Stella's release was no release at all.

They'd practically had to push her out, their big smiles showing too many teeth. They were shoving money into her fist and handing over the black plastic bin bag that contained everything that belonged to the departing Stella Moon; pushing her out into the world, her time done. The gates had squealed along on their metal rollers and clanked shut behind her. She'd stood there for a moment, looking about, feeling very small. Then she'd pulled the little blue suitcase out of the black bag, stuffed everything into it and pushed the empty black bag back through the bars of the gate. They could keep it. Stella stood tall and crossed the road to the bus stop.

Now, at the Beach Hut, Stella knows she should find something to eat. Or at least a hot drink. Stella knows this. But she doesn't move. She stays where she is, shivering and wrapped in the damp blanket. She stays close to the fire while outside the snow still falls.

For the first time since she left Holloway, Stella is missing Marcia with a longing that is deep and physical and makes the whole insides of her jagged and empty. The realisation that she has never really missed anyone before in her life comes as a shock. Some sort of shift is happening, tectonic plates bump and scrape and realign. Stella turns over, her back to the fire. She feels so sick, she wills sleep but she knows it won't come. She will get the note-book again and write some more.

Tell Marcia. Tell her what? That Home is a decrepit lodging house with boarded-up windows, fit only for rats and insects, stinking of vomit and Frank Fanshaw's rancid sweat? This isn't what Marcia wanted for Stella. Tell her about the poison cupboard? Death in every jar and bottle, death in the séance, death in the medical bag, aborted foetuses. Tell Marcia you killed Baby Keating as well as your own poor mother. See if Marcia's got any time for Stella when she hears all that. Memories are black stains creeping under the wallpaper, making hideous shapes. Look at them, they all look like Stella Moon.

At the Beach Hut, huddled beside the fire, Stella is in a prison a hundred times worse than Holloway.

Dearest Marcia,
I know how hard you tried to help me and I'm very grateful for all you did, but since I left Holloway everything's gone wrong and I've discovered even worse things and it's all gone belly-up and I'm never going to be able to have a normal life. I mean literally Never, so I'm saying goodbye now. Goodbye, dearest Marcia, and God bless you – and thanks again for everything, Marcia. It's me that's failed, not you.

Chapter Thirty-Four

The day the snow came, Gareth came too. He struggled more than five hours to get from Newcastle to the Beach Hut, though Stella didn't know much about that until later. The journey shouldn't have taken more than an hour, but on that day the snow blocked the A1 south of Morpeth and Gareth was diverted the long way round via Ashington and the coast – five hours in a long line of headlamps and tail lamps shuffling in single file behind the snow plough.

Gareth brought with him various newspapers, because there were bits in some of them about Stella. He didn't tell her then that someone from his own office had been yapping to the press. Gareth wanted Stella to leave the Beach Hut then and there, he said he could get her into some sort of safe house, where the press wouldn't be able to get at her. He talked about police protection, and about changing her identity and living as a completely different person. Her past – to all intents and purposes – erased. Stella could see Gareth meant well, that he was concerned for her. She couldn't think of how to tell him all that was beside the point, how to break it to him that there was another killing to be atoned for. And Stella knew that even if she went along with Gareth's plan, sooner or later she would still have to face up to what she had done, and the sooner she did it, the sooner it would be off her conscience. And as for changing her identity, Stella said an emphatic 'No' to that. Gareth didn't understand. He called her stubborn and ungrateful. Let him think what he likes. Stella's only just beginning to find out who she is: she's not going to start changing identity now.

Anyhow, the press didn't worry her, not now she'd decided to turn herself in. Having made that decision, Stella had somehow freed herself from a dead weight, and had started to write things down. She wanted to get that done, for Marcia – she owed it to her. She had a project now. Something she wanted to do for someone she cared about. Gareth was a distraction. He would get in the way.

The papers Gareth brought said nothing Stella hadn't seen or heard before – the likes of her shouldn't be running loose, should be permanently locked up, in the public interest, how could the public be expected to sleep soundly in their beds knowing people like her had the run of the place? The government's too soft on crime by half, etc. The fact that Macalinden wanted to unearth the truth about Baby Keating left Stella unmoved: she'd be giving it to Macalinden on a plate the minute she turned herself in to the police, which she was resolved to do as soon as she could get away. Stella couldn't quite take in what Gareth was so panicked about. She was resigned to everything.

There was a photograph in one of the papers, the same one from seven years ago. Gareth laughed at it, perhaps trying to be light-hearted. He kept saying he wanted to help her start again. Stella tried to laugh along with him. Couldn't bring herself to tell Gareth it was all far worse than he realised. She'd made up her mind to see this through, with or without Gareth's support. She'd give herself up, confess to killing Mrs Keating's baby and take whatever was coming to her. Gareth was oblivious. If she insisted on staying put, he said, he would coach her on how to speak to the press. He'd been on courses. The secret was not to be caught off guard, to say what you wanted to say, regardless of their questions. But hopefully, he said, they wouldn't find Stella – not just yet – not if she kept her head down. The snow was a good thing, it'd deter them from travelling any distance.

Gareth brought whisky – Glenfiddich, two bottles. He poured some into plastic beakers. Stella didn't want it but didn't like to disappoint him, so she sipped small sips every time Gareth did and said nothing when he topped her beaker up a second time, then a third. They talked about the freakish weather, Gareth's good fortune in getting through at all. He held up the *Chronicle* at arm's length and laughed at the photograph of Stella, compared it to her real face, laughed some more, drank some more, peered through the window and watched the snow, still falling. Over his shoulder he said Stella was 'his' case now, Geoff had handed her file over, Gareth would be looking after Stella from now on, responsible for her rehab. And he'd been thinking, he said, he might use her for his Case Study for his MSc dissertation, if she was agreeable? Watch this space, he said. Stella said nothing. Gareth was in a different world. Nothing of what he said touched her. Gareth came away from the window and sat down next to Stella. The *Chronicle* lay open on the floor with Stella's picture staring out. Gareth almost had his foot on her face.

'Here's to the future,' Gareth said, holding up his beaker and bumping it against Stella's, 'Here's to…'

Stella got up and walked over to the window.

She'd rather not look at that photograph. If Stella looked at it closely, she'd see not herself – not Stella Moon – but Muriel. She'd see her mother's horrid wide eyes and how crazy they looked. Stella Moon would disappear into the image, she'd fuse with Muriel, she'd be lost for good.

Stella cannot tell any of this to Gareth. She wishes he hadn't come. She has to leave Gareth sitting by the fire, his tie and his belt undone, pouring another drink, opening a packet of Cheddars and talking with his mouth half-full of cold pork pie. Gareth peering at the photograph, asking if there was a radio in the place, did Stella want another drink, should he put another log on the stove, did she have any other photographs from when she was small? It was like Gareth was on holiday, a weekend seaside break.

Stella slipped into the bathroom. She stood in front of the mirror. If she looked into the mirror she would see Muriel's eyes, she would see they were crazy. She would see why they made people afraid, why they made Stella afraid. She pulled the Wellington off her foot and hit it against the mirror, she hit it and hit it and hit it. She wanted the mirror to be shattered, for the wiry red hair and the wild wide eyes to be smashed in pieces.

Gareth was shouting through. 'What's going on in there? Stella, what are you doing?'

Stella does up the lock inside the bathroom door.

In Grandpa Worthy's room there was a long mirror. It was in the wardrobe door in the room they moved him to when he was taken poorly – the room where, not long after, Grandpa Worthy died.

It was a Wednesday. Muriel had collected Stella from the ballet class. She'd rushed Stella home because her father lay dying. She'd rushed out again, almost straight away.

'You stay with your Grandpa while I go and fetch Dr Burdon.' Stella listened as Muriel clattered down the stairs. 'Don't you budge from there,' Muriel shouted from the passage. 'Don't you so much as move an inch.' The porch door slammed and then the front door and then the gate.

The house went quiet. Apart from her grandfather's rasping breath, all Stella could hear was her own heart thumping. The eiderdown rose and dropped with each noisy heave of Grandpa Worthy's chest. As she watched, he pulled at his oxygen mask, clearly trying to get it off his face, Stella watching it all in the big long mirror. She watched it in the mirror because she did not want to look and see what was real, she did not want to bear witness to Grandpa Worthy's soul, which she knew was gathering itself, gathering itself up, his soul was rising out of him, and then it was flowing away. Even as Stella knew her dear Grandfather's death was happening, she could not bring herself to intervene to help him, to put the oxygen back on his face. She could not even bring herself to bear witness.

The long mirror in Grandpa Worthy's room had a crack in it – the start of a crack – in the bottom corner. Stella stared at it, she stared at it and as she stared she made it into a bigger one, and bigger, and bigger, until diagonally it cracked right across while Grandfather Worthy fumbled with unsteady fingers to pull at the elastic that kept the breathing mask on. By the time Muriel came back with Dr Burdon, Stella had made the crack in the mirror open up wide as a canyon, she had slipped inside, in through the crack, and she had disappeared.

Dr Burdon said they were too late. Where was Stella? Why didn't she put the mask back on? They said they didn't understand.

They said they would never forgive her.

In the bathroom at the Beach Hut, Stella throws herself at the mirror. Gareth is banging on the door. Stella hears him shouting her name. He's banging the door with a chair or something. Stella throws herself at the mirror again and again. She wants to drown out the sound of Muriel clattering up the back stairs with Dr Burdon, to drown out the sound of Muriel in hysterics screaming for her father, cursing Stella's name.

Then Gareth's voice is receding until all Stella can hear are echoes of her name as though down a thousand empty corridors. Stella has slipped in through the crack and is streaking fast along corridors of mirrors, losing herself among multiple images, multiple echoes, all clashing and collapsing into each other. In the distance, a baby is wailing. If Stella runs hard enough, she will run past the sound, she will run straight through it, she will leave behind a thousand fragments of Stella Moon in endless shards of mirror, all the Stellas running alongside her, all keeping pace with her, the baby's wailing echoes off the walls.

The baby wailing is the noise of Stella Moon. Stella falls to the bathroom floor, exhausted, bleeding.

Chapter Thirty-Five

Gareth has to go round the outside of the hut and smash the bathroom window in. He has to squeeze his body through the hole where there are still shards of glass that tear at his clothes and at the skin on his arms and make striations on his chest as if a lion has gouged him with its claws. He grabs hold of Stella and shakes her, yelling at her to stop the screaming, as if she could, by sheer force of will, stop the noise from coming out. Gareth says afterwards it was a wailing that came from somewhere he didn't know existed. He never wanted to know that place again, it scared the wits off him.

Gareth carries Stella into the main room while she is still screaming. She doesn't resist. He pulls a mattress through, lays her down on it and covers her over with the damp tartan blanket. She lies there with her mouth open, she keeps opening it wider, straining to get the sound out, the sound that needed to come out, till there was nothing left and she quiets and starts to sob, her body convulsing. He'd never seen a case like it. Stella would have said she wasn't a case if she'd had any voice left. Gareth tells her to sleep. She needs sleep. Says that he will wait up all night. Longer if he has to.

Now Stella's in bed, in her old room, in her old bed that creaks. Gareth had aired some sheets by the fire and made up the bed. He's stood Muriel's wellies side by side in the corner. He's put Stella's little blue suitcase at the bottom of her bed. She should be grateful. Snow still falling, lighter now. Everything quieted, just the soft sound of the sea, down beyond the dunes.

* * *

One winter, the snow came up high as the windows. You couldn't see out. It was like living on a cloud. Muriel was gleeful, more so when Grandma Willoughby couldn't get to the Beach Hut to fetch Stella back. They lived happily together that time, Stella and Muriel, eating ancient porridge with black treacle on when the Carnation milk ran out, and cheese footballs, gone tasteless, left over from some forgotten Christmas. Muriel trudged out up to her thighs in snow and had to dig her trapped pheasants out of the drifts. She didn't stuff those ones. She hung them by their scrawny feet from that beam there, in a line, then roasted them on a spit Frank Fanshaw had concocted out of an old bit of sheep wire.

* * *

Gareth's given Stella too many blankets. They weigh heavily, and the paraffin heater's too close to the bed for safety. But still, Stella cannot get warm. She's frozen inside her body. She's made of ice. Gareth has patched and wrapped her up, even though he too was cold and bleeding. This is the second time he's rescued her. She should be grateful. Stella wouldn't let him in. She couldn't. She needs to sleep. She'll think about everything tomorrow.

Gareth has had a glimpse of the real Stella Moon, the one who screams though no sound comes out. He's had a glimpse and he has not gone away.

Tell Gareth this, though. Tell him the real Stella Moon is worthless and selfish and evil and made of nothing but shame.

Stella Moon went with Frank Fanshaw. She betrayed herself and everyone. She's dirty and full of shame.

And she's an evil killer. Not once but twice. Not twice, but three times.

Stella Moon let her grandfather die a desperate death while she stood there looking into a crack in the mirror. She broke her grandmother's heart. She broke Muriel's heart.

Stella Moon killed an innocent baby and broke its mother's heart.

Stella Moon killed her own mother and broke her own heart.

Stella Moon is worthless and full of shame and guilty of crimes.

Stella writes it all down. She writes it in Marcia's lovely blue notebook. She laughs when she thinks that she might tell all that to Gareth. Tell him, Stella. See if he still stays on to look after you.

It's Gareth's job to stay. The snow keeps him at the Beach Hut. He's curious about Stella. He's fascinated. He's involved. He's in too deep. Whatever. He's not going away.

Stella doesn't know if she wants him there or not. Let him decide. Whatever. Sleep won't come, not proper sleep. She writes some more for Marcia. Writing it down for Marcia brings Marcia close.

Gareth brings Stella a mug of Cup-A-Soup. He says he's sorry, but there's no croutons to go with it. He laughs, sort of. Stella opens her eyes. She is resolved to turn herself in. She deserves to be punished. No punishment is big enough for Stella Moon. She will die of self-loathing. She deserves to rot in hell.

'No, no,' Gareth says. 'There now, there now. We can sort it out.' She turns away from him and faces the wall. 'You don't know what you're saying. You're exhausted, and you've been ill. It's all been too much for you.' He nudges up beside her on the bed, he pushes hair back from her damp forehead. He kisses her temple. The Cup-A-Soup goes cold.

Chapter Thirty-Six

Stella is still in bed. Still sleeping, thank God. Gareth is looking after her. He's made up his mind to do whatever it takes to rescue Stella Moon. Like Harry Callahan, Gareth will do whatever it takes. It's all down to him that she's calmer now. He walks over to the window, rubs a pane clear and looks out. It's stopped snowing but the sky's still heavy and there's a wind getting up. There'll be drifts – big ones. Gareth could be stuck here for the duration. In caring mode. Oh well. He hasn't got much option. It doesn't have to be all bad.

Gareth pulls the chair up close to the stove and sits, elbows on his knees and his head in his hands, listening to the roar of the fire as it rushes up the flue. By rights, he should be weary, exhausted, full of shame himself. But he's strangely awake, almost perky. He should take his chance now and sleep as well, but he won't. He needs to think, get things back in perspective. If Stella's mental state – or the snow, for that matter – keeps him at the Beach Hut, maybe for days, what will happen? What about supplies? What if the water freezes? Or the paraffin runs out? There's hardly any firewood left, not enough food – not enough of anything. Except Stella's madness: there's plenty of that. Gareth sees that now, now it's too late, way too late.

Fact is Gareth Davies, Probation Officer, Newcastle upon Tyne Probation Service, has committed the worse possible kind of error of judgement. Let's not say at this stage it's anything worse than an error of judgement. It could cost him his career. He's got to be careful – very, very careful – work out what's the best way forward.

Bottom line: Gareth's snowed up in a beach hut miles from anywhere with a madwoman who thinks she can talk to the dead and now says she's a multiple killer, having added a grandfather and some baby or other to her list of homicides. She's told him all of it. They'd been lying there, just lying there afterwards and smoking, like you do, and out she'd come with it. Gareth had laid there, hands under his head on the pillow. He'd just laid there, taking it all in, waiting for the full horror of his situation to sink in, while he acted like what she was saying was normal, like what she'd done was ordinary, his Master's in Criminology training kicking in, unfortunately way too late.

Bang goes the possibility of his Case Study on Matricide. What's done is done and can't be undone. Gareth's brain whirled, his body physically recoiled as he edged away so his shoulder was no longer touching her shoulder. He'd shifted his head on the pillow so that wild hair of hers was no longer dowsing his cheek, as his very self shrank with revulsion, for himself as well as for Stella.

Gareth Davies. What an idiot.

Gareth gets up and pours another whisky. He swishes it round his mouth till it burns his gums. He swallows the lot in a single gulp and pours another.

What a stupid bastard. He should never have touched her. Fuck knows what he was thinking of. There's no going back now, he shouldn't have done it. But he has and he did and now...

His defences were down, he'd had a drink, it was cold in that room, he'd felt sorry for her, she'd got his defences way down with those eyes of hers, and all that weeping, and those skinny little arms reaching out, reaching out for someone, anyone. Gareth isn't kidding himself that it was anything personal to do with him. All he'd done was respond to her, respond to her need. She'd wanted it. It had been her that wanted it.

Come on, Gareth. You've overstepped the mark. You're making lame excuses. The very moment Gareth most needs his professional self, it will not be summoned. This is as bad as it gets.

Gareth had fucked Stella with a desperation he didn't recognise belonged to him. He'd never been like that before. Stella had screamed for Marcia. Who the hell's Marcia? Someone else she's done away with? Gareth hasn't heard of any Marcia. She'd whimpered and pleaded for Gareth to hold her, and so he had. He'd held her for a long time while she shook and she sobbed and shrieked for Marcia, Marcia, Marcia. He'd felt the thin bones of her back through the thick sweater that smelled of mould and dust. Those bones had put him in mind of some little animal – half skinned, half alive, like one of her mother's taxidermy specimens, he couldn't tell what it was. Some skin-and-bone thing Gareth had rescued from a trap when he was ten. It was twitching. He didn't know what to do with it, he'd got sick of carrying it and he'd thrown it into the hedge before he got home. Now Stella reminded him of that lame, nameless thing.

Gareth had climbed into the single bunk next to Stella and squeezed himself up against her, holding her while she shook. The bed was damp, she was shivering cold, and he'd tried to warm her. She must have got the wrong idea. It was she who turned and kissed him first. She'd kissed like she meant to devour him. Her face was damp and hot and her hair was everywhere. His hands were caught up in it and he'd tried to pull her head back to get her off him. Then he'd felt his body responding. Gareth was shocked to find himself so full of desperation. It must have been the drink. They'd both had a drink. He'd unzipped his flies, tugged at her damp jeans till he got them half way down and registered she had no knickers on. It was over in seconds. She never stopped crying for Marcia.

Then, afterwards, he'd done his best to normalise. That's what they're always telling you in the training. Normalise. Normalise. So he'd lit them both a smoke and they'd laid there till, calm as anything, she'd told him all that shit. Multiple fucking murders.

Rule number one: don't get involved with clients. Emotionally or otherwise. Keep your distance.

These people are dangerous. They are mostly unhinged.

They can sue you if you're negligent or if you overstep the mark.

Keep the boundaries in place. Always keep the boundaries uppermost in your mind.

Gareth's career is over. Or soon will be. Stella wants to give herself up, she's intent on it. She'll confess to killing the baby, that's what she says she'll do. She needs to be punished, that's what she says, she wants to be punished, and it's what she deserves. Don't try and dissuade me, she says. It'll all come out, the whole rotten business. Plus, the press could come knocking on that door any minute; the minute the snow's gone they'll be knocking, and misdemeanors by Probation Officers, the very thing they'll be in ecstasies over. They'll think they've died and gone to bloody heaven.

Dirty Harry Callahan threw his badge away at the end of the first film. He'd achieved the end he was after, but he'd done it all wrong: he'd not done it by the book, and the means he'd used to get where he wanted to be were downright contrary to ordinary ethical principles. That's going to be Gareth. Throwing his metaphorical badge in the trash.

Gareth pours another drink, swishes it round in his mouth and gulps it down. He leans back in the chair and closes his eyes. He should go to sleep. Maybe it'll all look different after he has a rest. Maybe Stella will forget what's happened and they can carry on as before. He'll make an extra effort to be nice to her. Care for her till she gets well again. As long as it takes. If she doesn't forget, maybe she'll forgive.

Gareth wakes with a start, disoriented, thirsty and groggy with drink. How long has he been asleep? He has no idea. The paraffin lamp is still flickering and the stove still warm, but down to embers. It's pitch dark outside. The door is rattling. Gareth goes to the window. It's snowing again. Someone's knocking, banging, harder – a man's voice, Geordie accent, shouting for Stella.

The press. They've found her. In the middle of the fucking night. Gareth freezes, his head, still fuzzy with drink and asleep a moment ago, suddenly alert, suddenly sober. He wets his lips and swallows. His mouth is parched. Who is it and what do they want? Whoever it is, it sounds like they're going to have the damn door off its posts. Gareth rushes round the room, pulling curtains, not having them looking in this goldfish bowl. Now they're banging on the window, demanding to be in. Gareth will have to do something, say something. What should he say? They're shouting for Stella. Open the door, open the bloody door before they kick it in. It can't be the press. They wouldn't kick the door in, surely? Police.

It's the fucking police.

'Who is it?' Gareth stands behind the door and shouts. 'What do you want?'

'It's Fanshaw,' says the voice, 'Frank Fanshaw. I don't know who the hell you are, but you can tell Stella I'm here to see her. I know she's in there. Just tell her. She'll know what you're on about.'

Fanshaw. That's that weirdo bloke at the boarding house Stella told him about, all spittle and fingernails, can't keep his hands to himself. The one she's getting away from. No way is Gareth opening that door.

'What exactly do you want?' says Gareth.

'None of your business. Just open the door. And be quick about it.'

Gareth's brain won't think. Frank Fanshaw, banging on the door in the middle of nowhere, in the middle of the night, about to kick the door in. God knows how he's got here, through all that snow. He must be desperate. Or determined. What for, though? Kicking at the door...

'I know you've got her in there, whoever you are,' he's saying. 'Well, you can tell her I'll be straight to the papers, I'll tell them where she is if she doesn't open this bloody door and open it fast, cause I'm not standing here freezing my balls off, not for nobody.'

'Stella Moon is in my care, for the time being,' says Gareth in his most professional voice. 'I am her Probation Officer. And frankly, after what she's told me about you...'

'I don't care if you're the monkey's bloody uncle. She's not a bloody kid any more. She's a grown woman and fully capable of looking after herself and making up her own mind. Just tell her from me I've seen her grandmother and she's sent me here, so you'd better let me in. I don't intend to go on freezing my arse off out here to please some poncey Probation Officer.' Frank Fanshaw kicks the door so hard the wood in the bottom panel cracks. 'I mean it, I'll have this effing door in if you don't open it.'

'Alright, alright, there's no need for that. Say what exactly it is you want,' says Gareth, 'and I'll wake her up and ask her.'

'It happens to be confidential,' says Frank, 'as in between me and Stella. And old Mrs Willoughby,' he adds. 'Nothing to do with you. So you can mind your own business.' Frank puts his fist through the window next to the door and the shattered glass falls to the floor. 'Now are you going to open the frigging door? I'll smash the rest of those windows if I have to.' Frank goes back to the front door and starts kicking away at the cracked panel.

'How do I know you're who you say you are? You could be one of those press people for all I know…'

'I'm warning you.' Frank stands back and aims a heavy kick at the middle of the door. The wood splinters and the heel of Frank's boot is visible. 'Get Stella and she'll tell you.'

'Alright, alright, I'm opening it.' Gareth pulls the chair out of the way, turns the key and the door swings back on its hinges, letting in an icy blast of wind and snow.

'That's more like it,' says Frank, stepping inside and banging the door shut behind him. He stamps his feet on the mat. 'Where d'you say you've got Stella?' He shakes the snow off his hat and hangs it on the back of the door.

'Asleep,' says Gareth. 'She's asleep.'

'Well, go and wake her up, then.' Frank takes off his donkey jacket and shakes that as well before hanging it up. 'Evil out there, eh?' He picks his cigarettes and a box of matches out of the pocket, taps one out, lights it and inhales. 'If you're not getting her up, mate, I will.' Frank throws the still burning match down by the stove and goes towards the bedroom. 'Stella!'

'Let her alone,' Gareth says. 'Let her sleep a bit longer. She's had a hard time. If you'd seen her before… Here, sit down, have a drink.' Gareth pours some whisky into a plastic beaker and hands it to Frank.

Frank takes it, gulps it back and wipes his mouth on the back of his hand. 'Nice one. What did you say your name was?' He holds out the beaker and Gareth refills it.

'Davies, Gareth Davies. Probation Officer – part of the protocol when they're released. Idea was to get her settled in a hostel in Newcastle. But, well, one thing led to another, and it was here she wanted to be.'

'Protocol, you say?' a smirk spreads across Frank's face. 'Is that what they call it these days, protocol, eh?' He laughs and nods slowly. 'One thing led to another, eh? I'm getting the picture.' Frank lights another cigarette and flicks the match onto the hearth. 'Don't worry, official protocol man, Probation Officer Davies, your secret's safe with me.' Frank touches a forefinger to the side of his nose.

He's a sly bugger, this Frank. And a quick one. Gareth had better watch out. 'Yeah,' he says, sounding unconcerned, 'Stella mentioned she'd…er…bumped into you, at the boarding house place. I …er … Desperate to get away, she was, for more reasons than one, as I understand it…'

'Fact is,' Frank interrupts, 'I gotta see her. And I gotta see her quick. There's unfinished business, and time's running short.'

'You know about the press then…getting onto her story?' Gareth says.

Frank gets the crumpled Page 2 out of the donkey jacket pocket and smooths it out. 'Damn right.' He hands the paper to Gareth, 'That's the main reason I come looking for her.'

Gareth glances at the page. 'Bound to happen, sooner or later. Case like that.' He hands the page back to Frank.

'She's hiding out? Here?' Frank doesn't sound convinced. 'Bit stupid, if you don't mind me saying so. Beach Hut will be the first place they look.'

Gareth shrugs. 'It's what she wanted. I was only following orders.' Gareth riddles the stove a bit, 'This weather'll keep them away, for the time being, anyway. Tell me, though, what's it to you, Mr Fanshaw – Frank – whether they get to her or not? I'm not quite sure how you're fitting into this story. Why should you be bothered what the press does and does not do?'

'What's Stella told you, Probation Officer?' Frank asks. 'Lot of beans get spilled in pillow talk.'

'Did you say you'd seen the grandmother? Stella seemed to think she might be, well, passed away, like.'

'Oh, no, she's alive alright. Ruby Willoughby, strong as an ox. She'll see me out, that one, I shouldn't wonder. I just came from there. Like I said.'

'Stella didn't know what to make of it, the house all boarded up and what have you. She hasn't heard from her grandmother in years, not since…'

'You don't have to tell me,' Frank drains his beaker. 'Matter of fact,' he says, 'it was the old lady's idea I come up here. See Stella. Get things straightened out.' Frank gets to his feet again. 'So, Mr Probation Officer, I'll not be wasting any more of your time. If you'll just excuse me, Stella'll be awake by now. Stella!'

Gareth gets onto his feet and edges himself between Frank and the bedroom door. 'Hey, hey, wait a minute.' Gareth's on uncertain ground, as Frank's a much bigger man than he is. 'Stella said something, like you were "after her" or something. What's that all about?'

Frank shakes his head. 'What's she talking about? After her? Girl's paranoid. I'm not "after" no-one. Not like that, anyway.' Frank winks. 'I'll leave that to you, Mr Probation. I just need to talk to her, that's all. I've come with her grandmother's blessing. Then I'll make myself scarce. Leave you two to your own business.'

'Talk to her? What about? She's been inside seven years. What's so urgent that it can't wait a little while longer?'

Frank looks agitated, like his patience is about to run out.

'Look here, Frank. Stella's told me everything, all from when she was a kid. She's remembering a lot of stuff, since she's been out, and her mental health…'

'Mental health, my arse. I don't know what she's told you, Probation Officer lover boy, but I can tell you the girl's not reliable, never has been. Half the time she doesn't know her arse from her elbow, believe you me. That's been half the trouble. Half the things she remembers never actually happened. And things that do happen, she clean forgets. Ask the grandmother.'

Gareth's got Frank on the back foot. They come in handy, these training manouevres. Frank looks at Gareth, then goes over and throws a few more logs into the stove. 'I think we've just caught it,' he says, opening the vent, sitting back down. Gareth empties the bottle into the two beakers with a shakey hand. 'Time was, when

I lived here with Muriel…'

The two men sit talking well into the night, while Stella sleeps on.

'So you see, Gareth,' Frank says, 'I have to tell Stella the grand-mother says it was Muriel that killed the baby and not Stella at all. Muriel never was in full possession of her senses when it came to babies, and for good reason. Stella needs to tell me what she's done with the baby's body. We need to get it sorted before the reporters get here. Thank God for snow for once, eh?'

'I'd better get her up,' says Gareth.

Chapter Thirty-Seven

'Hello, Frank,' says Stella, her face pale, eyes huge and hair all over the place. She follows Gareth into the room, pulling the eider-down around her. 'Gareth says you've seen my grandmother? You know where she is…' On Stella's feet, a pair of old hiking socks, way too big.

'My socks!' Frank says, pointing and laughing.

Stella looks down. 'They're all I could find,' she says. She makes no attempt to return them. 'How's my grandmother? Where is she, can I see her?'

'I'm sure she'll see you, but we've got…er…things to be sorted first.' Frank glances at Gareth then looks at Stella. 'I mean, she's sent me here with strict instructions.'

'Sit here, Stella,' says Gareth, 'Have my chair, I'll get another.' Gareth stumbles a bit as he crosses the room and tries to laugh it off. Frank looks at Stella and shrugs. He nods his head sideways, indicating the empty bottle lying on the floor.

Frank looks up at Gareth as though he expects him to leave the room. Stella's good at picking up on cues. She's had to be. She's Muriel's daughter.

'He's alright,' says Stella, sitting down in Gareth's chair and pulling the eiderdown closer about her. 'I've told him. I've told him all of it, haven't I, Gareth?' She looks at Gareth. 'I think we can trust him. Are you to be trusted, Gareth?'

'I can make myself scarce, if you prefer…' Gareth articulates each word carefully. He puts the chair down at the other side of the room and plonks himself down on it, a silly grin spreads across his face.

'No need, as far as I'm concerned,' Stella is not bothered. 'Frank?'

Frank shrugs.

'Don't worry,' Stella says, 'Gareth already knows about the baby.'

'Bottom line is what you've done with the baby's body, Stella…' Frank says.

Stella interrupts, emphatic, 'I like that!' she says. 'Me? I haven't touched it. How don't you know where it is, since you're the one that buried it?'

Frank had feared the worst and now the worst was happening. Gareth leaves the room to fetch some firewood and as soon as he is gone, Frank leans over to Stella and says in a loud whisper, 'What if he talks? What exactly have you told him? You know he's under a professional duty.' Frank is very obviously trying not to get agitated. 'You know the papers are looking for you?' Frank fishes in his pocket and pulls out Page 2, hands it to Stella. She waves it away.

'I already know all that,' she says, 'and it's why Gareth came here. To warn me. To protect me.'

'They're on the scent, and that Macalinden is going on about the baby.'

'Well, what if they are? It's no secret that I've been released. It was bound to come out sooner or later.'

'Stella! You better not have dropped me in it.'

'Stop thinking about yourself, Frank. What is it about you blokes? You'd think you were the centre of the universe.' Stella sounds like Muriel, that tart edge to her voice. 'Anyway,' she says, adjusting her tone, 'I've already made up my mind. I'm giving myself up as regards the baby. As soon as this snow's gone, I'm turning myself in and, in the meantime, Gareth won't talk.' Stella is emphatic, 'I can absolutely assure you of that. I've made as certain as it's possible to be certain.'

Gareth comes back into the room, carrying a few bits of wood in the welt of his jumper. 'That really is the last of it,' he says. 'What were you saying, Stella? Did I hear my name?'

'Cold air seems to have sobered you up, man,' Frank says.

'I was saying you're not going to tell anybody anything, are you, Gareth? Frank here is worried, you being a Probation Officer and all. I told him you're not going to say a single thing to a single person, that you've no intention of doing anything of the sort. Isn't that right, Gareth?'

'I have nothing but your interests at heart, Stella. You know that.'

'There, that's settled.' Stella cups her hands to her face and blows on them.

'None of this settles the question of the baby's body,' Frank says. 'If the polis have already got that... Anyway, you don't need to be thinking of giving yourself up for that, Stella. That's not what your grandmother says. She says it was Muriel who killed Baby Keating. It wasn't you at all.'

Stella is silent for a few moments.

'But she said it was me. She said all along it was me. That night of the séance...'

'I didn't know till now, Stella, believe me,' Frank says. 'It was Muriel who killed the baby. Muriel lied to you. That's what your grandmother says. Muriel never let on to me – I swear it. She always maintained it was you.'

'Muriel? Why would Muriel have done that? Why did she make people – why did she make *me* – think I was to blame?' Gareth moves out of the chair to let Stella sit down. 'It all came back to me, Frank, that night at the Boarding House, about the séance and everything. To think I believed her, I really believed her. I thought I must be some kind of monster. I thought they should lock me away for good.'

'Is that why you dug up the body?'

'What? I never dug anything up.'

'That hole in the kitchen floor. I filled it in.'

'I never made that hole, Frank. It was there when I came here, on the day Muriel died.'

'Christ,' says Frank, 'was it there that long ago? So someone's had that body all this time. If it wasn't you, Stella, who the hell was it? Did Muriel get rid of it before she died? Is that what happened? But why the hell would she do that? Where would she have put it?'

'I don't know, Frank. All I know is that the hole was there the day I came here, the day I found everything ransacked and Muriel gone and out there on the cliff. When I went to find her, she kept wailing and saying the baby's gone and I didn't know what she was talking about, but I see now. She meant Baby Keating.'

Frank explains to Stella what Ruby's told him about Muriel's strange relationship with infants, how Billy took his own life after the teenage Muriel accused him of 'interfering' with her, how Muriel's father had saved her from a lifetime of shame by doing the abortion himself, how the family secrets had festered on across the years, one piling on top of the other, fragments of truth swamped by supposition.

'And now my grandmother's saying Muriel killed Baby Keating, killed him for the same reason she couldn't keep me? I can't take this in,' Stella says.

'Nobody knew what you knew, what you remembered.' Frank leans forward, rests a hand on Stella's shoulder.

'Murdering seems to run in my family…'

'Now, now, stop that. Stop it this minute. There's nothing to be gained by going down that road.'

Frank stands up and walks to the window and back again. It seems to him that the room's gone stuffy, despite the broken window. He goes back to the window and opens another. He has to bang it with the palm of his hand where the paint has stuck. Stella is sitting by the stove weeping quietly, wiping away tears with the cuff of her jumper. Frank has never seen her give into weeping before, not even when she was small.

'We'll never know all the whys and wherefores, Stella,' he says. 'Ruby was more interested in laying the whole thing to rest than finding out the truth, if such a thing can ever be found…'

'Quite right.' Gareth interrupts. 'And that's what we should be doing now, if I may say so. Drawing a line under all this, so we can each get on with our lives.'

Frank shakes his head. He wishes Gareth would shut his stupid, drunken mouth. He doesn't know what he's talking about. He doesn't know the half of it.

'You can put all that business about the baby to rest now, Stella,' Gareth is gabbing on. 'That's all in the past now, Stella. No more of this giving yourself up stuff, alright? Isn't that right, Frank? It's all over with.'

'Well, not exactly all over and done with.' Frank says.

'I want to see my grandmother. I want her to tell me all this herself,' Stella says.

'You can see her,' says Frank, 'but not yet. I know exactly where she is. I can take you. But not right now. First we have to… We've got other things to do, before we go on down to Brighton.'

'Like what other things?' says Gareth. 'I say we get gone from here as soon as the weather lets up. Eh, Stella?'

Stella looks up as Frank gets to his feet, scraping back his chair. She sees that look on his face, she knows this is not the end of anything. The eiderdown has slipped off her shoulders and she's shuddering, whether from cold or emotion, Frank can't tell.

'She's exhausted, man, can't you see?' Gareth says.

Frank paces the room, hands thrust deep into his pockets.

'I appreciate your concern, Gareth, it's very touching, but fact is we don't have the luxury of time. You know as well as I do that the press rats will be sniffing under every dung lump until they get what they want. Until we can find out for certain what happened to the baby's body, we're up to our necks, well and truly, up shit creek without a paddle. And I'm including you.'

Gareth interrupts. 'Now who's the paranoid one? If anyone was going to open their mouth about that, Frank, they'd have done it long before now. I mean, man, we're ten years on…'

'Because Stella's out, that's why. Wake up, Gareth. Anyone decides to mention the séance, or the baby, there's a load of juicy scoops those hacks – especially that Macalinden bloke – would give their right arms to get hold of…' Frank's voice tails off.

'What are you suggesting, then?'

'Hedy. Hedy Keating, the baby's mother,' Frank explains for Gareth's benefit, 'isn't that far from here, according to Ruby. I'm suggesting that we find her and warn her to keep her mouth shut. It's the very least we should do. She was in on it from the start, she's got as much to lose as the rest of us. The original story was that the baby disappeared from his pram outside the house. Hedy can confirm that and...'

'And how do you propose we persuade her to keep her story to herself, eh?' Gareth looks worried, 'Now look here, Frank. I can't afford to be getting involved in any dodgy goings on.'

'A bit late for that, Gareth,' Frank laughs. 'But seriously, I can make it worth Hedy's while. Ruby's got money. She says she'll hand some over to keep Hedy quiet. Take it or leave it, Gareth. But it seems to me you're not exactly in a position to pick and choose.'

Gareth shrugs.

'And that's about as much as we can do,' Frank says. 'After that, you'll be free to go.'

Gareth's in a corner. He's made a mistake – a big one – and he's going to have to do something to repair it. Harry Callahan might have thrown his badge away, but Gareth's not going down that road. With the material he's got, and the thinking he's done, Gareth knows he could write a brilliant Case Study, but he's not going down that road either. It's time to stand up and be counted. It's time to apologise. It's Gareth's turn to confess. He should go back to the office and tell Geoff everything and face the music, take whatever's coming to him. But Gareth can't even do that, not without making trouble for Stella, and for Frank. They've no idea of the turmoil he's in. All they think about is saving their own skins.

Chapter Thirty-Eight

It was the fifth of November when the snow cleared enough to allow them to leave the Beach Hut. Deal was, Gareth would take Stella and Frank as far as Alnton and Hedy Keating's last known address. After that, it was up to them. They were on their own. No more mention of anything on all sides, and Gareth would go back to work, minus any case study material, and take things from there.

Stella stuffed everything she wanted into the little blue suitcase, pulled the curtains to, jammed the front door shut, locked up and put the keys in her jeans pocket. They trudged off over the dunes in single file, Stella wearing Gareth's Barbour, head down against the wind, leading the column, snowdrifts still up to her thighs in places.

When they reached the car park, they had to borrow a shovel from the landlord at the pub to dig Gareth's car out. The landlord said he'd had no customers at all for the last three days and thank God a thaw was forecast. Snow was totally unheard of this early, let alone this amount: it would be death to his business, certain death, if this carried on. Stella sat in the back seat of the Zodiac, hiding behind her hair while Frank dug. She'd decided to have it all cut off and cropped short, Mia Farrow style, half an inch long all over. Gareth turned the engine over a few times and looked shocked when it actually started. He kept pulling on the choke and revving his foot on the accelerator, expecting the engine to cut out any moment. Frank finished digging round the wheels, scraped a path to the track and returned the shovel.

'No idea what the roads'll be like,' the landlord said, waving them off. 'Best of luck, pal.'

It took a good half-hour to drive the coast road to Alnton, a trip that normally took five minutes. The snow had turned to sleet. It splatted against the windscreen, sad grey dollops shunted back and forth by the wipers.

At Alnton, Gareth dropped them just before the bridge. It didn't look like cars could get any closer anyway: some were parked – abandoned – at all angles, marooned behind great piles of dirty snow that had been shoved to the sides by snow ploughs. Gareth stopped the car but left the engine running.

'So long, mate,' Frank said, slamming the door behind him.

'Let me know how it goes.'

Frank nodded. 'Will do.'

Stella got out the back and stood awkwardly, suitcase in hand. Gareth made a bit of a thing of turning the car in the tight space. Frank walked on ahead. Stella pulled Gareth's coat around her, tugged down the cuffs of her jumper, pulled her fists up inside the sleeves and buried her nose in the cuffs. The car now facing the other way, Gareth stopped where Stella was standing and wound the window down.

'Well, I'm off, then,' he said. 'Be seeing you, Stella. Take care of yourself, mind. Keep in touch. We'll get you sorted one way or another.'

'Gareth, you know what you were saying, about coming clean at work?'

Gareth nods. He'd hoped she wasn't going to bring up this particular subject.

'Well, I just want to say I don't think you should. If you do, I for one won't back you up. I won't testify against you. I'll refuse point blank. What happened, happened. I don't want it to ruin your career.'

'But you know better than anyone, Stella, when you've done something you know is wrong, it's best to come clean and face the consequences. Otherwise you're carrying a burden of guilt and shame around with you for the rest of your life. It was you who made all that very clear to me, and I thank you for it.'

'I know, Gareth. But only if the thing you've done is wrong. Don't you see? I genuinely believed I'd killed Mrs Keating's baby. I was determined to come clean, take what was due to me, and get it off my conscience. But look what's happened. You can't neces-sarily trust your perceptions, based on what other people think, or what they tell you. You have to make up your mind for yourself, Gareth. OK, technically what happened, *technically*, is a cardinal sin in your profession, I know all that. But what I'm saying is that there are wrongs and wrongs. Circumstances matter, and learning from your mistakes matters.'

'All the same,' Gareth said, 'I've decided to give up probation work anyway. I'm not cut out for it, never was. My heart's never really been in it.'

'What will you do instead, then?'

'Get my MSc finished, and maybe after that I'll try for a research post. Or I might do some lecturing. I'll have to see how it goes.'

'Bye, then, Gareth. I'll give you your coat back another time, if that's OK? And thanks for everything. Good luck with it all.'

Gareth smiled, looking suddenly shy. 'Thanks. It'll be OK. I'll say bye, then. Look after yourself.'

'Bye, Gareth.'

Chapter Thirty-Nine

Stella hurried on down the road to catch up with Frank, her feet sliding in the snow. She turned and waved one last time to Gareth as the Zodiac skidded then pulled away.

Stella and Frank walked into the village up the middle of the road, big piles of dirty, melting snow along either side, and only room for one vehicle.

'Where's the house, Frank?'

'Along here on the right, I think,' he said. 'Your grandmother said it was one of the bungalows, pebbledash. Yes, 21, that'll be it there, where the boat's outside.'

'She's got a boat?' said Stella.

'It could be anyone's. It's just there because there's room on the grass.'

'Can't imagine Hedy Keating sailing about in a boat, can you? Doesn't fit the picture, somehow. I wonder if she's still the same?'

Frank shrugs.

'Who's going to knock? Do we need to be worried about nets tweaking?' Stella nods towards the houses opposite, where there is already movement in the curtains.

'Probably best if we get a move on,' says Frank, 'just in case. But it's the fireworks, that'll be why people are looking out. There's a load of people heading over there towards the beach.'

'Bonfire night,' says Stella, 'I forgot. I lost track of time.'

'Probably best if I knock,' says Frank. 'She could get one hell of a shock if she sees you. Though, whether she'll remember me after this long...'

'Of course she'll remember you. What are you talking about?'

A small group of children, eight or nine years old, comes round the corner jostling and giggling with excitement. Two are squeezed together, bumping shoulders, each holding onto one handle of a

227

rusty old wheelbarrow with a wobbly wheel. Stella nudges Frank as they watch the little procession making its way up the street. A small horde of over-excited children is running to catch up with the barrow. 'Penny for the Guy!' the children shout, 'Penny for the Guy!'

Hedy Keating's door opens, and she comes out and chats to the children. She goes back in. The kids outside are hopping foot to foot till she comes back. This time she is carrying the Guy, dressed in old workmen's dungarees with a load of knotted yellow wool for hair sticking out from underneath a flat cap. She hands the Guy over and helps the kids get him propped upright in the wheelbarrow. The kids giggle and jump about in the cold, their breath visible in the night air. Frank and Stella watch.

The kids make their way towards the bonfire, the barrow wobbling along. The Guy keeps tilting and the children giggle some more and do their best to hold him up straight. Stella drops some coins into the tin can one child has round his neck on a string. Other people are doing the same. 'Penny for the Guy!' the kids shout.

'Yep. That's Hedy Keating alright. See, I was right about the house,' Frank says.

'Don't make it so obvious. She's gone fat, though, hasn't she?'

'It's her alright. I'd know her anywhere. Ten years, Stella – middle-age spread catches up with the best of us.' Frank pats his own belly and laughs. 'You'll get your turn.'

'Keep on walking,' says Stella. 'Don't make it obvious, until we've decided what to say.' Stella looks round as Hedy Keating goes back in and closes her front door. 'Shit, we might have missed our chance,' she says. 'She's gone back in. Go and knock now, Frank, strike while the iron's hot.'

'What'll we say?'

But Stella's already pushing Frank through the gate and following him down the path. Frank raps the knocker on the front door of Hedy Keating's bungalow. Stella bites the tip of her tongue so hard it hurts. She watches without blinking for the door to open. Hedy is taking a long time. Stella buries her nose in her cuffs. In the air, the smell of hot dogs and onions frying, and the crackling noise of someone trying to tune the ghetto blaster, the excited shrieks of children, a dog yap, yap, yapping.

Still Hedy does not come to the door. Frank raps the knocker again, then taps his knuckles on the window. Over by the bonfire, not yet lit, children are jumping up and down and waving sparklers, making swirly patterns, some of them trying to write their names in the air. Stella smells the smoky sizzle of the barbeque and hears the low hum of conversation, the slow rhythmic crash of waves on the shore, the Bee Gees now, 'Staying Alive'.

Then the door opens, and Hedy is standing there, a blank expression on her face. A group of teenagers go past, dragging a tarpaulin load of rubbish for the bonfire: chairs, a table, boxes, a sofa, a mattress, twigs and bushes. Hedy is still standing there looking at Frank and Stella as though she expected them, but now they are there, she can't quite take it in.

'You'd better come in,' she says, standing back to let them in. 'You've come at a good time,' she says, almost smiling, 'yes, a very good time.'

Half an hour later, they are back outside.

'I had a suspicion,' Frank says to Stella afterwards. They are walking down towards the bonfire. 'Yes, old Ruby thought as much as well. And we were right. So it was Hedy after all who took the baby, all those years ago. Took him on the very day Muriel died.'

'I feel bad she blames herself so much for Muriel's death,' Stella says. 'She shouldn't. That was down to me and nobody else.'

'Hedy didn't know any of the background, none of it. And neither did we,' Frank says.

'Family secrets, eh? But it's sad, though, isn't it? She had to dig up her own baby's body so she could give him a proper burial.'

'She never said how they did that,' says Frank.

'How could they give him a proper burial? When you come to think of it, they couldn't have done. It doesn't make sense. They would have needed a death certificate.'

'She's been terrified all this time that one of us would blurt out the truth…'

'The irony, don't you see, is nobody knows the truth. Nobody knows how or why the baby died. She thinks it was just one of those things. Could it just have been one of those things, Frank? Could it be that Muriel was innocent after all?'

'What the final truth is, we will never know. Ruby blamed Muriel. Muriel blamed you, Hedy didn't know what to think, and me neither. Once the whole thing started, and the story was told to the polis about the abduction and they started looking into that, we were all bound into that story, so to speak, and everyone was intent on covering up their own and everyone else's tracks. The truth gets lost, Stella, when there's too many people chasing it. It hides itself away.'

Stella sighs. 'I need a drink,' she says. 'It's been a long few days.'

'You and me both.' Frank buys two bottles of Newcastle Brown at the stall by the barbeque. They have the caps taken off and they drink from the bottle.

'Let's go down to the bonfire,' Stella says. 'I'm so cold, Frank. And do you know what? We're none the wiser. We still don't know where the baby is, where Hedy buried him.'

'She says we need have no worries on that score, Stella. Hedy swears she's not going to talk. And in her position, you wouldn't either.'

'Well, no. So that's that, then.'

Just then, a posse of excited children comes careering by, waving sparklers. A couple of dads are helping the kids hoist the Guy out of the wheelbarrow and heave him onto the top of the bonfire. He sits there all lopsided, cap askew, looking quite ridiculous, but only for a moment before the flames all around him catch and he topples forward. The bonfire blazes. A loud cheer as a bright plume of fire shoots into the air. The Guy is going up in flames.

Hedy Keating is standing by herself, hands in her coat pockets, staring into the bonfire. They hadn't seen her coming over.

They walk round the outside of the crowd to where Hedy is standing. For a minute or two, Stella and Hedy stand together, looking into the fire. As the Guy finally keels over and disintegrates, Hedy turns to Stella and looks into her eyes and takes both of her hands in her own. Stella sees Hedy's eyes are welling up, but perhaps it's just the smoke from the bonfire.

'Well, well, well, Stella Moon,' Hedy says. 'You'll be glad that's the last of it. That's him away now. God rest his poor wee soul.' Hedy crosses herself. She inclines her head towards the fire where the Guy is burning and crosses herself a second time.

Stella stares at her, trying to take it in. She looks at the blazing effigy, then back at Hedy. Hedy looks into the fire until the Guy is completely cremated, until there's nothing left of him at all. Then she crosses herself a third time, turns, and walks away towards the bungalow.

'I hope now you can do something with your life, Stella. And you too, Frank,' she says as she leaves.

Stella watches Hedy walking across the grass, knowing how very hard it must have been for her finally to do what she did, knowing that she did it for Stella, for Ruby, for Muriel's memory, and for Frank, as much as for herself.

Stella clicks open the little blue suitcase she's still clutching. She pulls out the bag of vomit-covered clothes – Muriel's silk dress, the sage green cardy, the gold lamé slippers – and tosses them onto the bonfire.

Time to move on.

'Just a minute Stella, love, there's one more thing,' Frank starts to say, 'before we go our separate ways…'

'Leave it, Frank,' Stella interrupts.

She knows what he's going to say and she doesn't want to hear it. If he's about to say Sorry, then Sorry is not enough and it's more than Stella can bear. Sorry would feel like yet another assault, yet another invasion, yet another onslaught. No more. Never again. Stella cannot forgive and she will not forgive and it is wrong of him even to think about asking: it's all part of the same vile, abusive thing.

'Leave it out, Frank,' Stella says, more emphatically. 'I mean it. I really don't want to know.'

Epilogue

The Warden's Flat
The Youth Hostel
Isle of Skye
Scotland

29 March 1979

Dearest Marcia,

Thank you *so* much for your letter. And here, in exchange, the blue notebook, filled up, as promised. Lots of crossings out (of which, more later!). Finally, after a lot of stopping and starting, finally it's done and, like you said, dearest Marcia, it's a ton weight lifted.

Only this morning did I clap the blue book shut, put the tired pen down, and straight away I opened your letter. I can't tell you the relief that came with reading the words you wrote. I see now why you insisted that I wait to open it. The waiting was torture, but worth it! I came so close, many times, to just ripping it open, but always the promise I made to you stopped me, kept me strong. Now, dearest Marcia, my story is there for you in the blue book.

Or is it?

I come back now to all the crossings out, all marginalised scribblings. In the words I wrote and revised and rewrote, you have what amounts to a new confession. I make it to you and only you, dearest Marcia. In the words in the book you will see the Stella you tell me in your letter you always knew was there.

Well, like you say, she's been in hiding, but she's come out now, and it's no small thanks to you. I've said it before, I know, and I'll say it a thousand times – I couldn't have got through that stint inside without you. And these few months outside, they've been worse, but I've pulled through. I've come out so much stronger. Your belief in me changed something inside me, Marcia. Truly, it has helped me find myself.

So, here you have my story, Marcia, and it comes to you with love and gratitude. It remains unfinished – as every auto-biographical tale must remain unfinished, always only true from the vantage point of the present, and the present shifts – oh, how it shifts! Hence the crossings out as I have gone back and back and tried to rework it. But finally, I have had to accept that in any case it's valid as far as it goes, and so here's an Epilogue that shifts the whole focus once again.

First, a job that Probation Officer Gareth found for me (you'll meet him in the blue book – don't be too hard on him, and he's not doing that job any longer). 'Youth Hostel Warden' in the Isle of Skye! It's a stunningly beautiful place, scenery-wise and weather-wise, very, very dramatic, and wild as you can get on these islands. Full of soul. You would love it. And for me, I can stop still here, take stock, earn my keep and take my writing forward. It is purely coincidental that Muriel had her honeymoon here, which was the beginning and end of her relationship with my father, whoever he was. Anyway, as I say, that aside, it's a great place, and ideal for you to take that 'break' from the Prison Service you talk about in your letter. Ideal for all your new projects, Marcia. Even for a tiny short time, it would be so good to see you. It's good to feel that I now have something I can offer to you.

Now, the final part of my Epilogue is more difficult. It's a bit of a bombshell, so you'd better sit down. As I said, a story of a life can only ever be true for a moment. Now I have some-thing to add which changes the colour of everything.

My grandmother gave me Muriel's diaries. I haven't read them hardly at all, I haven't been able to face them. Not after I read the final entry, written on the morning of the day Muriel died.

The last entry refers to the ransacking of the Beach Hut, which I told you I had seen. It also refers to the removal of the body of Baby Keating, which you will read about in the blue book. According to the diary, those events terrified Muriel completely.

But the hardest thing of all, Marcia, is that Muriel states quite clearly she intended to take her own life. She even describes the manner of her death, so close to the way it actually happened, the only real difference being that she intended to take me down with her when she jumped. It says in the diary she intended to cling on to me so that mother and daughter would never again be parted.

But Marcia, I know that Muriel changed her mind about that last bit. She must have changed it as a result of seeing me. Because she didn't take me with her, did she, Marcia? I remember her telling me to go. I can hear her begging me to leave her. But I loved her, I refused to budge without her, I was angry and abandoned and so wrapped up in my own feelings I couldn't see what was happening.

I know now that Muriel loved me, because she let me go. She spared me. I should have tried harder to save her.

Write soon, dearest friend.

Yours always,

Stella.

Acknowledgements

So many people have wittingly or unwittingly helped Stella and me. A massive THANK YOU to you all.

Chronologically:

Caron Freeborn told me I could write.

The late Gordon Burn told me I could write better.

Patrick Gale suggested I put Stella into a novel.

April Moon let me borrow her name.

Janette Jenkins took me aside.

Laura Degnan said I could do it.

Sean O'Brien, Gail-Nina Anderson and Chaz Brenchley – Phantoms at the Phil.

Jackie Kay taught me, inspired me and has always believed in me – very special thanks for supplies of magic dust.

Olivia Chapman and Claire Malcolm at New Writing North, and the family of the late Andrea Badenoch, recognised Stella's potential when she was only half formed. They gave me the award that changed my life. Their ongoing support has made all the difference.

Charles Boyle offered to read my scrappy first draft but in the end I didn't need to inflict it on him: the fact that he offered was amazing.

Lucy Ellman and Todd McEwen: sharp critics, always encouraging.

The Literary Consultancy – Helen Gordon and Becky Swift – gave editorial feedback, believed Stella had commercial potential and helped me find my agent.

Helen Ivory said Stella had stayed with her even after the book was closed.

Peggy Hughes and Ali Bowden and everyone then at the Edinburgh UNESCO City of Literature picked me to be one of their Emerging Writers in 2013 and gave me the opportunity to read at the Edinburgh International Book Festival.

Everyone at the Scottish Book Trust was generous and inclusive and helpful and kind.

Russel McLean suggested parings and re-orderings and caused mild panic.

AL Kennedy said fear was the only enemy I needed to be afraid of.

My agent Jenny Brown, whose unwavering belief in Stella kept me going as I revised and bit my fingernails and revised some more.

Sara Hunt at Saraband who fell for Stella and who has been so brilliant to work with. A very, very special thank you Jenny and to Sara, my excellent editor, Louise Hutcheson, and all the team at Saraband.

My friends, all of you, fellow writers, real friends and Facebook friends, my teachers and mentors at the NCLA Newcastle University and Edinburgh University, who've been rooting for me all the way. You know who you are, and I'm so very grateful.

Finally, my partner Andrew, and my kids Poppy and Nico, who've always been there with their love and their support and only the occasional dollop of disapproval.

Thank you so much, everyone!